The Truths We Told

Secrets & Truths Duet
Book Two

New York Times Bestselling Author

E. K. Blair

The Truths We Told
Copyright © 2020 E.K. Blair

ISBN: 9798606461417

Editor: Ashley Williams, AW Editing
Cover Designer: E.K. Blair
Interior Designer: Champagne Book Design

All rights reserved. No part of this publication may be reproduced or transmitted in any form, or by any means, electronic, mechanical, including photocopying, recording, or by any information storage and retrieval system, without the prior written permission in writing.

This is a work of fiction. Names, characters, places, brands, media, and incidents are either the products of the author's imagination or are used fictitiously, and any resemblance to any actual persons, living or dead, events, or locales is entirely coincidental.

The author acknowledges the trademarked status and trademark owners of various products referenced in this work of fiction, which have been used without permission. The publication/use of these trademarks is not authorized, associated with, or sponsored by the trademark owners.

The Truths We Told

KATE
One Year Later...

IN LIFE, WE ARE FORCED TO MAKE CHOICES WITHOUT EVER KNOWING HOW they will affect our future.

Nothing is guaranteed.

Nothing is fully in our power.

Life grants no promises.

All we can do is hope for the best.

When I looked through the peephole and saw Caleb standing outside of my condo, I made my choice when I backed away and refused to let him in. I tried my best to stay quiet so he wouldn't know I was there, but it was the middle of the night and he wouldn't stop banging on the door. Terror consumed me, and the fear that he would wake my neighbors or that someone would call the cops was a visceral thing. The moment I broke my silence and yelled at him to go away, he completely lost it. He was convinced Trent was inside with me since I had left the party with him. Threats were thrown my way as he hammered his fist into the door so hard I was sure he would bust right through. I wound up pushing my coffee table against it as a makeshift barricade.

A few seconds later, my neighbor started screaming at him and threatening to call the police if he didn't leave. That was all it took.

He was gone.

But I remained.

Sitting on the floor with my back pressed to the wall, my body trembled as I sobbed. It was only a handful of minutes before another knock came, sparking another rush of panic. But this time, it was Trent's voice on the other side of the door. Knowing he was with me, but not with me, helped in a way because I knew I was safe—because he was safe, yet the knot in my stomach didn't relent. I don't know how long he stood outside of my door, repeatedly calling and texting me, but I didn't move to let him in. I couldn't face him or myself or the truth.

Eventually, I went to my room, closed the door, and crawled into bed.

That was the choice I made.

I didn't know where that choice would lead me.

I was in so much denial that I was unable to think clearly.

It's been a year since that night, since my darkest secret was exposed to everyone around me. There was nothing I could do, no lie I could tell, no opinion I could sway. They saw it with their own eyes—the bruises, the blood, the utter disgrace. There wasn't a hole deep enough for me to crawl into that would hide me from the truth they saw.

I wish I could say that I never looked back and wondered if I'd made the right choice.

But I did.

Caleb came by my condo so many times, begging to talk to me. Countless texts and voice mails flooded my phone with his desperate apologies. And even though every text, every phone call, every knock on my door was ignored, a part of me wanted to fall back into his arms. I missed him, and I battled with so much guilt, but in the end, I knew I would never be enough to make him happy. No matter how hard I tried, I was constantly letting him down.

I was a failure to him.

I was a failure to *myself*.

I did everything I could to love him the way he needed me to, but I was always messing up.

His attempts to talk to me weren't the only ones I dodged. Ady, Trent, Brody, and a few other people who were at the party and saw what happened reached out to me. But how could I possibly face the very people I lied to time and time again? The shame was too much to bear, and I was scared to meet the consequences of my betrayal, so I sank deeper and deeper into the fabrications I wove for myself.

I was a liar, and they all knew it.

Two weeks later when I went home for Christmas break, I didn't come back. I hid away where no one could find me—I've been hiding for what feels like forever.

At first, my parents were extremely concerned about my moving back home. They asked questions I couldn't answer, so I lied. They knew Caleb and I had broken up, but that was it, and when it was all I would tell them, they eventually backed off.

To pacify their worries, I started taking online classes so that I didn't fall behind. That only served to isolate me more, and I knew it. But I couldn't blame Caleb for that. It was my choice. It was my doing. No matter how much I loved him, resentment grew, tempers flared, and slowly, we turned into the worst versions of ourselves. I never saw it coming; he was so perfect in the beginning.

And then it all changed.

Beneath my clothes were countless bruises, and beneath the bruises was inexplicable trauma. I wanted so badly to believe I was made of courage and strength, built to castle standards, sturdy and steadfast. Truth was, I was made of chaos and scars that bled and burned. I was a battleground of love and fear, of silence and rage.

I still am.

Looking back now, I thought I would have it all figured out, but I don't. My love for Caleb kept me devoted to him despite how dysfunctional we became. Fault lied with me, and no matter how much I tried to be better, do better, love better, I couldn't give him what he wanted, and it killed me. I failed him in so many ways. Every push, every slap, every hit broke away pieces of my heart. I blamed myself for constantly disappointing him by not being who he needed me to be. I still blame myself.

No matter how many times I thought about leaving him, I could never bring myself to turn my back. He needed me, and I refused to let him down the way his parents had. It wasn't his fault that he grew up at the mercy of his father's unrealistic expectations and bitter fury that resulted in years of violent abuse. How could I possibly blame him? Caleb wasn't the monster; he was merely the product of a monster.

I wish I could say we broke up because I fell out of love with him. That scenario would've lessened the pain that still lingers. Truth is, the split was inevitable. Even if I went back to him and forgave him, there was no way I was going to move to Chicago and there was no way he was ever going to stay in Miami.

We were doomed no matter what.

"Is this the last box?" my dad asks when he comes into my bedroom.

"Yeah."

"Are you about ready?"

I nod, and when he picks up the box, I tell him, "I'll be down in a minute."

"Okay, sweetheart."

It isn't the last box though—that was another lie.

As I look at the photo in my hands, my throat thickens and another memory softens my heart. I miss Caleb. The fibers of the photo paper weave together a precious moment in time. It was the Fourth of July, and we were at the beach. He was standing behind me with his arms wrapped around my shoulders and his cheek pressed to the side of mine. We both look so happy with our beaming smiles and the fireworks exploding in the sky above. I can remember being so hopeful that we could survive the obstacles that were in front of us.

A few days later, he fell back on another promise. The fight happened right before I was supposed to go home for my birthday, and he had bruised my ribs from kicking me so hard. I lied to my dad, told him I was sick and asked if we could postpone my birthday dinner until another time. It was a plausible excuse, one he didn't even question.

Despite all the horror, I was heartbroken when I made the tough decision to leave him. I thought moving back home would help, but it didn't. And when my sister moved out last semester to start college in Alabama, the loneliness was even more excruciating.

With my parents' growing concern about how I have been handling the breakup, I decided it would be best if I went back to Miami. They don't know the details of our dysfunction, but the shift in my mood was enough for them to figure out that things between Caleb and I weren't as stable as we tried to make them appear.

When I told them over the holidays that I was going to move back, they were supportive but leery, which is exactly why I know this is what's best for me. I can't fathom their reaction if they ever found out that I allowed Caleb to hurt me. I could never do that to them, but I can't do that to myself either. It's bad enough that all of my old friends know.

Taking the photo, I walk into my closet and pull down the box filled with so many wonderful memories of our love and drop the picture into it. I have no idea how it's going to feel being back in Miami. It's as if I'm starting over, only worse this time. At least I had Piper with me when I first moved there, but now I have no one.

That very thought punctures wounds that have yet to heal, and I take the picture back out, slip it into my rear pocket, and then shove the box onto the top shelf of my closet before walking from my room. I can't let go just yet, but I also want so badly to believe that I can pick up the shattered pieces of my heart and move forward.

I want to be hopeful, but hope is tangled in the wind, and half those broken pieces are no longer with me—I left them with Caleb.

"Are you off?" my mother questions as she gathers a stack of files in the living room.

"Yeah. Where's Dad?"

"Loading the last of your things in his truck."

She gives me a smile laced in sadness, and I walk over to give her a hug.

"Are you sure you're ready to go back?"

"Yes, Mom. I'm fine," I say, trying to ease her concern. "You worry too much."

Drawing back, she tilts her head. "You're my daughter; it's my job to worry. I just . . . I wish you would talk to me more." She then takes my hand, and I have to fight against the tears that ache behind my eyelids. "You've been locked away for months."

"I've been doing classwork. Online courses aren't as easy as ones on campus," I defend, but we both know that isn't the reason I was hiding away. "I promise, everything is fine."

"Okay then," she responds reluctantly.

"Everything's ready to go," my father announces when he comes inside, and I couldn't be more thankful for his interruption.

With another hug, I tell her goodbye and follow my dad outside. "You have the address?"

He walks over to his truck and opens the door, saying, "Yeah, I have it plugged into the GPS."

I slip into my car and back out of the driveway. With him following behind me, we make our way south to Miami and toward my new condo, which happens to be in the same building I was living in before.

When we arrive, we unload all the boxes before heading over to the storage unit I had rented and meeting the movers my dad hired. I watch while they load the furniture I left behind. It's a long day, but eventually, all my furniture is in my condo, the movers are gone, and it's just me and my dad in my new place.

He grabs one of the many boxes and opens it.

"Dad, you don't have to stay. I can unpack."

"You trying to kick your old man out?"

He looks at me from over his shoulder, and I smile and shake my head before he starts pulling the dishes out of the box. The two of us busy ourselves, and after a couple of hours, we manage to have most everything in its place.

As we flop down on the couch and dive into the pizza that was just delivered, my father asks, "Are you going to be okay when I leave?"

"Is that why you're sticking around? Because you're worried?"

He shrugs and takes a bite.

"Like I told Mom, I'm fine."

"I know you better than your mom does," he says, which is the truth. Our bond is our own. "I get that you don't want to talk—"

"Dad—"

"Just hear me out, okay?" I nod, and he continues. "Look, I

don't need to know the details of why you and Caleb broke up, but I heard you crying—I've been hearing it for a year now. So, you can sit there and tell me that everything is fine and that I have no reason to worry about you, but you know as well as I do that's a lie."

I hadn't known he had been able to hear me crying, and I shrink in on myself.

"I love you, and I want to do everything to protect you, but I also know that you aren't a kid anymore. You're twenty-one, and that puts me in a tough spot. I want to shield you from all the shit in this world, but I know I can't." He takes his napkin and wipes his mouth. "It isn't easy for me to sit back and watch you grow up. It's even harder to have to watch you get your heart broken."

I want to pretend that I'm a warrior on my own. That I don't need someone else to help me survive, but the truth is, I'm glad my dad is still here. In a way, I wish he'd stay forever because I'm not sure I'm ready to be on my own after everything that has happened. Two and a half years ago, I came here as a freshman and felt invincible, capable of making good choices, but now, I feel worthless.

He picks up his slice of pizza. "I'm proud of you for moving back, but I'm going to miss having you around. Now that your sister is in Alabama, I'm not sure what your mother and I are going to do in that big, empty house."

"Don't get all sappy on me now," I tease, trying to lighten the mood.

"You just wait until you become a parent."

I laugh and take a bite of a breadstick. "I'll be back home for spring break."

After we devour the entire pizza, there isn't any reason for him to stick around any longer. As I walk him out, he lectures me about keeping the doors locked at all times and carrying my pepper spray when I'm walking through the parking garage. I do my best to hold back my laughter, but he sees right through me.

"There are sickos all over the place," he asserts.

"Yes, Dad, I know."

"I'm serious."

"*I know*," I stress, secretly appreciating how protective he still is.

"If you need me, just call."

"I will, promise."

He gathers me into his arms, and I wrap mine around his waist. Not ready to be alone just yet, emotions bubble from deep within. I'm able to keep myself together by holding on to his dependable strength—I cling to it because I know that, once he walks out the door, I'm going to need it.

"I'm proud of you, sweetheart."

"Everything's going to be okay," I tell him again, more for my sake than his.

With a kiss to my head, he says goodbye, and the moment he's gone and the door is locked, I walk over to the kitchen. Picking up my phone from the bar, I click on Caleb's name and consider sending him a text. It's something I find myself doing from time to time; I'm not sure why. I know I need to move on and leave him in the past, but I'm struggling. The tears I've been holding back finally flood and spill over when I decide against reaching out to the other half of my heart.

Leaving the phone in the kitchen, I pull out the photo of the two of us before grabbing my pen from my purse and heading into the bedroom. With a heart too heavy, I crawl into bed and get high. The pot dulls my emotions, and I stare down at love lost as heartstrings slacken. These are the moments where I struggle the most. After the sun sets and the world stills, leaving me with nothing but space to reflect.

I miss Caleb far more than I should at this point, and the nights remind me that I'm weak and fucked in the head. I question my own sanity for wanting him still, despite all the brutality I endured at his hands.

I should hate him.

I should regret him.

I want to blame him solely, but I can't.

I'm to blame too because I was the cause, and I allowed it to happen.

I was so convinced that every hit, every strike of his fist, every blow I took was a touch of love. I often cry when I look at my naked body and find that no more bruises remain. It's a reminder that he's gone and that I'm no longer loved.

KATE

They say that a new year holds new promises. It's a notion I've been questioning lately, a notion I'm not sure will ever find its way to fruition.

January is supposed to be a month of resolutions that bring hope for a brighter tomorrow, yet all my tomorrows are still shrouded in dankness. I carry on, though, because that's all I can do. One foot in front of the other, but will they lead me toward the path of sanctitude?

There's no shaking the emptiness I feel from the moment I wake up until the moment I fall asleep. I drop tears every morning; I've never cried so much in my life. I used to be strong, and now . . . now, I'm just lost. I'm not even sure I know who I am anymore, but I want to find her—me—the girl who used to be filled with happiness and consumed with a freedom that breathed life into her veins.

But those veins are severed, and I don't know how to begin to heal them.

Maybe this is my first step—moving back here to Miami and returning to school. A part of me still wants to hide away, but I forced myself not to enroll in another online course. I need to be out here among the living, even though I feel lifeless.

It's strange being back on campus. Everything remains the same except for me. I've changed, and I'm even more unsure of my place here than what I was before.

Under the beaming sun, I make my way over to the student center to grab a coffee before my first class of the spring semester. With my head down, I stand in line as the people in front of me order their iced lattes or whatever fulfills their caffeine compulsions. The world moves from all around, voices and laughter surround me, plans for the weekend and which parties are going to be the best are discussed, but I'm on pause, nothing but a frozen image of white noise.

"Kate," the barista announces when he sets down my coffee.

"Thanks," I murmur, but the guy has already walked off to busy himself with another drink order. As I make my way outside, I take a sip and burn my tongue. "Shit."

My taste buds suffer as I walk into my digital marketing class and find a seat toward the back of the room. I slip my bag off my shoulders, situate myself in a desk, and wait for the professor to arrive. But it's who I see next that steals my attention.

Ady doesn't notice me when she walks in and finds a seat a few rows down next to a girl she immediately starts chatting with. I watch, nervous of what her reaction will be when she notices me. There are no hard feelings toward her on my end, but I'm sure they exist on hers. I allowed shame to control my actions, and I ditched her entirely, throwing our friendship away because I was too embarrassed to face her. Now that my secret was out, I knew she would also be upset that I'd blatantly lied to her each time she asked me if I was okay.

I'm struggling to understand myself.

I spend the next hour doing nothing to draw any attention

to myself as the professor goes over the semester's syllabus, and when our time is up, I toss my empty coffee cup and beeline it out of the door. It's childish, I know, but I just can't face her—not yet.

"Kate," she calls out as I'm trying to make my feeble escape. "Kate."

Anxiety rushes through my system. I can do one of two things: keep going and pretend I didn't hear her or turn around and deal with the ramifications of what I did. If I have any hope of taking that first real step forward, of proving that I'm not a coward, I know what I have to do.

I stop and face my old friend. As she catches up to me, I'm nervous. I have no idea what to expect from her. Anger for my being a total bitch and ignoring her is what I'm anticipating.

"Where have you been?"

"Umm . . ." Words fail me because, *where have I been?*

Before I can say anything else, she throws her arms around me in a hug that radiates relief. It's a confusing sentiment, and I reluctantly hug her back.

"I thought you fell off the face of the earth or something." She sighs heavily when she draws back.

"I, um . . . I've been around."

"No, you haven't," she counters. "I called and texted you for months."

And this I know. She tried to reach out to me every day until she, along with everyone else, gave up and faded away.

She waits for answers as she shakes her head, dumbfounded, and I don't blame her.

"I'm sorry," is all I can give because, how the hell do I even attempt to explain this to her? Knowing what she does about Caleb, I can guess how much she probably hates him, so there is no way she will understand. All I can do is wonder if that hate has been cast onto me. It wouldn't surprise me if that were the case. "I don't know what to say, I'm just . . . I'm sorry."

"You disappeared. All of us have been so worried about you."

It's an instant reminder of the truth they all know, and the urge to run and hide takes over. "I should probably get going. I have another class I need to get to."

"Wait." She grabs my arm as I start to walk away. "Did I do something?"

"No, you didn't do anything. It's . . ." I hang my head in defeat before telling her, "It's complicated."

Her hand slides down my arm until it's holding on to my hand. "Will you answer if I call you?"

"You're not mad at me?"

"Why would I be mad at you?"

My shoulders sag, and I let my hand fall from hers so I can grip the straps of my backpack. "I would understand if you were."

"Well, I'm not, but do you think we could get together and talk?"

The idea of having to explain myself and answer whatever questions she might have scares me, and I hesitate to respond.

"Come on," she presses. "We used to be good friends. I've missed having you around."

"I've missed you too," I tell her because it's the truth.

I miss all my friends, but I'm not sure I could ever look them in the eyes again without feeling a torrential amount of embarrassment. Ady wasn't there the night of the party, which is probably why I'm able to stand in front of her without crumbling under my mortification. But Brody, Micah, and Trent were. They saw everything.

"I have one more class today. Are you free later?"

Timidly, I nod.

"When I call, promise me you'll answer, okay?"

Even though my instinct is telling me to avoid her and everyone else, I give her what she's seeking. "I promise, but I have to run."

And with that, I rush across campus to my next class, all the while struggling to dislodge the knot stuck in my throat. The next hour drags on, and I try my best to focus on what the professor is saying, but I don't hear a word. I'm too lost in my head, replaying everything that happened freshman and sophomore year, and how quickly my life changed. And then I ask myself: If I could go back in time, would I forsake Caleb to keep the life I had before him intact?

It's a question that pains me to even consider.

I loved Caleb, but I hate the path of destruction he wrought on my life and my soul and my sense of self. Now, here I am—alone—forced to walk through the shambles. It wasn't as if I was delusional and thought that, at some point, I wouldn't have to face my old friends. I just didn't expect it would happen on the first day of class. I don't know why I didn't anticipate it knowing Ady and I share the same major.

After class, I have an hour break, which I use to grab a quick lunch from the student center. It's during this time that my phone chimes.

Ady: Just got back to the condo. Want to come over?

Too much too soon. There's no way I'm going over there and risking running into Trent or Micah.

Me: I still have another class. I should be home around 3:30. Want to meet me at my place?
Ady: Yeah, that works.

I send her my new address before tossing the rest of my food into the garbage. There's no question that I need to get this talk over with sooner rather than later, and the pressure of it all just killed my appetite.

I end up ditching out of my last lecture early, thinking the extra time will help settle my nerves before Ady comes over, but pacing around my condo only makes them worse. I wish I could simply sweep the past under the rug and resume our friendship with no questions asked, but I know if the tables were turned, I'd be hurt—to have a friend cut me off so easily. What I did wasn't okay, and I'll own it. She didn't deserve my shitty friendship.

When the knock finally comes, a part of me is relieved to end this agonizing waiting game, but it's short-lived when I open the door.

"Hey."

"Hey," I respond, and I can tell this is just as awkward for her as it is for me.

She walks in and looks around my new space. When I take a seat on the sofa, she slowly makes her way over and joins me, asking, "Why did you move out of your old unit?"

It's a benign question on her part, but not on mine. It has my palms sweating. "Because I moved back home for a while."

"You moved back home?"

I fidget as I nod.

"So, you haven't even been in Miami?"

I shake my head. "Not for a year."

Her brows lift in surprise. "When did you get back?"

"Two weeks ago."

"I can't believe I didn't even know you left," she says, and I can see in her eyes she wants to know more, but I'm not sure I can give her more.

"I'm sorry. It was kind of a . . . last-minute decision." I hope she understands that I'm not ready for her to push and ask why, but I steel myself against it just in case.

"It's okay." A beat passes between us, and then it's her turn to shrug. "Why does this feel so weird?"

"Because it *is* weird." I drop my head and then confess, "It's embarrassing for me."

"Do you want to talk about it?"

Hesitantly, I lift my eyes to hers. "I don't think I can." When she gives an accepting nod, I apologize again.

"Can I just ask you one thing?" When I don't move to respond, she continues, "Are you still with Caleb?"

"No."

Slowly, her lips move in a silent *good*.

"I couldn't stay here. I don't expect you to understand, I just—" No matter how much I don't want her to ask the questions I've been dreading, I still find myself trying to explain.

With softening eyes, she links our fingers together and tells me, "I might understand more than you think." Her hand trembles, and that in and of itself makes me think she just might.

"Are you okay?" I ask.

"I've never talked about this with anyone aside from Micah and my therapist, but I feel like you should know something about me."

Restlessly, she tugs her hand free and then tucks her long hair behind her ears, and I make myself sit still as she collects herself enough to speak again.

"I never told you the reason I left Tampa and moved in with Micah and Trent, but . . ." She takes in a deep breath and releases it slowly before revealing, "Someone hurt me too."

The moment her chin quivers, my eyes prick with tears that I quickly blink back.

"I know how hard it is for you to talk about this stuff because it's hard to talk about what happened to me. It's been two and a half years, and even though a big part of me wants to tell you, I can't."

My next blink sends a rogue drop of sadness down my cheek, and I quickly wipe it away.

"I just want you to know that I understand why you feel the need to keep saying you're sorry as if you've done something wrong when you haven't."

"But I did," I respond, my voice splintering against my pain. "I ran away and hid from everyone."

"So did I." Her shoulders drop. "You once asked me why I wasn't going back home to visit my mom for holidays and things . . . I was hiding from someone I was really close to because I was too ashamed to face him. I'm still hiding."

A few tears slip down her face as an unspoken understanding settles between us. Knowing that I'm not alone in this anguish that has imprisoned me is so overwhelming that I crack. The moment I drop my head and start weeping quietly in my hands, Ady scoots closer and pulls me into her arms.

Grief seeps through the fractures Caleb left me with, and I hug her back with a tearful, "Thank you."

She asks nothing else because she gets it. The gift she just gave me, letting me know that I'm not alone and that we share more than I ever thought, is the most precious thing anyone has ever given me, and I cry harder. The details of our circumstances don't need to be outlined . . . maybe one day we'll share our stories with each other, but for now, this is enough.

Three

TRENT

"You here for the rest of the night?" Micah asks from my doorway.

"Yeah, man. My classes are done for the day. I was just about to run out and grab dinner. You want anything?"

"I'll pick something up later. I have that night class, remember?"

"Dude, that fucking blows."

"Yeah," he responds. "It was the only time slot that had an open seat."

"Early surf still on for tomorrow morning?"

He nods. "Six o'clock, right?"

"Bright and early. Smack 'em and yack 'em."

The front door sounds, and when Ady calls his name, he ducks out, asking, "Where have you been?"

"You'll never guess who I ran into today," Ady tells him.

"Who?"

"Kate," she says, and all my senses go on high alert as I sit up to eavesdrop on whatever else she says. "I was just over at her place."

"Shit, are you serious? How is she?"

"How you would assume . . . not that great."

Ady's words pull me off the bed and out of my room.

"Where has she been?" Micah asks, but before she can respond, I walk into the kitchen.

"You saw Kate?"

"Yeah."

There's a solid rotation in my chest—a tumbling of emotions. It was just over a year ago when I last saw or spoke to her. Like a phantom, she fucking vanished in the middle of the night, broken and bruised, and no one has heard from her since. Not that I didn't try to find her—I did. I called, texted, and went to her condo countless times, but she was gone. As time passed, my attempts to get in touch with her dwindled until, eventually, I gave up.

"So, what did she say?" I ask.

"We just talked."

"About?"

"About things."

Her vagueness irritates me. I can still recall every detail about that fucked-up night. Kate's terrifying screams for help have never left me, and the fire within me that ignited wasn't anything I'd ever felt before. When I ran into that room and found that motherfucker pinning her to the floor with his knee in her spine and his hands pulling her head back, ripping her hair out, I lost all control. I wish I could say that was the worst of it, but when I saw her without her shirt on, it was so, so much worse. The bruises that dickfuck put on her told the story of more than one instance of abuse. He had been beating the shit out of her for a long time. The idea that she didn't feel like she could trust any of us to help her, that she simply had to endure his fists until he decided to stop, gnawed my gut—it still does. At least that night, Brody, Micah, and I were there to put a stop to it, but all the other times, she was alone.

When Ady opens the fridge to grab a soda, I ask again, "Seriously, Ady, what did she say?"

She pops the tab and takes a sip. "She didn't say much."

"Then what did you talk about?"

"Not a lot," she responds, pushing off my questions. "She just needs space. I'm sure, with a little time, she'll come around."

"Time? It's been a year."

"Dude? What's up with you?" Micah questions, and I back off, realizing I'm coming off too strong.

Ady picks up her backpack, and with her drink in hand, she tells me, "Maybe try reaching out to her," before she and Micah make their way to his bedroom.

I head back to my room and kick the door closed before I grab my cellphone. It's been a long time since I've pulled up her contact information, but when I find her name, I don't even think twice before I tap her number and call.

I'm eager to hear her voice and to find out where the hell she's been this whole time, but all I get is the recording of her voice mail. I hang up without leaving a message and decide to send a text, but then I waver on what to say. I want answers, but I also don't want to scare her away. It's a high wire on which I walk, so I opt to play it chill.

> **Me:** Hey, I hope you're not planning on ignoring me for a lifetime. Still missing you.

I hit send, take a seat on the bed, and wait. A spark of hope strikes when I see that she still has her read receipts on her phone turned on. She's read it, but that ember wanes when minutes pass with no response.

Going back and forth, I debate whether I should just go knock on her door. The last thing I want to do is put her in an awkward position. I mean . . . if she were interested in talking to me, she would simply talk to me. But there's an urgency inside that I can't ignore. The last time I saw her, she was battered and bleeding, and I have to know, even after all this time, that she's safe and that Caleb isn't still in the picture. The thought of that piece of ass shit negates all hesitation, and I'm out of here.

With my keys in hand, I head down to my car and make the short drive over to her condo building. A rush of nerves wreak havoc as the elevator ascends, and when I'm standing in front of her door, I can't get my damn hands to stop shaking. Maybe it's uncertainty that has me so unsettled, but I don't rest on it for too long before I knock.

Restless are the feet beneath me, and when the door opens, I'm surprised to see a guy around my age answer.

Who the fuck is this new dipshit?

"Can I help you?" he asks when I don't say anything.

"Sorry, man. Is Kate here?"

His brows furrow. "Who?"

"Kate," I repeat. "Is she here?"

Slowly, he shakes his head, and when I peer over his shoulder and see that none of the furniture is the same, I realize she no longer lives here.

"You got the wrong place, man."

"Do you know the girl who used to live here?"

"No."

I take a step back, shut out once again. "Sorry to bother you."

"No worries," the guy says as I walk back to the elevators.

The drive home seems much longer than the drive there as I wade through the swarm of questions and confusion. All it took was the mere mention of her name to take me right back to a year ago and all the moments before. Never has a girl, or anyone for that matter, been able to get to me like she did. It took no effort for the two of us to fall into a friendship. Shit, Kate was able to get me to open up in ways no one else has managed to do. Not that I exposed much, but what little I did bonded us.

It wasn't until she got together with Caleb that I noticed the tug in my chest that I couldn't get rid of. As time passed, that feeling became more and more tangible in the most puzzling way. Maybe it was my manifesting anger toward her boyfriend or the unspoken awareness that something wasn't right. I don't know, but the sensation is back and more ferocious than before.

In the time it takes me to return to the condo, defeat has morphed into anger, and I walk straight to Micah's room.

"Where is she?"

Ady's mouth gapes when she sits up.

"I went to her condo, but she doesn't live there anymore."

"Trent—"

"You said you were at her place today."

Micah picks up the remote and turns the television off. "You went over there?"

There's no time for me to respond before Ady tells me, "When I said reach out to her, I didn't mean go over there. I told you she needs space."

"But she's ready to be around *you*?" I press when I step deeper into the room. "Come on, Ady. Just tell me where she lives."

"Why don't you try calling her?"

"Why are you being so secretive?"

"Dude, easy," Micah says when my voice sharpens, but I don't expect him to understand where I'm coming from.

"I'm not being secretive." Her tone matches mine as her eyes intensify. "Just leave her alone."

Leave her alone? What the fuck?

"Stop hounding her, man," Micah says in defense of Ady, who has tears building in her eyes. "What's your problem?"

"What's *my* problem?" I turn to Ady and throw it back to her. "What's *your* problem? Why won't you just tell me?"

"Because!" she snaps, her outburst shocking me. "I know how she feels right now."

"What's that supposed to mean?"

"Back off, Trent," Micah warns.

"No, tell me."

"Because someone hurt me too!" she shouts and then catches herself, pressing her lips together.

It's a punch to my gut.

"Fuck, Ady," I breathe regretfully. "I'm sorry."

"Dude, just get out."

I don't say another word, even though my conscience is telling me to go over to her and make things right. Instead, I turn on my heel, walk to the living room, and collapse onto the sofa.

I'm staring at the ceiling as things begin to crystalize from all angles, each one forming a clarity that's difficult to digest. My focus shifts to Ady as I go back in my head and recall how she secluded herself from everything and everyone for months after she came to Miami. It was an abrupt move on her part, and I'll never forget the day I walked in on her crying hysterically and looking at me as if I were a ghost.

There are so many instances that start making sense, and I have to wonder if Kate is now a reflection of who Ady used to be. If Kate is as unrecognizable as Ady was when she first moved here.

I feel sick to my stomach for how I just behaved—it isn't who I am, but this entire situation has me completely wound up. For years, I've been in my own world, living free with little to no care, all the while unable to see that the people who mean the most to me have been going through some serious shit.

Micah steps out of his room and shuts the door behind him.

"Dude, I'm sorry."

"What the fuck is wrong with you?" he questions when he walks over to me.

With a heavy sigh, I admit, "Honestly, I don't know." It's so out of my character to get riled up like that. "Is she pissed at me?"

"No, but today kind of dug up some shit for her, and she doesn't need your shit too." He picks up his backpack and slings it over his shoulders. "I have to get to class. Try to lie low, man."

"Yeah, I hear you."

But how can I lie low, knowing that I upset her? After Micah leaves, I make my way to his room and tap on the door.

"It's open," she says, and when I step in and catch sight of her splotchy face, I drop my eyes in shame.

"I'm an asshole," I say as I go over and sit next to her on the bed. "I'm sorry." I don't hesitate before I pull her in for a hug, and I'm relieved when she doesn't resist.

"It's okay. I'm sorry I yelled at you."

Drawing back, I look at the girl who has become a little sister to me in a sense, and silently berate myself for acting like a jerk.

"Was there something going on between you two?" she asks. "I've never seen you get so upset."

Shaking my head, I admit, "No. I just . . ." I'm at a loss for words, because I don't know how to make sense of whatever the fuck is going on with me. "I just care about her."

"I do too."

"I know. Can you at least tell me if she's okay?"

"It's hard to say. From the outside, she looked fine, I guess—too thin, but fine." Ady gives me a small smile. "I don't want to go behind her back and say things I doubt she wants me telling anyone."

"No, I get it," I respond. "I'm sorry."

"You don't need to keep apologizing. The whole situation is messed up, but I know she'll pull herself back together, she just needs time."

I get what she's saying, but it doesn't quell my pressing impulse to go find Kate, to see for myself that she's okay, and talk to her. Right now, it weighs so heavily on me that it aches. It's a foreign feeling I don't know what to do with or how to manage. Truthfully, it's damn near killing me to know she's close enough for Ady to see but still so far out of my reach, as if it's a personal rejection. But what pains me the most is the possibility that she's going through what Ady went through and that she's all alone. It's enough to breed an infestation of torment inside me.

KATE

W ARMTH SEEPS INTO THE PALMS OF MY HANDS AS I CRADLE MY cup of coffee. There's a comfort to be discovered while sitting in a coffee shop. The aroma of freshly ground coffee beans—smoky and nutty with a hint of vanilla—has the ability to make you forget what lies outside the doors. It's actually funny how a smell can alter your thoughts and emotions or wrap you in memories of the past, consoling you or upsetting you, possibly triggering you and forcing a physical reaction.

I've sat here in the student center, in this very spot, many times since freshman year, but today, I'm met with the glint of a silver lining—that glint being Ady. I've found myself leaning on her over the last two weeks, whether it be a text, a phone call, or asking her to meet me for coffee between classes. Ady asks for no explanations, no apologies, no details of the past whatsoever, and for that, I am so thankful for her presence in my life. It also makes me feel guilty for how intrusive I used to be with her . . . if only I had known. But even if I had, would I have understood?

"Hey, girl," she exhausts as she drops her bag on the floor and plops down in the seat across from me. "Sorry I'm late."

"Don't worry about it."

"Can I have a taste?"

I hand my drink over, and she takes a sip, closing her eyes in delight as she does. "I can wait while you order something."

She hands the paper cup back to me. "No, I'm fine. I'm trying to cut back on my caffeine. I got addicted to those energy drinks last semester."

"Those are the worst."

"Tell me about it, but my course load had me so stressed out. There weren't enough hours in the day," she says, and I nod in understanding. Even though I wasn't here, the online classes I was taking had me completely overwhelmed. "So, what's going on? What did you want to talk about?"

"Nothing really," I confess.

"You seriously had me run my butt all the way across campus for nothing? Girl, I thought you were in crisis mode." Her face is pinched in mock annoyance, and I laugh.

Most days feel as if I *am* in crisis mode, but surprisingly, today isn't one of them.

"For real, though, is everything okay?"

"Sometimes it's hard to be alone but not want to be around people at the same time." I shake my head. "I know it doesn't make any sense."

"It makes complete sense."

Her understanding is a relief. The last thing I want to do is try to dissect these unexplainable emotions that feel like a never-ending rollercoaster.

"Do you want to talk about it?"

"Not really."

"You know I'm always here for you if you ever change your mind."

"I know."

She gives a sympathetic nod before a smile starts to tug its way onto her lips. "You'll never believe what happened last night."

"What?"

"So, Micah and I were hanging out, while Trent was on the balcony, talking on his phone. When he came back inside, he left the door open and a damn mockingbird got into the condo."

"Are you serious?"

"The harder Micah tried to get the bird out, the more frantically it flew around."

I start laughing. "What did you do?"

"I was freaking out, running around and closing all the doors while Trent was completely worthless."

"What was he doing?"

"He was stoned, so all he could do was laugh. At one point, he literally offered the bird the freaking salute from *The Hunger Games*."

"Oh my god, that isn't even the same bird."

"I know!"

I'm laughing so hard I have tears in my eyes because I can picture this whole scenario, but beneath my laughter is a pinch of sadness. Last night while they were all dealing with this very comical situation, I was on my sofa beneath a cloud of depression until I fell into a night of fitful sleep.

"How did you get the bird out?"

"When Micah started cussing out Trent, Trent grabbed a broom and knocked the life out of the bird and destroyed the flat screen in our living room."

"Are you serious?"

"I can't make this stuff up," she says.

"So, the bird died?"

She nods. "And we have to buy a new television because he completely shattered the screen."

"That's crazy."

"Tell me about it."

I hold my smile until it pains me. As the moment of levity subsides and veers into something more lamenting, my lips drop. It's a shift I come across from time to time. I find pieces of life around me that grant me a sliver of joy, only to have it pass as quickly as dust in the wind. Ady gives me glimpses of my life before Caleb, and there's a longing to have that back again, but it's gone. There's too much space between then and now, and it's the now that has me trapped.

"He called me," I murmur out of the blue, and when I see her confusion, I clarify, "Trent."

With a slow nod, she says, "I know."

"You know? You told him I was back?"

"I told Micah, and he overheard."

Flushed with insecurity, I ask, "What did you say?"

"Nothing. I just told him that I ran into you and that we talked, but I didn't say about what, and Micah didn't ask. He isn't nosy like that."

"And Trent?"

She sighs. "I told him to give you time and maybe to reach out to you."

I fret because hanging out with Ady is one thing, but I'm not ready to face Trent—not after how I left him that night.

"Kate, I promise. There hasn't been anything for me to even say because you haven't told me anything."

She's right, but just being aware that Trent knows I'm back has me on edge.

"Can I ask you something?"

"Do I have a choice?" I ask with a slip of humor.

"Why won't you talk to Trent?"

Mindlessly, I pick at the cardboard sleeve on my coffee cup before pinching my eyes shut. "Because I'm embarrassed."

"He was upset," she tells me. "When he heard that I had seen you, he got really upset. I've never seen him like that before."

"Really?" I want to ask her if he was upset because she'd seen me and he hadn't or if he was upset that I was back.

"He went to your old condo, and when he found out you no longer lived there, he demanded that I tell him your new address."

"You didn't, did you?"

"No," she responds emphatically. "It ticked him off that I wouldn't. Even Micah was surprised by Trent's reaction."

I think about that night I snuck out of their condo, how he called me nonstop, and how I ignored him when he showed up at my door.

I felt horrible—I still do.

I can't even imagine what that did to him.

No doubt he was pissed, but the next day, he started calling again. That was when I blocked his number because I couldn't take it anymore. It was easier to just avoid that whole situation, so I did.

Still, there were times I missed him. Trent was my friend, and I carried so much guilt for how I threw it all away with no explanation. There was so much regret for never thanking him for getting me away from that party and helping me, and eventually, I unblocked his number. I told myself that, if he were to contact me, I would respond, but he never did. Each day that passed, I became more and more sure that he had given up on me, not that I expected him to still be trying to call. Then, when he does call me, I'm too chicken to pick up.

"He genuinely cares about you," she adds after a long pause, and I care about him too.

"I'm just not ready."

She lets out a breathless chuckle I can't ignore.

"What?"

"I remember telling Micah the same thing, how I wasn't ready to face the truth of my situation," she says before looking right into my eyes. "He said I would never be ready, but that I couldn't let that stop me from trying."

"That's a lot easier said than done."

"I know," she says, and I wait for the *but* that never comes, and I appreciate her not pushing.

When Ady has to leave for her next class, I decide to take a drive to clear my head before going back to my place. It's difficult to be here with no distractions from my thoughts, and I've been going stir crazy lately. Tonight is no different. Dinner passed a while ago, but there's no point in feeding this misery of mine, so I skipped eating, opting to do what I swore I never would.

Sitting in bed with my laptop open, I take a hit off my pen to relax before logging into my social media account and typing in Caleb's name. I know better than to be doing this, but I can't help myself. Nights are lonely, and all I have to hold on to are the memories that still live so vibrantly inside me.

Vibrancy snuffs when I see the first photo in his feed.

My hands turn to ice, and it's heartbreak all over again when I look at the girl on his arm and the beaming smiles they both wear as they stand on the red carpet at some event. I would read the caption, but I can't move my eyes away from his face.

He's just as perfect as always, and the girl next to him is perfection too. She's nothing like me. Her brown hair is flawless, tucked in a low bun at the nape of her neck. Poised and proper, she's everything his parents would expect.

I was never good enough for them, and Caleb knew it. All of us did.

After closing the lid to the computer, I pick up my cell and tap on his name to text him, but what do I say? Would it even matter?

I wonder if he's already fallen in love with her. I'm sure he has, and I'm sure she doesn't let him down and make him hit her the way I always did.

I don't want to cry, so I take another hit to dull the misery brewing underneath my ribs. It's a storm filled with sadness, anger, and jealousy that kicks my self-esteem behind the knees. How is it that he's moved on when I'm still suffering?

One question breeds two more in its wake, and before I lose all control and break down, I shoot a message to Ady.

Me: Just saw a photo of Caleb with a girl.

With another pull off my pen, I'm taken from chill to completely stoned.

Ady: I'm coming over.

I try to text her back, but my head refuses to work in conjunction with my fingers, and I can't type anything out correctly.

Damn it.

I decide to call her instead, and after only one ring, she answers.

"Hey. How are you?"

"It's cool. I'm cool. I mean . . . Shit, what?"

"Are you high?"

Closing my eyes, I drop my head back against the pillow I'm propped against, but my equilibrium is thrown off. It has me on a tilt-a-whirl, forcing me to open my lids to regain my balance. But was I even off balance?

"Are you there?" she asks.

"Wait, what were we talking about?"

"I asked if you were high, but it's obvious that you are."

"I mean . . . maybe a little."

Then I hear Micah in the background asking, "Who are you talking to?"

"Kate."

"Don't tell him!" I snap. "Oh my god, now he knows."

"He already knows we talk, girl." She starts laughing. "How much did you smoke?"

"My life suuuucks," I whine.

"It doesn't. Just take it easy, I'll be over in a bit."

With that, she hangs up, and I realize I totally forgot to tell her not to come over, which was the whole point of my calling. Before any more of this high sets in, I hop out of bed and unlock the front door. I'm so blasted, and I'm grateful for the relief it brings. I used to have a higher tolerance, but when Caleb asked me to stop, I did with no questions asked. I didn't pick the stuff back up until a few weeks ago.

After a while, a knock sounds, and I call out, "It's open."

"I could've been a crazed killer," Ady scolds when she lets herself in. "You didn't even ask who it was."

"At least they would've put me out of my misery."

"Ha ha. Not funny." She walks over to where I'm lying on the couch and stares down at me. "Open your eyes."

"They are open," I tell her.

"Is this what you've been doing all afternoon? Getting high?"

Slowly, I sit up with a groan. "No."

"Uh-huh. So, who's this girl?"

I stand and drag myself into the bedroom as she follows. Flopping down on my bed, I hand over the laptop. "Open it and see for yourself."

She sits next to me, lifts the lid, and after a second, she asks, "Why are you trolling his social media?"

Cocking my head, I confess, "Because I'm a loser."

"Do you know who she is?"

I shake my head. "She's pretty."

"No, I'm not going to let you do this to yourself." She closes the laptop and sets it aside.

"You think he loves her?"

"Kate, stop."

"Do you know he deleted all of our pictures?"

"You can't do this," she says gently but firmly. "You can't live in the past."

"I know it's been a year, but I can't believe he's already with someone else."

"What does it even matter? she stresses. "You're moving on."

"Am I? Because to me, it feels like I'm stuck."

"I know it feels like you are. It might even feel like you're drowning, but I assure you, you aren't."

A sadness so deeply rooted inside me exposes itself, and my throat tightens in its presence.

"You're doing exactly what you should be doing," she says, adding on the sly, "Aside from stalking him on the internet. But that's beside the point."

"I don't feel like I'm doing anything."

"You came back," she states firmly. "That's a huge step, but you need to start letting go of him."

The thought doesn't sit well with me.

"I'm not sure I know who I am without him," I reveal, my voice softening under the weight of gloom.

"I think you do. I think you're just scared."

I am. I'm terrified, and I'm not even sure of what, but the fear is there. There's a mountain of emotions I need to work through, but I don't know where to start or how to begin.

"I still love him," I confess shamefully because I shouldn't care about him at all after what he did to me.

"I know you do, but this won't last forever."

Rolling my head back with a heavy sigh, I breathe, "I hate this."

"Come on," she says, taking me by the arms to get my attention. "Look at yourself. You don't see him hiding away, and I seriously doubt he's moping around like this, so you shouldn't be either."

I lean to the side and tip over. Lying on the bed, I drape my arm over my forehead with a whiny, "Why did I even get involved with a guy? I knew better."

"We all do things we know better than to do. That's life. But, if you really want to start moving past this, the first thing you need to do is unfollow him and, if you haven't already deleted his number from your phone, you need to do that as well."

Slipping my arm off my face, I give her a look that screams *are you crazy?*

"I'm serious. I had to do the same thing when it came to my ex. I held on to him for far too long, but if I hadn't let him go, I never would've fallen in love with Micah."

"Micah loves you so much," I mumble. "It makes me sick."

Ady rolls her eyes. "You're blasted."

"I know." I giggle as I reach out for her hand so she can pull me up. "It's better than sitting around crying, right?"

"I wouldn't know. I've never tried it."

My mouth falls. "Are you serious? You've never gotten high?" She shakes her head.

"But you live with two stoners. Hell, you're dating one."

"Doesn't mean I partake."

"Like, never?" I ask, shocked that she's more straitlaced than I thought.

"I'm too scared of not being in control," she reveals, and there's something in her expression that tells me this most likely stems from whatever it was she went through.

The last thing I want to do is make her feel uncomfortable, so I let it drop. I have no clue what she's suffered, but if it's anything like what I'm coming out of, she doesn't need my judgment.

Plus, I know what it feels like not to have control. How quickly I would lose it when Caleb got angry. There wasn't a thing I could do or say to stop his rage once he lost his temper. I've never felt a greater love than when I was with him, but at the same time, I've never felt as much terror. My fear ran rampant, but I still stayed, and I've spent a lot of time trying to make sense of that. Logic tells me I should've left the first time he put his hands on me in anger, but I didn't—I cared for Caleb too much to turn my back on him.

But eventually, I did.

Maybe the reason seeing that picture hurts so much is because it's proof that he has finally turned his back on me as well—on our love.

"I can't do it," I say when I pick up the laptop and hand it over. "You want me to?"

I nod and then sit and watch as she removes him from my friend's list, and when I say, "The phone too," she grabs my cell and deletes his contact information. If it weren't for the pot, I'd be in tears, but I remind myself that I still have the picture of Caleb and me tucked in the drawer of my nightstand. If I need him, he's still there.

Five

KATE

"What the hell was I thinking?" I mutter under my breath as I stare at Caleb's profile screen that shows nothing but a message box that reads: This account is private.

If I had been straight that night, I never would have given her permission to delete him from my friend's list. I can't take it back and send him another request because then I would look like a psycho ex-girlfriend. He doesn't need to know my craving to cyber-stalk him and his new girlfriend.

It's the weekend, and I have nothing to do. I would hit the beach and kill time in the water, but that would put me at risk of running into old friends and their curious eyes. Instead, I sit around my condo as the walls slowly close in on me.

A month has passed since I moved back, and although Ady has been a huge source of support, I worry my neediness for her company might start to annoy her, so I try to keep an appropriate distance. It's difficult to be alone, the space grants freedom for my mind to roam into dark territories.

All I have is time.

Time to think, time to dissect, time to question.

Time to examine my own judgment.

Lately, I've been asking myself why I didn't leave him and why I was okay with him putting his hands on me. The answer comes quickly and is wholly unsatisfying: I loved him. It makes me wonder if it comes so quickly because it's the easiest answer. And if it's the easiest answer, does that mean it's the shallowest, and if it's the shallowest, is it meaningless?

It's a turnstile of questions that cause my head to spin so rapidly that it's impossible for me to think straight.

I'm going insane.

Loving Caleb was tumultuous—extraordinary on the hips of a hurricane. We could've devastated worlds with the way we loved each other, churning and bursting inside vicious winds—like a disaster.

And then another question reveals itself: Am I confusing disaster with love?

Shoving my laptop to the side, I crawl out of bed and exchange it for the couch. I find the remote and turn the television on to some random daytime movie I'm not the least bit interested in, but it serves to numb my thoughts, and I zone out.

Halfway paying attention, I'm yanked out of my reverie when someone knocks. I shut the television off before walking over to the door and pushing onto my tiptoes to see through the peephole. Trent is on the other side.

I draw back as my heart pounds loudly in the silence of the room.

Another round of knocking needles my anxiety, and with my hands pressed against the door, I slowly lean in and take another look, noticing the scruff he now wears on his face. I wait for him to leave, but he isn't budging.

"Kate," he says, his voice puncturing through the delicate fibers of my heart. "I know you're home, I heard the TV."

Shit!

"You can't keep avoiding me."

Resting my forehead against the door, I stare at the floor as my stomach knots.

I'm not ready to face him.

Opening my mouth, I hope to inhale courage, but there isn't any to be found, and when I speak, my voice trembles. "I can't do this right now."

I look through the peephole again and find his head is down and his hands are braced on either side of the door. He appears to be angry, but when he looks up, there are lines of sadness etched across his forehead.

"How did you even find where I live?"

"I stole the address from Ady's phone," he reveals.

She should really put a password on her cell.

"Come on, Kate. Let me in."

His words plead gently, tugging on my emotions. There's a desperation in his tone that moves my hand to the lock. I hesitate and then turn it. The click is loud enough for him to hear, and when his arms drop at the invitation I cowardly gave him, I take a few steps back.

A second passes, and when he opens the door and comes inside, a swarm of chaos combusts inside my chest. The door closes, and all I can do is stare at him. It's funny how a year can change someone. Along with the scruff, his hair now hangs below his ears, and the muscles roped along his shoulders and arms are more defined. But the one constant are his distinctive dual-colored eyes—one hazel, one blue.

They're soft as they scan over my face, eliciting everything I felt from the last time I saw him. Flashes of horror from that night cripple my heart: Caleb slamming his knuckles into my face, Micah and Brody attacking him, Trent rushing me out of the house as everyone stares in horror. It's a night I force myself not to think about, a memory I've fought hard to bury but haven't been able to.

Trent takes a step toward me, and fear causes me to take a step away. He takes another; so do I. Panic has me turning my back to him as my feet stumble beneath me, but before I can get away, he wraps his arms around me from behind, hugging me close to his chest. The touch is profound and too much for me to handle. Out of nowhere, all the walls I've worked carefully to construct around me start to crack.

The pressure mounting inside me becomes too much, and I grip tightly on to his forearms that are bound against my chest. His head falls to the side of mine, and no matter how hard I fight to keep myself from crying, I choke on my pent-up anguish and break. Tears fall, and when I slump over, he holds me tighter. His chest vibrates against my back with such intensity it scares me. I don't know what it is he's feeling—anger would be my best guess.

I'm not ready to face the consequences of my actions, but I don't have a choice when he softly asks, "Why did you leave my bed that night?"

My head shakes because I know he won't understand.

"Where did you go?" he continues, the strain in his voice cutting through old wounds.

"Trent, please."

"You went back to him, didn't you?" His heavy breaths mingle with my soft whimpers. "Just put it to rest for me and tell me the truth."

I shake my head, and when he sighs in relief, I jerk from within his hold. His arms release me, and I quickly step away.

"Talk to me, Kate."

I run my hands along my cheeks, collecting tears before I finally turn to face him. My shoulders sink in humiliation, but I take a second to look into his eyes, to really look into them, and when

I do, I can't find a glint of anger or judgment or condemnation over this whole situation. "Aren't you mad at me?"

"Mad? Why would I be mad at you?"

I'm stunned because I assumed his reaction to be completely different from what he's giving me. "Because I ran from you."

"I've been fucking worried," he admits as he steps closer, but this time, I don't move away or try to escape. "You vanished on me."

Tears resurface, weakening my cheap façade and spinning him into swirls of watercolor. "I'm sorry," I weep, and when he gathers me into his arms again, I go freely.

His hand cups the back of my head, pressing me close to his heart, which beats fiercely against my ear, and I cry. We stand in the center of my living room as I try to make sense of it all, but there's no sense to be made out of this.

His touch is too much, too forgiving and too understanding, and I can't take it. I step out of his arms before walking over to the sofa and taking a seat. Trent remains standing, looking at me as if he's waiting for me to speak.

"I don't know what you want me to say."

Running a hand through his hair, he asks. "Why were you ever with him?"

The air I breathe thickens with the stench of shame while a tear slips between my lips, its bitterness swallowing me whole.

"Because," is all I give, my voice trembling in meekness. Perhaps there will come a day when I'll be able to trust him with my truth, but I'm not ready. I may never be ready.

And yet, there's a part of me that wants to confess everything just to free myself of it.

He walks over and sits next to me, imploring, "Because why?"

Doubting he'll drop this, I go ahead and break off a piece of the truth. "Because I loved him."

He exposes the anger I knew existed. His eyes burn with it, and his jaw flexes before he grits out, "He fucking hit you, Kate. He had you pinned to the ground with his knee jammed into your spine—"

"Stop."

"He hit you in the face—"

"Stop!" I beg, my hands fist against the tingling spikes of anxiety as he throws haunting reminders at me. "You don't even know what you're talking about."

"Are you seriously going to defend that dickfuck?" he fumes. "And you're right, I don't know what I'm talking about because I know that what I saw that night was only a *fraction* of what he put you through."

My head falls into my hands as painful memories carve their existence down my cheeks, leaving me with scars that won't ever let me forget the nightmare I lived. But those nightmares were embedded between moments of pure love.

His hand presses softly against my back. "I'm sorry."

"You act like you know everything," I accuse when I raise my head. "Like you're so perfect."

"I never claimed to be perfect."

Sadness hits steel and recoils into anger. It's a shift so sudden that there's no time to second-guess myself before I'm lashing out and telling him, "Then why are you sitting here, acting as if you didn't have a hand in any of this?"

"What are you talking about?"

"You knew you were provoking him, even when I told you to back off, you kept pushing. You made everything worse!"

"Fuck that," he counters. "Are you seriously blaming me for what that bastard did?"

"I'm just sick of you acting like you have all the answers when you don't have a clue!" I yell and then stand because I need distance from him. "You think you're so much better?"

Trent lurches off the couch, heated and defending, "Do I think I'm better than the guy who beat the shit out of you? Yes! Yes, I think that. No fucking question about it. He's a pussy and can lick my nine for all I fucking care!"

"Get out!" I shout. With my emotions running on high, overflowing and spewing out in animosity, I stalk over to the door, open it, and yell, "I'm done."

He stands, as if to test me, but I'm too tired for his games.

"Leave!"

This time, he sees the ferocity in my eyes and can hear it in my voice—hell, it's so overpowering he can probably taste it. With no more to say, he stalks across the room, right past me, and out of my condo. When he slams the door behind him, all I'm left with are more crumbled pieces and a pounding heart that sends me straight to the floor.

Six

KATE

"So, I talked to Micah, and he offered to let us use the reservations he made for tonight," Ady tells me over the phone.

"What are you talking about?"

"Girls' night!"

Looking down at my mismatched sweats, I shake my head. "No way." My hair is in a ratty bun, and I'm already halfway through the red heart-shaped box of chocolates that I picked up from the drug store last night. No joke, there are tiny paper wrappers everywhere.

It's utterly pathetic.

"Oh, come on."

"I'm busy," I tell her, not bothering to come up with a better excuse because there's no way in hell am I going out tonight.

"No, you're not."

"I have to clean my condo."

"You're a neat freak."

"Ady, no!" I stress, pushing the nearly empty box of Valentine's chocolates off my lap. "This is not the night I want to go out."

"This is the perfect night to go out," she counters with too much pep in her tone. "It'll be fun! No boys at all," she adds as if that will be enough to tempt me. It isn't. "You can't leave me hanging, girl. I just let my boyfriend off the Valentine's Day hook tonight. He's already made other plans with his friends."

"Tell him you changed your mind. He loves you; he'll drop his plans in a heartbeat to take you out."

"No." She's stern and demanding now. "You're going out, so be ready by seven. I'll pick you up. Reservations are at eight," she states and then hangs up before I can argue.

I rush to call her back.

One ring is all it takes for her to answer. "You better look fierce," is the only thing she says before hanging up on me once more.

Irritated but secretly humored, I call again, only to receive another dose of her sass. "Nails, hair, hips, heels."

"What?"

"Play it, girl. I'll be over later."

"Ady—"

Another hang up.

"Ugh." I groan as I toss my phone into the sea of chocolate wrappers. Clearly, this past year has served Ady well, because I've never seen this side of her—feisty and a hell of a lot more confident. I wonder if this is who she has always been, but whatever she went through stifled it.

It brings me joy to see her so light when she used to be so hidden and uptight. It's that very thought that tells me to cut my shit and give her what she wants. She deserves a fun night out, and maybe I do too.

Despite my self-inflicted tummy ache, I get off the couch, clean up the candy wrappers, and turn off the crappy romance movie I was watching before dragging my pitiful self to the bathroom. One look in the mirror has me cringing. I literally have a string of caramel hanging off my chin.

After a long shower, I do my hair and makeup, going the extra mile—because, why not? It's been forever since I've gone out with a girlfriend, and the whole process of pulling myself together has me excited.

Sure, it's Valentine's Day, the worst day ever to be single, and an even worse day to try to mend a broken heart, but I'm ready to put all that aside for the night. I add another layer of mascara to my lashes before turning up the music I have playing throughout the condo. The bass thumps as I walk over to my closet, and I dance along to the song.

As the music feeds my energy, I pull a short, sparkly dress off a hanger and toss it onto my bed before selecting a pair of strappy heels.

By the time Ady knocks on my door, I'm still in my robe, but I run to let her in anyway.

With an over-the-top strut, she enters my living room, doing a slow turn to show off her deep purple dress, which has a nice swing to the skirt, and I laugh. "Damn."

"I know, right?" When she notices my bathrobe, her enthusiasm drops. She motions her hand out with a snarky, "This wasn't what I was talking about when I said fierce."

"I was just about to change."

She follows me into the bedroom, and when she sees my dress lying out, she gives a spirited, "Yes!"

I untie the robe and toss it aside while Ady leans against the doorjamb. "So, what have you been doing all day?"

"You don't want to know." After stepping into the dress, I shimmy it up my body as I add, "It was a depressing day."

"Well, we're going to turn that around."

"Promise me there will be no talk of boys tonight." I walk

over to her, turn so she can zip my dress for me, and then take a seat on the bed to slip my heels on. "I think I've reached my limit."

"You have my word."

Good. The last thing I want to discuss is boys. I know Ady would never mention Caleb because she always steers clear of him unless I bring him up first, but Trent is another story. She will ask about him, but honestly, there's nothing to tell. I haven't spoken to or heard from him since I threw him out two weeks ago. I figured he would've reached out, but he hasn't, and I don't blame him. I was way harsh, but after I had time to calm down, I realized how out of line I was. Still, I haven't had the guts to apologize, even though I should.

"You ready?" she asks.

"Where are we going that we need an hour to get there?"

"South Beach."

"This isn't like a super romantic place, is it?"

"No," she responds.

"Thank God."

"Wait," she says, holding her hand up to stop me from walking out of the room.

I look down the front of my dress to see what's wrong. "What is it?"

She points to my neck. "You're not wearing that."

My hand comes to my collarbone and the diamond necklace Caleb surprised me with nearly a year and a half ago. I had forgotten it was there because I never take it off.

"It's pretty, but, no."

Of course, she's right. Just because I miss Caleb, I don't need him dangling around my neck tonight, knowing he's most likely out with his new girlfriend, spoiling her rotten the way he used to spoil me.

I walk over to my dresser, unfasten the clasp, and drop the delicate necklace into my jewelry box.

"Better?"

"Much." She smiles. "Let's go."

We hop into her car, and she turns on the stereo before we start driving north to South Beach. After we battle the traffic, we finally cross the bridge that takes us straight into the glitzy nightlife that's second to none. Glamorous is an understatement because, when the sun sets along this coast, bikinis and flip-flops are replaced with the trendiest designer labels. I'd be hard-pressed to pull off the looks worn here in any other part of the country, but no one even bats an eye. There's no such thing as being overdressed.

This is home to the hottest and most infamous nightclubs, and I'm shocked that Micah would bring a girl like Ady here on a Valentine's Day date, considering how reserved she normally is, but when she turns off A1A, I realize we aren't partying at all.

"You told me we weren't going anywhere romantic."

She grins as she pulls up to Casa Tua. "Don't complain."

The valet opens my door, takes my hand, and helps me out of the car. We walk into the restaurant, and while Ady checks in with the hostess, I do my best to ignore all the lovely-dovey couples enjoying their expensive meals. I'm only slightly relieved when the hostess leads us outside to the secluded lush garden that glows beneath the many lantern-lit trees. This is the epitome of romance and only marginally better than the main dining room.

"You lied," I whisper from across the small, intimate, candle-lit table.

"How was I supposed to know?"

She's evil as she grins because she knew exactly what she was dragging me into.

"I'm going to need a drink," I mutter when I pick up the wine list. "I can't believe Micah brings you to places like this."

"Oh please," she says with a roll of her eyes. "Like Caleb never wined and dined you and took you to red-carpet events."

All it takes is the mere mention of his name for me to feel the tightening in my chest, but she's quick to backpedal. "I'm sorry. I didn't mean to bring him up."

"It's okay." I pick up the water goblet and take a sip. "To be honest, I always felt really out of place."

"Understandable," she notes. "And Micah doesn't usually take me to places like this. I'm honestly kind of shocked he had booked us dinner here."

"I hope he wasn't upset that you bailed on him."

"Actually, it was his idea."

She's lucky to have someone like Micah. I've always known him to be a great guy, and I envy their relationship. It's something I've yet to find for myself. "By the way, we suck at the no-boy talk."

Our waitress stops by to take our drink orders, and when she returns with my wine and Ady's iced tea, she tells us about the night's specials, which we both decline before ordering off the main menu.

The two of us go on to talk about the classes we are taking this semester and our distaste for our digital marketing professor, and before long, the waitress is back with our food.

"Here you go," she says to Ady when she sets down the honey-seared duck that looks so good my mouth waters.

"That looks amazing."

As my food is placed in front of me, she compliments, "Your girlfriend has excellent taste. It's one of our more popular dishes."

Ady blinks wide eyes at me and I have to hold back my laughter.

"Is there anything else I can get the two of you?"

"No," Ady answers, clearly about to lose her composure. "Everything looks great."

As our waitress disappears back inside, Ady looks at me. "Did I hear her right?"

"Hear what?"

She stretches her neck toward me to get my attention.

"What?"

"She thinks we're lesbians." Sitting back, she quickly scans around the garden, only to catch a couple of people looking our way as if we're the cutest couple in this place. "Oh my god. The people here think you're my girlfriend."

"Is that a problem? What . . . I'm not good enough to be your girlfriend?"

"News flash, we're not gay."

I drop my fork loud enough to garner a few side-glances before reaching across the small table and taking her hand. "Am I not your type?" But it's when I kiss her knuckles that I can't contain my laughter.

"Oh, stop." She yanks her hand away. "I guess it's better to be mistaken as a lesbian who has a date on Valentine's Day than to be single."

"Ouch. Insulting much?" I pick my fork back up with a smug smile on my lips. "You should be proud to have a girl like me on your arm. You should be showing me off."

She shakes her head, before taking a bite of her duck. "This is good." She moans in delight.

"You're telling me. I've never eaten lamb this delicious before." I then cut a piece. "Want a taste?"

She nods as she finishes chewing and waits for me to put it on her plate, but instead, I hold the fork out to her with a smirk.

"What are you doing?"

"Waiting for my baby to take a bite," I tease.

"You need to stop with all that."

"Oh, come on. Don't make me beg."

Pressing her lips together, she admonishes me with a glare before leaning in and sliding the lamb off the fork with her mouth as I giggle.

"Payback is coming," she threatens as she chews. "Just you wait."

"Feisty."

"Speaking of feisty, I'm curious . . . have you ever kissed a girl?"

"Just once," I tell her.

"Spill it. All the dirty details."

"There are no dirty details, perv." I dig my fork into the risotto and scoop a little up. "When I was thirteen, I was at a slumber party with bunch of friends. We were playing truth or dare and someone dared me to kiss one of the other girls. That's all."

"And?" she asks, elongating the word.

"And what?"

"Any tongue action?"

"No, I was thirteen," I defend. "I wasn't kissing anyone with my tongue. It lasted all of a split-second."

"That's a disappointing story." She takes a sip of her tea.

"Okay, your turn. Tell me all about your girl-on-girl kiss."

"Never had one."

"Are you serious? Then why are you making fun of me?"

"For the same reason you're acting like I'm your girlfriend. Because it's funny."

Our banter continues through the dessert course, which I insist we share just to play up our supposed romance. As we devour the orange crème brûlée, I feel an overwhelming sense of gratitude toward Ady. She didn't have to give up this special night with Micah for me, but she did, and it was completely selfless on her part.

I didn't even want to come out tonight, but I'm so glad I did. I needed to feel human again, and if only for a moment, to let go and smile. Somehow, she's managed to help me see that I'm still the girl I was two years ago and that maybe I'm not beyond repair.

"I really appreciate you forcing me to come out tonight," I tell her as I set my spoon down. "I didn't know how much I needed this."

"I needed it too. It's been a long time since I've had this much fun with a girlfriend."

"Tell Micah *thank you* for letting me have you for the night."

"Sorry to interrupt," our waitress says when she stops by our table. "I just wanted to let you know that your dinner has been taken care of."

Ady looks shocked. "By who?"

"A gentleman by the name of Micah."

"Thank you," Ady tells her, and when the lady walks away, Ady pulls out her cell to shoot Micah a text, thanking him for the lovely meal and adding my sentiments as well.

She takes the last bite before asking, "Do you feel like you're getting any closer to coming over and seeing the guys?"

After my fight with Trent, I have no idea how to answer that question. All I can do is give her a shrug. "I don't know, but it's something I really want to work toward."

She gives a reassuring smile. "You'll get there."

I need to hang on to her optimism because I miss this feeling of normalcy, of just being me and having fun and laughing with a good friend. Ady is the only thing that's keeping me grounded at this point. With her soft strength, she's showing me there are possibilities within the impossible, and although there are times I want to run back to West Palm Beach and hide, I'm starting to find morsels of courage to keep moving forward. So, that's what I plan to do.

Seven

KATE

"Hey, sweetheart," my father greets when he answers his phone. "How's everything going?"

Meandering around my kitchen, I pull a bowl down from the cabinet and grab a spoon. "Good. I've been spending time with Ady, and I'm starting to feel settled in."

"Was it as difficult as you were anticipating?"

"Not really. Ady made it easier," I tell him as I open a box of cereal and pour myself a bowl before getting the milk.

"I'm happy you two were able to get your friendship back on track."

"Yeah, me too."

"And how is school?"

Setting my breakfast down at the bar, I take a seat and respond, "It's been busy, but I'm managing As and Bs."

"When are midterms?"

"In two weeks, but I'm not too stressed about them. My course load is pretty manageable this semester." I then shove a spoonful of cereal into my mouth.

"Are you still coming home for spring break?"

"Uh-huh," I mumble as I chew.

"Have you been getting in some time on the water?"

He asks this every time we talk, and I respond with the same, "Not yet."

He sighs into the phone. "What's going on, Kate? Whenever I ask you about surfing, you give me the same push off," he says. "You just told me that school isn't too time-consuming right now, so what gives?"

"Nothing, I just haven't made it out."

"Surfing is your life, so I'm not buying that you can't carve out some time for it."

"Dad."

"Whatever it is that's keeping you out of the water, don't let it," he tells me. "Nothing is worth sacrificing the things that make you happy, you hear?"

"I know. How's mom doing?" I ask, attempting to bring the surf talk to an immediate halt.

Dad chuckles. "You really need to work on your segues."

I laugh as I shovel another spoonful of cereal in my mouth.

"You enjoying your breakfast?" he teases over the loud crunching. "Why do you always call me when you're eating?"

"Because I know how much it annoys you," I joke.

"I have to get back to work, and you should get back into the water."

"Yeah, yeah."

We say our I love yous, and after I hang up, I debate whether I should suck up my hesitations and hit the beach. My dad is right—this is the longest I've ever gone without being in the water. It's the first of March, and when I bring up the surf report on my phone, it shows to be a pretty decent day.

Looking over my shoulder, I eye my board, which is leaning against the wall by the sliding doors that open up to the balcony, untouched since the day I moved in here. I consider all the excuses

I've been using to avoid the very thing my father just pointed out—the one thing that brings me the most happiness.

I miss feeling happy.

Being a Tuesday morning, I doubt I would run the risk of seeing anyone I know, but the fear is still there. Going against what my gut is telling me to do, which is to stay cooped up in this condo, I decide to drive to one of the small local beaches and check it out. Even if it winds up being nothing more than a drive-by, at least it's progress.

After I finish my breakfast, I rinse my bowl and load it into the dishwasher before throwing on a bikini. As I pack my surf bag and go through my old routine, I get a slight tingling of excitement. My father is right, I live for the rush of surfing and the peace it brings along with it. I even find myself smiling as I lug all my belongings down to the parking garage and load my hatchback.

Before I pull out of my spot, I grab my cell, take a selfie with my board hanging out the back window, and text it to my dad. As I'm on my way over to the often-empty beach, my father texts me back.

Dad: That's my girl.

I breathe a huge sigh of relief when I turn my car into the small parking lot and find the place completely deserted. Shutting off the engine, I look down toward the water, and suddenly, I realize how much I've missed coming out here. I can't believe I've gone so long without getting in the water because just being here fills me with a sense of empowerment. My fear was never of simply coming, it was of having to face everyone, but I do recognize that, although this isn't a huge step, it is still a step.

After shrugging on my long-sleeved rash guard, I toss my backpack over my shoulders and slide my board out from the hatchback. A smile creeps on my lips again when I hit the warm beach and my feet sink into the rough, shelled sand. It's a short distance to the water, and I find a spot to drop my things and prep my board. When I'm all ready to go, I tie my hair up and jog out into the ocean. Salt kisses my skin, and I'm at home as I paddle toward the rising sun. Alone within the water my soul feeds on, I ride the unobtrusive waves.

They are subtle and relaxing, exactly what I need after being absent for so long. Reacquainting myself, I enjoy everything I've been avoiding. My lungs fill with the sea air, and I catch another wave, popping up and gently falling down the smooth face that glides me effortlessly across the water until it dies and I'm forced to kick out and sink under the surface.

As the hour passes, storm clouds roll in from the south, which have the waves ramping up. I decide to call it a day, and as I start packing up my gear, a couple of cars pull into the lot. It isn't surprising that people are showing up. The promise of a storm always brings out the surfers, so it's good that I got my time in when I did.

After slipping out of my rash guard, I towel off, throw on an old T-shirt over my bikini, and head toward my car. As I'm loading my board, a rumble catches my attention, and when I look over my shoulder, I see a Jeep turning into the lot.

I toss my backpack through the opened hatchback window before getting in. The Jeep pulls around and parks one spot away on my left. When I glance over, my stomach coils when I see Trent in the driver's seat.

Shit.

I shove the key into the ignition and turn it, but my engine only gives a pitiful groan.

"You've got to be kidding me?" I mutter as I crank it again to the same result, and I know my car battery is dead.

Trent gets out of the Jeep and approaches my door.

This is exactly what I was hoping to avoid.

With my heart thumping, I take a rough swallow and slide down my window.

"Car won't start?"

Avoiding eye contact because I'm too cowardly to face him head-on, I respond with, "Battery is dead."

Thunder rumbles from overhead.

Without invitation, he opens my door and leans in across me to look at the gages. The back of his shoulder touches my chest, his over-grown hair brushes along my arm, and I swear my heart just lurched into my throat. It's been a month since I saw him, since we last spoke, since I threw him out of my condo. There has been so much strain between us, and I hate myself for all the damage I've done.

He turns the key, and nothing sounds this time. "It isn't the battery." When he draws back, putting space between us, he says, "You're out of gas."

Looking down at the fuel dial, I cringe. I didn't even notice that I was running low.

"Come on. There's a station down the street."

I cannot believe I'm stuck in this situation.

As he walks back to his Jeep, I reach behind my shoulder and pull my board over the front seats so I can close the rear window before locking my car. Raindrops are just beginning to fall as I slip into his passenger seat, but he doesn't move to kick it into reverse.

"Are we going?" I ask as his keys dangle from the ignition.

Leaning back against his seat, he stares at me, and I'm stuck staring at him. The pelting of the rain against the roof grows to an uncomfortable level that borders on torture.

"What are you doing?" I ask.

"Wondering when we're going to cut all this bullshit between us."

My head falls.

"I'm serious, Kate. I'm not taking you anywhere until we talk this out."

His voice holds an undeniable sincerity that touches upon a tender spot inside. There's so much I want to say, but I don't know how. Trent and I have always had an unexplainable tension within our friendship, something intangible but readily present, yet there's a closeness that's been there from the very beginning. Nothing between us has ever been simple, but that doesn't take away from the fact that the very tension that parts us also melds us.

"I'm sorry." It's as good of a place to start as any. After having time to calm down after our fight, I've been carrying around guilt for blaming him for Caleb's actions. It wasn't fair of me to put that on him. "I was out of line to accuse you of—"

"You were right," he interrupts, his eyes dropping as he does.

"I wasn't."

"I keep looking back, and I knew . . . I knew something was off with that guy, and when I saw him put his hands on you the first time . . ."

"Trent," I say, needing him to stop because I'm not ready to have this conversation. I doubt I'll ever be ready.

"I should have tried harder." His voice cracks, and he quickly turns away from me, looking out of his side window. "I could have done so much more."

The heaviness of his conscience fills the air around us, and I hate that he feels like any of this should weigh on his shoulders.

"I sat back and allowed that fucker to put you through hell because I was afraid that, if I came down too hard on you, you'd run. But you ran anyway."

My lids fall shut against the pain my actions have caused. I was foolish to believe that it only existed between Caleb and me, and I have been so blind that I haven't been able to see what it's done to Trent too. And if it's done this to Trent, what has it done to Ady and everyone else?

"This isn't your fault."

Slowly, he turns back to me with eyes glazed in burden, and it pierces through a pain so complex that I can't even begin to break it down into digestible pieces.

"I wasn't thinking straight," he reveals. "I had no idea how bad it was, and you're right, I ignored all your warnings and I made it worse."

"You didn't. I never should've blamed you for any of that," I tell him. "I'm the only one who needs to apologize. All the lies—" The words get stuck, choking me up, but I manage to force the rest of them out. "I could see how mad I was making you with every lie I told, and I'm so sorry."

"You think I'm angry over the lies?" he questions as if the idea is absurd. "I forgave all your lies the moment I knew what he was doing to you." He shifts to face me straight on before adding fervently, "I was never mad at you, Kate. *Never.*"

I take an agonizing swallow and hang my head, lost in a labyrinth of confusion and regret.

He then takes my hand in his, and with worry etched across his face, he asks, "You don't still talk to him, do you?"

I shake my head, and I can hear his sigh of relief. A part of me hates that everyone around me feels this way when I'm still so heartbroken—even after all this time. Even when I know I never should have been at all.

"There's so much I want to ask you—"

"Don't," I tell him.

"Have you talked to anyone about this?"

Again, I shake my head. "I can't."

He leans into me, bracing his elbow on the center console that separates us. There's a lot I want to ask him too. I want to know how he's been and how his mom is doing. I miss all the fun we used to have, and I'm scared we'll never get that back.

Running his thumb over my knuckles, he questions, "Have I fucked this up?"

My fingers tighten slightly around his hand, and I give him my honesty when I say, "No, but I'm worried that I have."

He slips his other hand behind my neck and pulls me closer to him. Resting my forehead against his shoulder, I bite the inside of my cheek to keep myself from crying because I feel so undeserving of his compassion. He should be mad at me, blame me, be appalled by me—by the deceitful woman I became when I was with Caleb. More than anything, he should be disappointed in me.

"You haven't," he assures.

"I'm so sorry." When I pull back and look at him, he shakes his head.

"You did nothing wrong. I'm the one who fucked up." His brows furrow, and I can see the regret he holds festering through his mismatched eyes.

"There's a lot I did wrong and a lot that I need to apologize for," I admit. "It's really hard for me though."

"Why?"

"Because it's humiliating."

"Look," he says as he tucks back a lock of my wet hair that's fallen out my hair tie. "If you don't want to talk about it, that's fine, but I don't want you to feel like you need to apologize to me, because you don't."

I appreciate him saying that, and if I could just move on and go back to how things used to be without having it constantly hanging over my head, I would appreciate it even more.

And as the storm rages on, pouring down so hard it obstructs everything around us, he folds his arms around me in a consoling hug I'm unworthy of, but I don't dare tell him that. He would dismiss the thought the moment I put it out there. So, I hold on to the hope that this is our turning point, and that mending this fracture between us will somehow help me untangle the knots of this nightmare. Because, no matter how much destruction I caused, I can still clearly see the parts of him I love—mostly his veiled sincerity. The gentle moments of purity . . . those are the parts I've missed the most.

Eight

KATE

"I SWEAR, THOSE LECTURES ARE GOING TO BE THE DEATH OF ME," Ady complains as we walk out of class.

"Tell me about it. The guy talks like a constipated robot."

"Thank God spring break is coming up," she says. "By the way, do you have any plans?"

"Nothing exciting; just going home for the week to lie low. You?"

"Micah and I were thinking about doing the same back in Tampa," she says as we walk across the lawn.

"Yeah, Trent mentioned possibly going back home too."

"So, how is everything between the two of you?"

"Good. We've hung out a couple of times since our talk at the beach." My phone vibrates from my backpack, and I pull it out to see Trent's name. "Speaking of the devil," I say before answering, "Hey."

"What's up? Where you at?"

"On campus. Just got out of class, why?"

"I wanted to talk to you about something."

"Give me a sec," I respond and then turn to Ady. "I'll catch up with you later, okay?"

"Yeah, no problem."

As we part ways, I head toward my next class and lift the phone back to my ear. "Sorry about that. So, what did you want to talk about?"

"A party."

"Trent." I sigh, not liking where this is going.

"Just hear me out before you turn me down," he says. "It's Brody's birthday."

I have yet to talk to Brody, and the longer I put it off, the harder it is for me to gear up to make that call. Still, it doesn't feel right that I've mended my relationships with both Ady and Trent, but not with him. So, to know that it's his birthday sends a wave of guilt through me.

"He's having a party tonight to celebrate," he adds.

"What kind of a party?"

"The kind he always throws."

Dragging my feet, I hesitate with a heavy, "I don't know."

"Come on, it's his birthday, and I kind of already promised that I would bring you."

"What? Why?"

"Because he's your friend," he states. "Stop harshing my mellow and say you'll come."

When I reach the building of my next class, I take a seat on the bench out front and try to calm the anxiety bubbling inside me.

"I'm not trying to be a buzz kill; I just haven't been out in a really long time," I tell him, hoping he understands the gravity of what he's asking me to do. The last party I went to ended in utter mayhem. It's been almost a year and a half since that night and, in many ways, I still haven't recovered from the devastation of it all.

"It's Brody."

"I know."

"He misses you," he adds, unintentionally throwing me more guilt. "Just make an appearance."

Truth is, I miss Brody too, and my not going would only add another nail into the coffin that holds our friendship, so I go against my gut and give in. "Okay, I'll go. But I'm not staying all night."

"I'm finally getting you off your log cutter!"

"Why do you have to be so gross?" I complain as I stand from the bench and make my way into the classroom.

"You know you love it. See you at Brody's!"

As the day passes, I find myself wrestling over tonight. In a way, I'm motivated to put another fear to rest, but fears are a huge battle for a girl like me. Cowering is easy and safe—I should know, I've been doing it for quite some time now. There's no doubt that, if I bail, Trent will be disappointed in me. Hell, I'll be disappointed in myself.

If anything, I need to show Brody that our friendship is worthy of me putting my issues aside for him. He was the first friend I made when I moved here my freshman year, and he deserves better than what I've been giving him, which is nothing. I turned my back on him . . . on everyone for that matter, and it wasn't right.

The sun set a while ago, and Trent just texted me to let me know that he's already at the party, so I message him back to let him know I'm on my way.

Despite all my unease, I head down to my car and make the drive to Brody's house, blasting music in an effort to drown out the thoughts that try to creep in. When I pull onto his street and see all the cars lining the curb, my anxiety kicks into full gear. It isn't like I didn't know there would be a ton of people here, but to see it, to actually be doing this, has me in a bit of a tailspin.

I'm able to find a spot that isn't too far out of the way, and as I walk along the sidewalk, I start getting flashbacks of the last party. Visions from that night filter in, and the closer I get to the house, the more my courage wanes. Thumping music echoes, and when I'm only a few houses down, I chicken out. The knots in my stomach twist too tightly. Turning on my heel, I start heading back to my car, feeling like a complete failure.

"Kate," Trent calls from behind me, and when I look over my shoulder, I see him jogging my way.

The wimp in me screams to run, but I'm not bold enough to do that. Instead, I stop in my tracks and stand with my head hanging while Trent catches up to me.

"Where are you going?"

In my defeat, all I give him is a shrug.

"You're not bailing, are you?"

I lift my arms and then drop them lifelessly.

"Come here," he says, taking my hand and pulling me over to the front stoop of the random house we're in front of. We sit on the steps before he says, "Talk to me."

"I don't know what to say."

Leaning forward, he clasps his hands together. "Why are you trying to leave?"

"Because . . ."

"Because why?"

Releasing an uncomfortable sigh, I admit, "Because I'm scared."

"Of what?"

"Of who'll be there," I tell him as I nervously fiddle with the delicate bracelet around my wrist. "It's embarrassing."

He shakes his head, refuting my words. "You have no reason to be. I doubt they even remember that night."

I give him a side glare. "You're full of shit."

Chuckling under his breath, he defends, "I'm not. I promise you. Trust me, every few days, there's new gossip or something else that catches everyone's attention. What happened that night was so long ago."

"It doesn't feel that long ago."

"But that's in your head, not theirs," he says. "And it isn't like you have to walk in alone; you have me."

I consider what he's telling me. The thing is that I've been trapped inside my head for so long that I've convinced myself that my thoughts mirror everyone else's. That if that night is still so vivid in my memory, then it's vivid in everyone else's too.

"Plus," he adds, "Brody will have my dick if he found out I let you bail."

He then holds out his hand, and despite all the reluctance in me, I go ahead and take it before he stands and pulls me up.

"You're worrying over nothing." He tries to assure me, but I find myself gripping his hand a little tighter the closer we get.

There're a few people standing outside the house, and when we get inside, the music is loud and the place is packed. Nervous about catching eyes, I keep my chin tucked down

"Come on," Trent hollers over all the noise.

I bump into people with every step I take, but my hand never leaves Trent's until we enter the kitchen. Looking up, I spot Brody on the opposite side of the island.

"Holy shit!" he exclaims loudly, holding his hands up in worship. "I thought Trent was talking out of his ass when he said you were coming."

His excitement to see me quells my nerves, and I smile as I walk over to his out-stretched arms.

"Hey, Brody."

He pulls me into a bear hug, whispering in my ear for no one else to hear, "Damn, girl, I've missed you."

So many words hit my tongue, but I'm too overwhelmed that

I don't know which to choose, so when he draws back, I simply smile up at him.

"You just made my whole fucking night."

"Well, I couldn't miss your birthday," I tell him as Trent hands me a plastic cup.

The two of them hold out their drinks, and when I raise mine, we toast the night. My intent is to take a sip, but I wind up gulping the vodka down because, damn, all this stress I've been dealing with today has taken its toll on me and I'm ready to take the edge off.

"Yeah," Trent encourages before grabbing the bottle to give me a refill.

The three of us hang out for a while, and Brody never once asks me where I've been or how I've been doing. And to my greatest relief, he also never mentions Caleb or anything that went down that night.

It feels like old times, and I start to think that maybe Trent was right, that I have built things up too high in my head. Finishing my second cup, I'm skirting the line between tipsy and drunk, and after dancing with Brody, I start working on my third.

Trent slides in close from behind as I dance by myself and leans in. "You having fun?"

Turning around, I stumble in my footing, and he laughs, answering for me, "Yeah, you're having fun."

It's at this point that the two of us start dancing in the middle of the room, surrounded by people I might recognize if their faces weren't all blurred together. When the song switches to one of my favorites, I throw my arms up, spilling half my drink down my arm and all over my top, but I don't care because I need this. Need the numbness from the alcohol, need the music to deafen my thoughts, and need the reassurance that, although Caleb destroyed me, he didn't destroy everything else around me.

In the throng of people, I feel entirely free as I dance with my best friend, tossing all my heartaches aside as we let loose. Sweat trickles down my spine, and out of nowhere, Trent scoops me up off the floor. With my free hand, I grip his shoulder as he smiles up at me. "You're fucking wearing me out."

"You're tired?"

"You've had me dancing all night."

He lowers me back down, and when my feet touch, I ask, "How long have we been here?"

"I don't know, but it's already after one."

"How is that possible? I'm only on my third drink," I shout over the music.

Trent laughs and tells me, "You're fucking wasted. You were on your third drink hours ago."

Looking down into my cup, I see double. "What number is this?"

"Fuck if I know. But you've been sucking them down like it's tit milk."

Laughter bursts out of me and tips me off balance, knocking me into his chest. He grabs on to my elbows to steady me and then leads me out of the room.

"Where are we going?"

"I'm sweating my dick off," he complains, and when he pulls me outside, we run into Brody, who's hanging out with a couple of familiar faces.

"You guys heading out?"

"Yeah, man," Trent tells him as they clap hands. "Kate's wasted."

"I can hear you."

"I'm glad you came," Brody says, giving me a side hug. "Am I gonna see you in the water any time soon?"

"I'll get her ass out there," Trent answers for me.

As I start to sway, he's quick to catch me before I fall down the steps.

"See you later," he tells Brody before helping me down to the sidewalk.

I hug his waist and, after a few seconds, I start smacking my tongue against the roof of my mouth when I notice how dry it is.

"What the hell are you doing?"

"I'm thirsty," I whine.

"We'll grab you some water."

"Water is boring."

Each step becomes more difficult than the one before, and the next thing I know, I have all my body weight leaning against him. He's practically dragging me down the sidewalk at this point, and I break out into a fit of laughter.

"What's so funny?"

"I'm drunk."

"Ya think?" he teases before stopping. "Come on. Get that little ass of yours in."

"This," I state, touching my finger to the window of his Jeep, "is not my car."

"No shit."

"Where is your old SUV?"

"Traded it in a few months ago."

He opens the door, and I literally crawl in like an animal, and when it takes too long for Trent's patience, he lays a hand right on my ass and pushes me in, tipping me forward and over the console. With my legs in the passenger seat and my head in the driver's seat, another burst of giggles consumes me.

"What the . . ."

Popping my head up, Trent stands in front of me with his door open.

"Scoot over, woman."

When I manage to settle in my seat, he reaches across me and fastens my seatbelt.

"Safety first!" I announce with a pep of energy.

As he pulls away from the curb, he laughs, "Damn, you are ham-dogged."

He drives out of the neighborhood, onto the main road, and it only takes a block or two—I can't even count at this point—to come up on a drive-thru.

"Ooh, stop and grab some food."

He scores us a bag of tacos, and it's only a few minutes later that he turns into the parking garage of his building.

"Where are we going?"

"My place. You can sleep off all that potato juice, and I'll take you to your car in the morning."

"You just want to get me in bed, don't you?"

After he parks, he shoots me a wink, asking, "You ever been corkscrewed?"

"Eww, no!"

He gets out, walks around the front of the Jeep, and opens my door. "Well, I've corkscrewed a chick before, and let me tell you, I won't ever do that shit again."

After he helps me out, we head inside. Once we're on the elevator, I have to brace against the wall because the movement tampers with my balance.

"Why is this thing going so fast?" I fuss. "It's like a rocket ship."

When we make it off the elevator and into his condo, I go straight to his bedroom, kick off my shoes, and fall belly-first onto the bed.

"Ahh, this feels so good," I garble into the pillow.

Trent tosses the sack of tacos next to me and then grabs a T-shirt and a pair of sleep pants. "Here," he says, and I lift my head. "Change into these before you pass out on me."

Taking the clothes, I roll a couple of times until I'm off the bed. Closing the bathroom door behind me, I quickly change and head back out.

Trent is already sitting on the bed, wearing nothing but a pair of athletic shorts as he digs into the food.

"I grabbed you a water."

Picking up the bottle from the nightstand, I guzzle half of it before hopping onto the bed next to him, crawling beneath the warm covers, and fishing a taco out of the bag.

"Mmm," I moan as I unfold the paper and take a bite.

"Damn, girl," he laughs. "Don't molest the damn thing."

Shreds of lettuce fall from my mouth. "This is so good."

As I devour taco after taco, Trent takes a few hits off his pen, but I decline. I'm already trashed as it is, I don't need to get stoned on top of it.

"I can't believe you just ate all that."

I toss my napkin, down the remainder of the water, and lie back. With a stuffed belly, I relax into the softness of his bed and let out a deep exhale. My head falls to the side, and I look up at Trent as he takes another hit, and when he releases a plume of smoke, I notice that his scruff is all gone.

"You shaved."

"What?" His hand runs along his smooth jaw. "Yeah, I got rid of it this morning."

I like him better without it.

I don't even realize I'm staring until he jokes, "Like what you see?"

"Maybe," I respond with absolutely no filter.

He leans back against the headboard while I sink deeper into the mattress.

Out of nowhere, the words, "I used to have the biggest crush on you," spill out, followed by a light chuckle when I think back to how I used to obsess over him.

"I must be way fucking stoned."

"It's true," I say lazily as I fully relax. "Remember that night at the dance club in Boca?"

"Hmm," he languidly acknowledges as he nods.

I hold up my hundred-pound arm and almost pinch my thumb and forefinger together, leaving a very narrow slit of space between them. "I was *this* close to sleeping with you that night."

His eyes pop open as wide as they possibly can since he's high as a kite. "Shut the fuck up."

I laugh. "No, I'm serious."

"Dude, are you kidding? So, what the hell happened?"

"Ehh," I joke.

"Man," he sighs. "I had no clue I actually had a shot with you."

In my foggy state, I mindlessly reach over and slip the pen out from between is fingers. After I take a long pull, he sinks down under the covers and rests his head on the pillow next to me. "So, you used to have a crush on me."

Blowing out the fumes, I turn my head and start to giggle because, now, I'm so far beyond blasted. "Yep. It's those damn eyes of yours."

"These fucked-up eyes?"

"Fucked up?"

"I hate them," he says, and I'm surprised because they're fascinating.

"Really?"

"Yeah, kids used to make fun of me when I was little."

"Hmm," is all that's left in me as I start to fade.

"You passing out?"

My eyes fall shut, and I give him a slow nod.

"Let me ask one more thing," he says, and I'm barely hanging on when he adds, "Seriously though, why weren't you okay with hooking up?"

Somehow, right before I drift completely, I manage to mumble, "Because I would've wanted more."

The next time my eyes open, I'm blinded by the piercing rays of the morning sun and force my lids to close again. As the cloud in my head dissolves, the room dip-dives and I have to open my eyes to regain my equilibrium. It's now that I realize I'm not in my bed. It takes a few seconds for recollection to appear, reminding me that I came home with Trent last night.

Rolling over, I discover I'm alone, and I breathe a huge sigh of relief when I lift the covers to see I'm still clothed.

"Oh, thank god," I murmur to myself.

While I'm attempting to sit up, Ady walks past the open bedroom door. She glances in, sees me, and comes to an abrupt halt.

Her eyes widen in disbelief, and she silently mouths, *What are you doing?*

I assume she isn't saying anything aloud because Trent is out there, so I mouth back, *I don't know*, before shamefully pulling the covers halfway over my face.

Not a second later, Trent appears with a bowl of cereal in his hand. "What's up, Ady?" he says nonchalantly as he walks right past her and straight over to me. "Morning, sunshine."

Oh my god, I want to die.

He crawls into bed next to me and shovels a spoonful of cereal into his mouth, and when I look back to Ady, she's gone.

"How do you feel?"

"Like crap," I mumble.

"Dude, you got so wasted last night. I can't imagine the hell you must be in."

Laying my head back down, I freak out on the inside when I try to recall what happened.

"You even remember anything?"

I shake my head. "What happened?"

He laughs and then takes another bite.

"What's so funny?"

"Nothing."

"You wouldn't be laughing if I didn't say or do something stupid."

"Don't be so paranoid. You didn't do anything stupid."

I don't believe him though. As I lie here, fretting over what that laugh meant, my stomach begins to churn, and I break out into a cold sweat.

"Dude," Trent says when he looks down at me. "You don't look so good."

The moment my tummy convulses, I launch off the bed and bolt to the bathroom. I almost miss the toilet when the contents of my stomach barrels up.

"Shit," is all I can hear of Trent as I puke. My body heaves, causing all my muscles to constrict, and I hit a new low when Trent comes in and holds my hair back.

I'm far past mortified, swatting my hand back, urging him to leave. I can't believe he's witnessing this monstrosity.

"Relax," he says before another expulsion hits.

When all is said and done, I'm nothing but a cold, clammy ball curled up on his bathroom floor. The flush of the toilet sounds a couple of times before a warm, wet washcloth runs across my forehead and down the side of my face. All I can do is groan in absolute misery.

"I feel like I'm dying."

He slips a hand beneath my shoulders and helps me sit up. "Here, swish this."

I take the small cup of mouthwash, and when I spit out the

minty blue liquid into the toilet, I reach up to flush before he gets me back to bed.

"I hope you don't have any plans today," he says in humor.

I can't believe how chill he's being. I'm sure the last thing he wants to be dealing with is a hungover girl barfing in his bathroom.

He gives me a couple of aspirin and then surprises me when he crawls in and pulls me toward him. I'm too weak to protest, but I manage to conjure enough energy to mutter, "If there were ever anything beyond the realm of mortification, this would be it."

"That was some serious carnival salsa you just spewed, I'm not even gonna lie."

"Oh god," I grumble.

"You're fine. Don't even worry about it," he assures me. "I have nowhere to be, so just chill and sleep it off."

And that's exactly what I do. Closing my eyes, I spend the rest of the day fighting one of the worst hangovers of my life.

Nine

TRENT

MARCH WAS THE MONTH THINGS SHIFTED, AND I'VE BEEN FUCKED ever since. March was the month Kate got wasted and confessed that she once had feelings for me. March was the month I began reevaluating everything I thought I knew about our friendship. It's now May, and somehow, I've managed not to slip in the puddles of awkwardness she escaped simply by being too drunk to remember telling me what she did.

I've been trying not to question myself too much since I know I don't have the answers. It would only cripple my head more than what it already is.

The two of us have been able to restore our friendship after it felt like there wasn't anything left of it to restore. We've been hanging out more, partying more, and surfing more. It feels great to have her back, and yet, that feeling perplexes me because none of my other friendships mirror the one I have with her. It's weird in its uniqueness, but that's because she's the first girl I've had *this* close of a bond with. My friends, no matter dudes or chicks, are kept on the other side of the barriers I put up. There is no need to throw my personal shit on them, and I'm not really one to want their shit being thrown on to me either.

Kate is different though. She pushed to want to know about my junk, and in turn, I give her pieces of it. The same can be said for the flip side as well. There's a tugging inside that has me wanting to know more about her. The thing is, ever since she came back, she's more cautious to open up than she was before. I can't fault her for that, but it only piques my curiosity about what's inside her head.

It's what has me texting her late at night.

It's what has me calling her more.

It's what has me out with her today.

"Did you see that foam climb?" she hollers as she floats in the water and hangs on to her board.

I shoot her a shaka. "We should probably head in. I'm seeing lightning."

When we make it to the shore, we kick back in the sand, drink some water, and watch the dark clouds as they roll closer to land.

"Looks like it's going to be a bad storm," she says.

"Made for some good waves though."

"Too bad Brody had to bail early. He really has a crappy class schedule this semester."

"No kidding."

The wind kicks up, sending a mist of sea spray in our direction.

"Give me your extra band," I tell her.

She slips it off her wrist and hands it to me. I comb my fingers through my hair, tie it back, and throw on a fresh T-shirt from my bag.

"You ready?"

She nods, and we gather our things. It isn't long until we're headed back to her place. Fortunately, neither of us have classes on Thursdays, so we've made a habit of wasting this day away together each week.

"If you want to hit the shower first, I'll get the coffee going," she offers.

Taking my backpack into her room, I toss it onto her bed before pulling out my clothes and closing myself inside her bathroom. It only takes me five minutes to clean up, and then I stroll into the kitchen to find she already has a cup of black coffee waiting for me.

"Give me fifteen," she says, taking her mug with her.

I make myself comfortable on her couch, grab the remote, and attempt to turn on the television, but it doesn't respond. The batteries are dead. I return to the kitchen and rifle through her junk drawer for new ones, figuring that's where people keep shit like that. When I turn up empty, I go in search of batteries in her room. The shower is still running as I open the drawer to one of her nightstands and find nothing but an old package of gum and some lip balm. It's the other drawer that throws me—next to her stash of cannabis cartridges and pen is a photo. It sickens me to see she has this here next to her bed, so close to her every day. The fact tears at something inside me, sending a strange sensation through my chest as I look at the smile on her face, but my chest constricts when I shift my attention to the fucker who's holding her. That piece of shit smiles and has his hands on her, the same hands he used to beat the shit out of her with for god only knows how many times.

I can't understand why she would hold on to this when there are no other signs of Caleb around her condo. She never even talks about him, at least not to me.

"What are you doing?"

Her voice comes out of nowhere, and when I glance over my shoulder, she's walking toward me, curious as to what has my attention. I hold up the photo, and she freezes.

"Why do you have that?" she questions timidly.

My instinct tells me to back down so I don't upset her, but we've been skating around this topic for months, which is too long. "Why do *you* have it?"

In three steps, she's close enough to snatch it out of my hand before dropping it back in the drawer and closing it.

"Why are you in here snooping?"

"The remote's dead. I was looking for batteries," I explain and then ask again, "Why do you have that photo?"

I watch her jaw flex as she bites down, and I can see the defensiveness building in her eyes before she says, "It's none of your business."

The last thing I want to do is slip backwards with her, so I take a seat on the edge of her bed and collect my thoughts for a moment. "I feel like we should talk about this."

"I don't want to."

"I know you don't, but that doesn't mean you shouldn't."

She turns and walks over to her dresser as she ties her wet hair back.

"The batteries are in the laundry room," she says, putting a stop to the conversation and then walking out.

I hate that she shuts down so quickly, and when I step out of the room, I find her fiddling with the remote. When she aims it at the television and it turns on, she smiles a fake smile. "There. It works again."

Flopping down on the couch, she starts skipping through the channels, and when I round the sofa and sit next to her, I swipe the remote from her and shut the television off.

"I don't want to talk," she states.

"I know, but we're going to." She throws me a harsh look, and I can't hide the smirk it causes me to have. "You can give me that nasty eye all you want, but I'm serious. It bothers me that you have that picture."

"Why?"

"Because that guy was an asshole to you."

She shakes her head as if I'm full of shit, and it ticks me off, but I force myself to stay calm and not be too aggressive.

"If I'm wrong to think that, I need you to tell me why."

"You hated him from the start," she snaps.

"Then explain to me why I shouldn't have, because I can't figure out how you and I see him in entirely different ways."

She leans back and sulks into the cushions, and it's written all over her face how much she doesn't want to be doing this. But she's never going to get past this if she's still hung up on him.

Shifting to face her, I let her know, "I want to be able to understand."

"I fell in love with him." Her voice comes out weak—almost sad, and to hear her say it sends another current through my ribs that can't be ignored. "He never meant to hurt me."

"What does that even mean?" I try so hard to keep my voice soft and nonjudgmental.

"I know you want to paint him with one broad stroke as the bad guy, but he wasn't." She won't even look at me as she talks. She just keeps her chin down as she picks nervously at her nails.

"He put his hands on you. I don't know how that doesn't make him the bad guy here."

Silence stretches before she says, "It was my fault."

I run an angry hand down the side of my face and around the back of my neck to keep my temper in check. I can't believe she would think she had anything to do with what he did. But at the same time, I don't want to diminish her reasoning and make her feel stupid, so I choose my words wisely.

"I need you to explain this to me, because, I'm sorry, I can't begin to understand how this could possibly be your fault."

She isn't quick to respond, so I sit and wait while she finds whatever strength she needs to speak again. When words fail her and a small tear slips down her face, I start questioning if I'm doing the right thing by forcing this conversation on her.

She doesn't bother to wipe it away, and my only guess is that I've made her so uncomfortable that she's too nervous to make a movement as she sits next to me—frozen.

Reaching over, I drag my thumb along her cheek.

With her eyes downcast, she admits, "I was always disappointing him. He would only get mad when I did something I knew I shouldn't have. He never did anything that I didn't provoke."

The fact that she actually believes this shit is her fault is so far beyond fucked up that I'm about to boil over with anger. Clenching my fists, I do everything I can not to lose my shit.

"I'm so fucking mad right now," I let her know, and when she still refuses to acknowledge me, I touch her chin. "I need you to look at me." And when she does, I'm fervent in my tone when I tell her, "You can't understand how pissed I am right now. There is no way in hell I could ever lay a hand on a woman, no matter how angry she made me."

"You don't understand—"

"There isn't anything you could possibly do or say that would ever make it okay for anyone to hurt you."

Her eyes fall shut and more tears break free. "I wasn't good enough," she whispers. "I knew it wasn't okay, but . . ." She then looks at me as her face turns splotchy and says, "I just kept trying to be better."

At that, I pull her over to me and hold on to her tightly, as if my strength alone could be enough to keep her together. "It wasn't your fault, Kate."

"Truth is the truth though. If I didn't upset him, he wouldn't have lost control. It *was* my fault."

I drop my head on top of hers as she continues to talk. I want to shut her up from all the nonsense, but I bite my tongue because she's finally talking. Bullshit or not, at least she's talking.

"I did everything I could to make him happy, but it was never enough—*I* was never enough."

In her mind, everything bad that came out of that relationship was her fault. It kills me to know that this is what she believes and that Caleb's the one who probably convinced her of it. For years, she's been thinking she holds all the blame.

With my arms around her, she cries, and it's so hard for me to listen to. But I hold her and allow her time to just release it because all I want to do in this moment is help her get rid of all the shit she's been bottling up inside. It's so clear she isn't over what happened, not that it's something easy to just put aside.

Her tears dampen my shirt, and the heaviness that's pressing against my ribs is a pain I've never encountered before. This is the shit I'm always trying to avoid, yet here I am, seeking it out with her. Fuck if it's not playing with my heart right now.

The urge to protect her is fierce, but the urge to ensure that bastard never gets the chance to come near her again is even more so. He left so much of her in shambles, tore her down, burned bridges, and damned her self-esteem to the point she actually believes she was deserving of the shit he put her through. Unfortunately, destruction is easy; it's the rebuilding that's the hard part, but I want to do whatever I can to help her get there, starting with me letting her know, "He manipulated you."

Against my chest, she denies my words as she shakes her head.

"He took advantage of your feelings and fucked with your head, Kate."

Before she can refute what I'm saying, I take her face in my hands and angle her to look at me when I tell her sternly, "He manipulated you to make you believe you were the cause. You weren't. There isn't anything you can tell me or anyone else that will ever change that. He filled your head with lies."

"He loved me."

"No, he didn't."

"He did," she presses.

"What he did to you . . . I know that isn't your idea of love."

"There were so many other moments though—good ones."

"That's how he manipulated you, by giving you those moments. They might have meant something to you, but I promise, they didn't mean the same thing to him."

She pulls back, away from my touch and the truths I'm giving her, and turns her head. I know she's thinking about what I just said. I only hope it's getting through to her, but if not, I take another step when I add, "Think about it. If I asked you, right here and now, if you would be okay having a boyfriend—anyone other than Caleb—who threw you into walls and hit you, what would you say? Would you even consider that love?" Her chin starts quivering, but I don't stop there. I need her to see the truth through all the lies he clouded her with. "Turn it on me. What would you think if I had a girlfriend who I hit? If I hurt her so badly that her entire body was covered in bruises? Would there be any way you could rationalize or excuse what I had done?"

The moment she lets go of a wretched sob, I know, for the first time, she's seeing Caleb for who he really is. It's the hardest thing to know I'm the one that's igniting all her tears, but I also know that she needs to have this clarity so she'll stop blaming herself.

"But I really loved him." She cries into her palms.

Tucking her back against me, I hold her tightly. "You didn't fall in love with him; you fell in love with his betrayal."

"I don't even know what to think."

"I just need you to believe me when I say that none of this was ever your fault."

"I'm . . . I don't know anything right now. It's all so confusing."

It can't be easy to think that everything you thought you knew was nothing but a lie. She's going to have a lot of shit to sort through to figure it all out for herself, but at least I know that she won't have to do it alone. I'll always be here for her. In this moment, I want to tell her that, but I'm not sure how. I just hope that she can feel everything I'm unable to say. There has never been a person in my life who I've been so drawn to like I'm drawn to her. All I know is there is no place I would rather be right now than here with her—tears and all.

Ten

KATE

These past two weeks haven't been the best. There's so much I've been examining, including myself. Talking to Trent hurt—it hurt so much—and hearing his perspective wasn't easy. It was what I needed though. After I was able to talk about it, I felt lighter—minimally lighter, but still lighter, as if the walls were no longer closing in on me. Since then, I've been trying to figure out the part I played in my relationship with Caleb and what that says about me. I keep questioning how I could've let someone do what he did to me. How could I have been so blind and foolish?

When Trent asked me how I would feel if he had done to a girl what Caleb was doing to me, my answer was clear: There would be no excuse that would make his behavior okay. So, why was it okay for Caleb? Why couldn't I see what was happening to me?

The questions don't stop there. Day by day, more come to surface, confusing me even further, but they also help me understand better. It's weird how that happens—clarity birthing perplexity and vice versa.

Trent has been there, a silent support, this whole time, and I don't think he knows how much I needed that. So, when summer break rolled around and he invited me to Tampa with him,

I jumped on board. Micah and Ady would be there to attend his mother's fiftieth birthday party, so she suggested I stay with her at her mom's place.

Ady and Micah left early this morning and had already made it to Tampa before Trent and I hit the road. The four of us won't be hanging out until tomorrow because they're busy with Micah's parents.

As Trent drives over the Sunshine Skyway Bridge, my tummy growls. "I'm getting hungry."

"We're almost there; about another thirty minutes."

When Trent talked to his mother earlier, she mentioned already having plans for tonight, but I'll still be able to meet her before she leaves. I've been so interested to meet the woman who raised a guy like Trent. His sense of humor is something I thought would fade over the years, but it's who he is, and although he has changed in other ways, the crudeness is most likely here to stay.

It's creeping up on seven o'clock when he pulls into the drive of the lavish, two-story, Mediterranean-style home with an impeccably manicured lawn. I don't know what I was expecting, but it wasn't this.

"Is this the house you grew up in?"

"Yeah," he responds before parking under a large palm tree that glows above the in-ground lights.

He leaves my suitcase in the Jeep for when I go to Ady's later but grabs his own before leading me up the brick drive toward the extravagant arched doorway. I snicker.

"What's so funny?"

"I just had no idea you grew up so fancy," I tease.

Trent is the furthest thing from fancy. I don't think I can recall ever seeing him in anything other than flip-flops and surf-branded T-shirts.

"Half your pantry is filled with your shoes because you have too many to fit in your closet," he points out before adding, "You're so fancy, I bet you call blow jobs fellatio."

"Gross," I scold, slapping his arm as he laughs. "I'm not *that* fancy," I defend, holding out my arms to accentuate the fact that I'm wearing flip-flops, running shorts, and an old UM T-shirt.

"Whatever you say." He then opens the door. "Mom," he calls out, and his voice echoes through the home that boasts an impressive foyer. To the left is a large, winding staircase with wrought iron features, but my focus shifts when his mother walks in.

"I was wondering when you'd get here," she says, and I smile as the two of them hug. When she pulls back, she rustles her fingers through his long hair. "Are you ever going to cut this?"

He ducks his head away from her and smooths his hair before gesturing to me. "This is Kate, Mom."

The smile on her face grows, and it resembles Trent's. She wears her long hair in soft curls, making her appear younger than what she is. She's stunning even in her casual long black maxi dress and sandals.

"It's good to meet you," I say before she gives me a welcoming hug.

"It's good to meet you too." She takes a step back. "You can call me Laura."

With a polite nod, I follow her and Trent through the house and back to the kitchen, which opens to the large living room and an amazing view of their pristine backyard.

"How was the drive?"

I take a seat next to Trent on the sofa as she sits across from us.

"Boring," he responds. "Kate was worthless entertainment. She slept for most of the way."

"It was your idea for us to go clubbing in South Beach last night," I defend. "I was tired."

"I managed to stay awake."

"You were driving."

"Just ignore him," his mother says. "It's what I have to do about ninety percent of the time."

"Good to know, Mom."

"So, are you hungry, Kate?"

"Yeah. Trent wouldn't stop at the McDonald's when we passed it."

"I'm not eating there. That shit is nasty," he says. "Hell, I'd rather eat a wooden dick."

My eyes shift to his mom, who only rolls her eyes. At least I know that Trent is exactly who he is no matter who he's around.

"I think there's some leftover fajitas in the fridge."

"You didn't cook it, did you?"

His mother narrows her eyes. "And if I did?"

"Then we'd definitely be eating out."

"Trent," I reprimand.

"Dude, trust me."

"I'm not that bad of a cook," she defends.

"You are so rude."

He smiles at me. "She knows I'm just bustin' her balls."

"In his defense," she says, "I've had my fair share of tragedies in the kitchen, but I'm getting better."

"See, even she knows it's true. But seriously, I'm starving," he tells me. "What do you want?"

"What's around?"

"Everything." He then stands and looks at me. "You coming?"

With an exhausting sigh, I hold out my hand for him to pull me up, but then his mother suggests, "Why don't you stay and visit before I have to run off?"

"Do you mind?" I ask him. "I'm really sick of being in the car."

"It's cool."

"Just pick up whatever you want. I'll eat anything."

When I sit back on the couch, he takes a few steps backward and points to his mother, saying, "Don't be talking any shit about me."

"Go get this girl some food and leave us alone."

I laugh under my breath when he turns and heads out of the house.

"I don't know how you got through that drive without slapping him silly."

"I'm not easily offended," I tell her.

"Well, that's good. You seem like a sweet girl; I'd hate for him to scare you away." She then comes to sit next to me, which puts me a little more at ease since she's no longer talking to me from across the room. "Forgive me, but I don't know anything about you other than you're Trent's friend. He isn't much for talking about himself."

I laugh. "Yeah, I know. I feel like I have to pull information out of him at times."

"The two of you go to college together?"

I nod and then tell her about how I met her son, what I think of school, and what I'm majoring in. She asks about where I grew up and she tells me that she's a born and raised Florida girl too, who surprisingly has never stepped foot on a board.

"So, who taught Trent how to surf?"

"He taught himself," she says. "Trent went through a phase in middle school where he didn't come home very much and surfing sort of became a place of healing for him."

I nod, not having a clue as to what she's talking about. Never has he mentioned anything like that to me, but like she said, he isn't one who talks about himself very much. In fact, I don't know a whole lot about his past other than he felt as if this house was a never-ending revolving door of men coming in and out of his life. I can only assume what she is hinting at has something to do with that.

"Grub time!" Trent announces, cutting our conversation short.

Laura places a hand on my knee. "I should probably get going. It was really nice meeting you."

"Same here."

When she walks into the kitchen, she grabs her purse and kisses Trent on the cheek. "I'll see you tomorrow?"

"Yeah, we'll be in and out for the next few days."

After she leaves, I go into the kitchen and take a seat at the oversized island. "What did you get?"

He slides a flat box from the large brown bag. "Donuts." Then he practically salivates when he lifts the lid, revealing a dozen chocolate covered donuts.

"How is this dinner?"

"Hey, you said you'd eat anything."

"Yeah, anything of nutritional value."

"This shit's on the food pyramid," he defends before shoving half a donut into his mouth.

"That's not even a thing anymore," I tell him as I walk over to the fridge.

"It isn't?"

Opening the door, I go in search of the fajitas. "I think it's, like, a food plate thing now." I find a takeout box with the fajitas inside and pull it out.

"You're seriously not going to eat the donuts?"

"Yes, but I'm going to have this too."

"Don't hog it all," he says. "I want some."

The two of us hang out while we eat fajitas and donuts, and when we're stuffed, he shows me around the house, eventually taking me upstairs to his bedroom.

"You have a lot of skimboards." A lot is an understatement since there are tons of them stacked against the wall.

"I'm getting your ass on one of them tomorrow," he says when he kicks off his shoes and jumps on top of the bed. "We're all going to Indian Rocks."

"What's Indian Rocks."

"Just a local beach. You'll be the only kook there," he jokes as I step out of my flip-flops and lie down next to him.

His cell phone rings, and when he picks it up, he murmurs, "It's Ady," before answering, "What's up?" He then holds the cell out to me. "She wants to talk to you."

"Hello?"

"Hey, so, don't kill me, but—"

"What?" I question wearily.

"I had no idea that Micah's parents were chartering a yacht for the party, so we're out here on the water, and I have no idea when we're going to be docking. I can only assume it's going to be late."

"Hold on," I tell her, and then turn to Trent. "Apparently, the party is on a boat and Ady won't be home until late."

"It's cool. Just stay here."

"Are you sure that's okay?"

"Yeah, it's not a problem."

When I bring the phone back to my ear, I tell Ady, "I'll just crash at Trent's."

"I'm so sorry," she says, and I can tell by her tone she feels really bad.

"It's no big deal. Don't worry about it."

"Thanks. I'll see you tomorrow."

I hand him back the phone, and after he sets it on his nightstand, he grabs the remote and turns on the large television hanging on his wall. His childhood bedroom feels so much different from his room back in Miami, and it's weird to be hanging out in it. There aren't as many clues to who he is at his condo as there are here. I lift my eyes to the surfboard that's broken into two pieces and mounted above his headboard.

"Is that real?"

He looks up and nods. "Yeah."

"What happened?"

"My brother and I were spring breaking in Huntington Beach. I took a fall and a damn wave came straight down on the board and snapped it."

I laugh. "That's a lame story."

"Not all of us have righteous tales of face-planting into the reefs of Hawaii like you."

Reaching down, I grab the blanket that's folded along the foot of his bed and pull it over myself.

"You cold?"

"Yeah."

"Come here," he says, slipping his arm underneath my neck and pulling me close.

I use his chest as a pillow while we watch a random movie; although, I'm having a hard time focusing. I keep thinking back to what his mother said. I want to ask him about it, but knowing how private he is, I waver on whether I should mention anything. The last thing I want to do is tip the boat when everything has been going so smoothly with us lately.

Almost too smoothly.

I'm well aware that I need to sort my shit out and not reignite this hopeless crush on Trent. But, at the same time, it isn't just my relationship with Caleb that I'm trying to sort through, I'm also trying to figure out my relationship with Trent. Since we started talking again, I'm feeling things that I haven't felt in a while—not since we first met—not since Caleb came into my life. When Trent isn't around, he's on my mind, and it's clear that I'm treading down a path I have no business being on. I know Trent well, I recognize exactly what it is he's looking for, and it isn't commitment or anything close to that idea.

But I don't want that either—at least I don't think I do. After all, Caleb burned me in the worst way possible, and it's left me too fragile to pretend that I'm ready for another relationship. Really, it's an asinine idea I shouldn't be entertaining.

But here I am, once again, lying in his arms, entertaining it.

Something about this feels different than what it did when we were freshman. I consider everything we've been through, and after all this time, we're bonded in a way we weren't back then.

My emotions are a mess, and so is my head, but the more time we spend together, the more my heart wanders—the same stupid heart that led me right into the arms of Caleb and kept me there. I shouldn't trust it.

It's a scary feeling not to trust myself, but that's where I am. I'm incapable of making right decisions when it comes to guys. That I'm starting to have feelings for someone like Trent is another example of my ill judgment. He's sweet and loyal but completely against commitment.

I'm not even sure why I'm giving these thoughts my attention. Even after all this time, the wounds Caleb left me with are still so raw.

When I lift my chin and glance up at Trent, I find he's already looking at me.

"You got quiet on me."

I should say something—anything aside from everything my heart is screaming at me. He shifts down to meet me eye to eye, but I wish he hadn't because now I'm questioning my questioning. A new thought I hadn't considered perplexes me further: If my judgment is so off, and I'm telling myself not to cross any lines with Trent, does that mean I shouldn't listen to myself? Should I do the exact opposite?

Shit, what is he thinking, staring at me the way he is?

Then I wonder if there's a chance he might be on the same page as I am. If I really think about it, it's clear that, when we go to parties, he no longer tries to score chicks to take back to his place. At the beach, he no longer chases after bunnies. When he has free time, he gives it to me.

Damn, this boy has my head spinning.

Unable to take the silence for any longer, I push past my rankled nerves to speak. "I don't know what to say."

"What do you want to say?"

He has me in tangles right now, and he knows it. How could he not? I don't even realize my fingers are fidgeting along the collar of my shirt until he pulls them away and slowly laces his fingers through mine.

My eyes fall shut when I softly beg, "Don't do this." God, I want him to, but under all the indecision and worry and doubt about my life, I know that I'm still the same girl at the core. I still can't be a passing fling.

"Why?"

"Because I'm not that girl."

When my eyes reach his again, I wait for him to say something, but all I see is his confliction.

"Say something," I request.

His eyes drift down to our hands, and it takes him a moment before he confesses, "I think I'm falling for you."

It's the last thing I ever expected him to say, and I can barely hold on to myself as excitement and fear battle it out. His words are leading me to the edge, but if I jump, I don't know if I can trust that he'll catch me.

"Now you say something."

Choosing to be upfront, I tell him, "This scares me."

"Same."

I can't do this.

Pulling my hand out from his, I sit up. "What are we doing?" I question. "This is crazy, and you know it."

Sitting up next to me, he turns off the television and tosses the remote aside. "Is it really that crazy?"

"Yeah, it is," I respond. "I mean . . . it's you. Do you even know what you're doing?"

"Do you?"

His question shuts me up, because no, I have no idea what I'm doing.

"Answer me," he presses.

"No, but I don't want to be some hookup for you."

He takes my head into his hands, and I've never seen him look so serious. "I don't want that either. And yeah, I don't know what the fuck I'm doing here, but I do know how I feel when I'm with you, and I'm having a really hard time keeping you at a distance."

"I don't know if I can trust you."

"Let me show you that you can," he says.

I want to let him prove it to me, if only because I feel the same way. When I'm around him, I always want more. No matter how much I've tried to ignore it, that pull is there, and it isn't leaving.

His hand slips past my cheek, around my neck, and into my hair. "Just give me a chance to show you."

Locked on to his mismatched eyes, I wonder if we're mismatched too, but what if we aren't? "This really scares me."

"I know it does," he says before pulling me closer and kissing me.

It isn't the first time his lips have touched mine, but it's the first time I know it isn't a mistake on his part. He's soft and slow, purposeful and cautious. It's something I wouldn't have expected from him, but it's the care that he takes with me that has my doubts about this diminishing.

When my hands get lost in his hair, he lowers us onto the bed. Parting my lips, he drags his tongue along mine, and I swear I can taste the life he's breathing back into me. It's an overwhelming sensation I never want to end, and when his hand drops to the small of my back, I go freely as he presses me closer to him. Comfort surrounds in his touch, a comfort I've been searching for. I just never thought it existed within him.

My past has left me with knots the size of cannonballs all over me, but with the weight of Trent on top of me right now, he rubs some of them out. I just hope it doesn't take a lifetime to untangle what he didn't tie. It shocks me to know he's willing to take these broken pieces of mine, take them willingly and soak them with every brush of his lips, with every caress of his tongue. He pulls back for a moment, his forehead resting against mine, and I can't believe the taste of my damaged heart didn't just burn a hole straight through him.

His chest beats against mine as I wonder if it isn't him I'm afraid of, but rather, maybe I'm afraid of the realness. Fearful that, for the first time in my life, I know I'm incapable of walking away from something—him. Maybe that is the very thing that scares the shit out of me. It still isn't enough to make me push him away, so I pull instead, bringing his lips back down to mine.

Eleven

KATE

Warmth cocoons me as I stir awake. Selfishly, I keep my eyes closed because to be wrapped in Trent's arms like this feels too good to give up. Last night, nothing happened beyond kissing, but damn, the kissing felt amazing. Right now, my only worry is having to face the inevitable awkwardness.

It's one thing to meet a guy you have an instant connection with and start dating, but it's another to be friends for three years before ever crossing that line. In a way, it's comforting because we already know and trust each other, but still—it's Trent.

His arm constricts around me as he begins to stir, but the heat of his skin continues to relax me. Finally opening my eyes, I roll over, and he pulls me in close, tucking my head under his chin.

"Did you sleep okay?"

I nod as I nervously drag my finger along the edge of the waistband of his shorts. When I hit a certain spot, his abs flex, and he flinches. "Damn, girl."

"Does that tickle?" I tease before running my finger along the spot again.

This time, he catches my wrist. "You're about to wake up the big man downstairs if you're not careful."

I giggle, but it catches in my throat just as there's a knock on his door.

"Yeah?" Trent says, and his mother walks in.

I jump out of his arms and put a decent amount of space between us.

She takes a quick glance my way. "Oh, I'm sorry, I didn't know you spent the night."

I want to die, like, literally die as I sink down into the covers.

"What do you want, Mom?"

"Just heading to my office to catch up on some patient files. Are you going to be home for dinner tonight?"

"I don't know. I'll text you."

"Okay," she says. "You guys have a good day. I'll see you later."

After the door closes behind her, I yank the covers completely over my head with a mortified, "Oh my god."

Trent laughs, but I remain hidden. Next thing I know, he rips the sheets away from me, asking, "What's the problem?"

"Umm, your mother just saw us in bed together."

"So? At least you aren't naked." With a sexy grin, he rolls on top of me. "But we can fix that."

I goose him in the ribs, but the moment his lips capture mine, I give up and kiss him back. I've waited so long to finally have this with him. I was a fool to think that my feelings for him had ever faded. They just went quiet for a period of time.

He finally drags his lips away from mine, and I look up into his eyes as he stares down at me. A lock of his long hair falls over his brows and lands on my forehead before I run my hand through it, pushing it back, the smooth strands gliding between my fingers.

His expression is intent, focused solely on me as if he's trying to read my thoughts. "Is this weird for you?"

I nod. It's a very strange feeling to have spent nearly the entire night kissing him. To shift from friends to . . . well, I'm not even sure what the hell we are, is extremely awkward, but it is in no way unwanted. "What about you?"

He slides off me and lies at my side as I shift over onto my hip. "All of this is weird to me," he admits. "But at the same time, it isn't, you know what I mean?"

"Yeah." I think about the two of us having to spend the day together with Ady and Micah, and it only makes me more uncomfortable. I don't know how I'm supposed to act with Trent when we're around them. There's a big part of me that's afraid of being judged and scrutinized for possibly making another huge mistake. Plus, this just happened, and with neither of us knowing exactly what we're doing or where this is going, I'm not ready to share this with anyone. "Can I ask you something?"

"What is it?"

"Can we not say anything to Ady or Micah about this? I just . . . I just don't want them to know yet."

I worry he might take offense, but he immediately quells that when he grins. "I've never been someone's dirty little secret before."

"Shut up." His sarcasm makes me smile. "Is that okay, though?"

"Yeah," he agrees. "We'll just keep it between us for now."

I'm sure he probably has the same reservations I do. It isn't as if he's ever gotten involved with anyone, and once people find out about us—if there even is an us—there's no doubt opinions will follow.

We bide our time through the morning, not quick to get out of bed. We're nothing more than restless lips, and there isn't a single moment I have to tell him to go slow because he isn't pushing at all. It's another surprise he gifts to me. Last night, he was cautious and unhurried, and this morning, he allows me to lead. Trent is used to getting what he wants from girls, but in this moment, right now . . . between us . . . it's as if the only thing he wants is what I'm willing to give him.

I could stay in this bed with him all day, but someone keeps calling his cell over and over, he throws a curse before answering it with an annoyed, "Dude, why're you blowing me up like a barnacle bitch?"

I can hear Micah's faint voice on the other end.

"Yeah, I'll see you in a bit."

Trent tosses his phone aside. "They're already there."

Once we throw on our beach gear, he grabs a couple of his skimboards before we head down to his Jeep and toss everything into the back. The humidity is thick, and as I'm buckling in, my skin is already dewy. While I shoot Ady a text to let her know we are finally heading out, Trent hops in the driver's seat and hits the button to open the convertible top, exposing us to the elements.

With the wind whipping through my hair, I throw on my sunglasses as he drives over the Gandy Bridge that takes us to Indian Rocks Beach. After we park and head to the sand, I spot Micah and Ady with a couple of guys.

"Who are they with?" I ask Trent.

"Looks like Brogan and Brandon," he tells me. "Micah and I used to hang out with them all the time when we lived here. They're chill."

"There you guys are," Ady announces when she sees us. "What took you so long?"

"Your girl wouldn't get off my nuts this morning," Trent tells her, and for a split second, I freak out on the inside. Then I realize no one is taking him seriously because they're so numb to the crap that comes out of his mouth.

I'm quickly introduced to Brogan and Brandon before Micah nods to the boards we brought. "You getting on today?"

"Going to try."

"You've never been on a board?" Brogan questions.

"Surf, but never a skim. I grew up on the east coast."

"She's a Palm Beach tart," Trent tells them.

I slug him in the arm and correct for the hundredth time. "*West* Palm Beach."

Brogan quirks a brow. "Is there a difference?"

"Do I look like a Palm Beach girl?" I question, sweeping a hand down my body to emphasize my racer top bikini and my hair that is pulled into a ratty knot on top of my head.

He eyes me for a second before grabbing his board and slinging his arm around my neck with a smirk. "Come on, you don't want that assjack teaching you how to skim," he says, shooting Trent a grin as he leads me away from the group.

I welcome his distraction because I'm paranoid that, if I'm too close to Trent, everyone will be able to see right through the façade we agreed to hold on to.

Brogan and I reach the edge of the water, and he guides me through the basics. "You're going to hold on like this." He demonstrates holding his board in front of him with one hand on the tail and the other hand on the side. "So, you want to wait until just after a wave rolls out—when the sand is coated with just a film of water—to begin your run. Once you're at a decent speed, drop the board flat on the wet sand, directly in front of you, and get on. Don't jump on, just run on top of it."

He covers a few more points before I'm ready to give it a go. As a wave rushes in, I begin my run and drop the board as the water rolls back out. Focusing on the weight distribution, I step onto the board, only to kick it out from under my feet and nearly topple forward. Thankfully, I'm able to catch myself from eating sand. From afar, I hear a collective applause, and when I see Trent and everyone else laughing, I flip them off.

"You were leaning too far forward," Brogan says as he grabs my board.

From over his shoulder, I find Trent jogging our way with his board under his arm. "I've got this, man."

When Brogan heads back to the group, he echoes what his friend just told me, saying, "You're leaning forward too much. You have to steady your weight because you don't have any fins." He shows me how to drop it. "Lean down with it before you let go and try to stay on the thinner part of the water."

I continue to practice launching and mounting the board, and after a handful of times, I'm finally able to get a decent ride.

"How'd that feel?" he asks as I jog back to him.

"I think I'm getting the hang of it."

The two of us stay off on our own for a little while longer before we go back to the group. When Trent joins the guys, I take a seat next to Ady on her towel.

"You picked that up pretty quick," she says as she watches Micah throw down a couple of tricks.

"It's nothing like surfing at all." I dig a bottle of water out of my backpack, and as I'm unscrewing the lid, I catch Ady staring at me. "What?"

She shrugs. "You tell me."

I take a long sip as her eyes linger. "Tell you what?"

"Whatever it is that's going on between you and Trent?" She starts laughing when I choke on my water.

"What are you talking about? Why would you think something was going on?"

"Because he can't keep his eyes off you."

"Umm, that's because he's teaching me how to skim."

"Even before that," she says. "I don't know, seems like you're not telling me something."

"Because there's nothing to tell."

She cocks her head, and I fold like a paper house doused in water.

"Okay, fine," I say, and the girl lights up as if she's about to get the best gossip of her life. "Wipe the obnoxious grin off your face first."

"Spill it."

"You can't say anything," I warn.

"Promise."

"I'm serious."

"So am I," she asserts. "Now dish."

"Last night, he admitted to catching feelings for me."

"I knew it," she chirps. "So, has anything happened?"

"We're just . . . I don't know, figuring it out, I guess."

"Figuring it out?"

"It's Trent," I say, stating the obvious.

She gives a slow nod as she lifts her brows. "I'm surprised."

"Yeah, me too."

"I never thought he'd show an interest in anyone. What all did he say?"

"Basically, just that," I tell her.

I run the back of my hand along the sweat beads forming along my brow and watch Trent as he runs onto the board and does a kickflip. I can't deny how much I'm drawn to him, and after last night, the reasons have only multiplied.

"What are you going to do?"

"I don't know. I'm still trying to deal with all the shit Caleb left me with." And that's the truth. I question if I should even entertain the idea of whatever is going on between Trent and me, but at the same time, I'm trying not to get too hung up on it. "Honestly, though . . . Trent scares me."

"Yeah, he's a risky person to throw your heart at, but at the same time, he's calmed down a lot over the past year," she tells me.

And she's absolutely right. He used to come with so many red flags I could barely see through the barrage of them all. But day by day, I find them fading to white—bright white, blinding me from all the reasons why I should push him away. Instead, I only pull him closer. So, when Ady asks, "Do you want to stay with him again tonight?" I want to say yes, but I don't.

"No, it's fine."

"Are you sure?"

"Yeah, I don't want you to have to be by yourself," I tell her, aware that Micah's parents are old-fashioned and aren't okay with Ady staying the night with their son. "Plus, I've been looking forward to having some time together without the guys around."

She smiles, and I can tell she feels the same. I'm sure it can get old living with both Trent and Micah and never having any space from them. So, after we all decide to call it a day, I take a quick rinse under the beach shower before walking over to where Trent is waiting for me.

"Hey, we have to run back to your house so I can grab my bag."

"Where are you going?" he asks as he tosses me a dry towel.

"I'm staying with Ady, remember?"

He doesn't put up a fight when I tell him this, he only teases me by saying, "I didn't expect you to hop off my jock so fast."

"I was never on your jock."

"You could've been," he flirts as I shake my head.

After we grab my things from his place, he drives me over to Ady's house, which is just as impressive as his. Trent grabs my hand and starts tugging me in, but I wouldn't put it past Ady to be inside spying on us, so I dodge his kiss and quickly hop out of his Jeep with a casual, "See you later."

"That was cold, Kate," he hollers as I rush up to her front door. "You owe me a titty text later!"

I refuse to turn and show him my laughter and the huge smile he just put on my face, but Ady gets it the moment she opens the door.

"What's got you so happy?" she asks as she peers over my shoulder at Trent, who's still parked in her wrap-around drive.

I give in, and when I peek back over, he's shooting the two of us the middle finger, in jest, before driving off.

Ady rolls her eyes. "Come in."

Her mom is out of town, so we have the place to ourselves. It's a huge home with a remarkable pool out back, and we spend the rest of the afternoon, lying out and soaking in the sun before ordering in dinner. When night falls, we crawl into her bed, and I listen as she gabs about Micah and their relationship.

"What do you think will happen after graduation?" I ask.

"I don't really know. He's been talking about moving to San Diego."

"For surfing?"

"Yeah."

Micah recently snagged a sports agent who has been guiding his surfing career toward the professional circuit.

"Would you go with him?"

"If he wanted me to, I would. I honestly can't imagine not being with him."

"And I can't imagine not having you in Miami," I tell her right back. I would hate to lose her to California, but I totally understand where she's coming from. She and Micah have been dating for two years, and they are still going strong. You would think living together would put a strain on the relationship, but it doesn't seem to impact them at all.

As we wind down and grow tired, Ady lets go of a heavy yawn. After we turn out the lights, it isn't long until she passes out. I'm exhausted too, but my mind won't let me sleep with Trent running through it. The light from the pool below casts its veiny reflection onto the ceiling, and I stare up at the glowing webs floating around and get lost in them.

A buzzing from the nightstand causes me to startle, and I grab it fast before it wakes up Ady.

Trent: I can't sleep. Are you still up?

Looking at the time on my phone, I see it's almost one o'clock.

Me: Yes. Why can't you sleep?

When Ady stirs, I press the phone against my chest to snuff the light. It takes a few seconds until she settles back down and her breathing evens out. Rolling over on to my side, I tap the screen to light it back up, but Trent still hasn't responded. I wonder what's taking him so long. I want to text him back, but I also don't want him to know how eager he makes me, so I play it cool, even though I'm not cool at all.

After a few minutes of nothing, I give up and set the cell down on the nightstand, perplexed as to why he isn't answering my message. Shifting on to my back again, my focus returns to the streaks of lights dancing along the ceiling.

Maybe this is a bad idea.

Is Trent really someone I should be considering getting involved with?

My heart lurches in my chest when my phone vibrates, and I can't pick it up fast enough.

Trent: Because I can't stop thinking about you.

Twelve

KATE

"What are you going to do while I'm gone?"

Sitting on Trent's bed, I catch a few T-shirts he tosses to me as I help him pack. "Waste away my youth, I guess." I stack the shirts and set them in the suitcase. "It'll be quiet with everyone gone."

"Well, if you get bored at your place, you can always come over here."

"And do what? Nobody will be here."

"I don't know," he mumbles as he throws a few pairs of board shorts into his luggage. When a smirk grows, he adds, "You could drop by and do dirty things to yourself in my bed."

"You're such a pervert."

We've only been back from Tampa for a couple of weeks, and in that time, we've been hanging out a lot more. Although we're growing closer, we still haven't talked about what we are to each other. We're still wading in the gray, which isn't a bad place to be. It's nice to take things slow without the pressure of having to define or label whatever this relationship is that we've been falling into.

With Trent, there's no conformity—there's no mold he

attempts to fit into. He's nothing like Caleb and doesn't act as if he needs to win me over by taking me out to fancy places or planning special events. Even though we've crossed over the friendship line, we've yet to go on an actual date, and we are both completely happy with simply hanging out. It's refreshing that we can still be exactly who we were a few weeks ago and don't feel like this shift has to change us.

With all that, it'll still be strange not to have him around. He's packing to go meet up with his older brother in La Jolla for a guys' trip. On top of that, Micah and Ady left yesterday to the Pacific Northwest for the next two weeks. I'm not quite sure what I'm going to do to fill the time aside from the few plans I've made to hang out with Brody while everyone is away.

"Are you sure you don't want me to drive you to the airport in the morning?"

"No, it's cool," he says from deep within his closet. He pulls down his board coffin and sets it on the bed next to me. "I have to be there around six thirty, so that means I need to leave here at the ass crack of dawn."

"Why did you book such an early flight?"

"Because Garrett has a buddy who just moved there, and he's throwing a party at his new house tomorrow night. He wanted me to fly out early so we have time to chill beforehand." He grabs his shortboard and slips it into his travel coffin before asking, "Would you go into Micah's room and get my hybrid?"

Micah has a vast collection of boards in his room, but I easily spot Trent's teal Cannibal board and bring it back to him. "Here you go," I say as I hand it over.

I stand and watch him zip up the coffin before he props it against the wall and an unforeseen zing of jealousy creeps in. Trent's about to spend a week around all the west coast bunnies, and I'm going to be here. It's a strange feeling because I have no idea where his head is at exactly with us, but it also seems way too premature to ask him. I have no clue if we're just casual and still free to do our own thing. Not that I have any interest in talking to anyone else, but what if he does?

Maybe gray isn't where I want to be.

"Is Garrett single?" I ask in my curiosity.

"Yeah, why?"

With a shake of my head and a shrug, I respond as casually as possible. "Just wondering."

After he tosses in a few pairs of flip-flops, he closes the suitcase and wheels it next to the boards. When he turns back to me, he gives me a peculiar look. "You thinking about ditching me for him or something?"

Pushing my fingers through my hair, I ask, "Are you even mine to ditch?"

There's a shift in his eyes, and I instantly regret asking. There is no doubt he just saw right through me. "Is something worrying you about this trip?"

"No," I defend, but it comes out too quick and too sharp.

The corners of his lips lift as he steps closer. "You seem unsettled. Almost as if you might be a little insecure."

"Oh my god. Insecure about what?"

"The thought that I might hookup with someone while I'm there."

I open my mouth to say something, to press further, but I get hung up and stall.

"You tongue-tied?" he taunts.

"No."

With a cock of his head, he keeps goading. "If there's something you want to ask me, just ask."

"There's nothing I want to ask you."

His lips pull into a full smile, and I bite my cheek to keep from cracking my own.

Two more steps, and he's standing right in front of me. "Are you sure about that?"

I fold my arms across my chest and throw the ball back into his court. "What do you think I want to ask you?"

He peers down at me with his perfectly imperfect eyes that make my tummy somersault. "I think you want to know if we're solid or if we're casual."

A swell of nerves builds around me, and he has me on needles. Trent's a free-spirited guy, one who avoids strings at all costs, and to expect anything other than that would be dumb of me.

"Well, since you brought it up . . ."

He slips his hands along my jaw as he chuckles lightly. "You have nothing to worry about," he says, soothing the insecurity he knew was there. "I'm solid with you."

Relief washes over me.

"Is that what you wanted to hear?"

I give him a bashful nod, and he gives me a reassuring kiss before smacking my ass.

"Ouch!" I screech as I push him away. He only laughs as he approaches again.

His eyes grow deviously playful as he taunts me step for step. Holding out my arms in front of me, I backup but with no escape.

"Don't pretend like you don't want me."

"I don't," I try asserting through a fit of giggles as he closes in.

I launch to my right, but he's quick to block me. My laughter only grows when I bolt to my left, only to fake him out and dart back to the right. As I charge away from him, he loops his arms around my waist, capturing me against his chest from behind. I squeal happily while he ravages my neck, tickling me with his kisses as I squirm in his hold.

Bursts of laughter barrel out of me as his arms constrict, making it impossible for me to free myself. My skin breaks out in goose bumps, and I grow short of breath. Grabbing on to his forearms, something inside me snaps, and suddenly, my smile hurts and I can't breathe.

Panic crashes over me like a tidal wave, shooting my heart into my throat. He has me trapped, and the moment I close my eyes, I get a flash of Caleb's rage.

"Stop," I attempt to scream, but it comes out too weak because I'm winded and can't take in a decent breath.

Trent's laughter gets buried beneath the screaming in my head, and I freak out. The weight of him is smothering. Tears spring from my eyes as fear takes me captive, and I don't even realize that I'm free from his hold until I'm halfway across the room with a heart hammering against my ribs.

Trent stares at me in horror. "Shit," he breathes heavily. "I'm sorry, Kate."

He takes a step toward me, and this time, when I hold my arms out, he stops.

I try to catch my breath, but the sudden rush of fright that just came out of nowhere is startling and slightly disorienting, but somehow, I manage to mutter a faint, "I'm sorry."

All the joy this room just held is sucked out in an instant because of me. Embarrassment scorches my neck as the alarm stays rooted in Trent's expression.

With a heart that won't stop terrorizing me, I'm on the brink of crying, so I quickly mutter, "Just give me a minute," before rushing out of the room and shutting the door behind me.

On wobbly knees, I lean against the wall and hunch over. I don't know how to make sense out of what just happened. I've never experienced anything like that before. Taking in a few deep breaths, I feel my pulse slow to a steadier pace, which helps bring my senses back to life. As my head clears, my emotions become too ripe, and I lower myself to the floor. With my knees pulled to my chest and my forehead pressed against them, I tell myself to calm down, that everything is fine, and that Trent would never . . . never hurt me, but my confusion makes it difficult to compose myself.

When the door opens, I lift my head, and Trent steps out into the hall before kneeling in front of me. He doesn't say anything as he lays his hands on my knees, but he sees the tears, which are reflections of bad memories, on my face.

"Are you okay?" he asks gently, but I'm not sure how to answer him.

The question is more complex than it sounds. Truth is, I'm a mix of peace and chaos, torn between two spheres. It reminds me that I still have issues I need to deal with. The majority of the time, I feel okay, but right now, it's as if I'm caged by my own flesh and bone in a swarm of petrifying memories.

"I'm sorry," I whisper. "I don't know what happened."

Slipping his feet out from under him, he sits by my side, the two of us facing each other when he asks, "Does this have something to do with Caleb?"

His name is like a razor digging through scars I wish would heal, but they won't because he silently haunts me. I wipe my damp cheeks and shamefully nod. "I'm sorry," I tell him again.

"Why are you sorry?"

"Because you shouldn't have to deal with this."

"Hey." The word is barely a breath of sound as he scoots closer to me and pushes my loose hair behind my ear. "You say that as if you're a burden."

It's exactly what I feel like I am—a burden.

When I don't respond, he assures, "You're not."

I look at him and the veracity in his eyes—something Caleb's never held, something I didn't know I needed until now. It's as if looking at Trent is like looking up at the infinite sky in wonderment of what all it holds and if it's holding it for me alone.

"I need to ask you something you might not want to talk about."

My stomach curls into itself, and even though I want to run and push him away, the need to grab on to him is stronger.

"What happened that night . . ." He starts and then hesitates before finishing. "Had it ever been worse than that?"

My head drops, and I hug my knees a little tighter. These are the moments I've worked hard to avoid thinking about. It's a pain I'm still trying to cope with—a pain I always assumed came from a place of love, but now know it didn't. I'm not even sure if love was ever there on his end. I *want* to believe that it was because to think that he didn't love me at all would hurt me even more—to know that I endured all of that for nothing.

Trent lays a tender hand on my back, and when I lift my head to answer, remembrance salts the secrets I've held on to and I hesitate.

"Was it ever worse?" he presses, furrowing his brows as if he's bracing himself for the impact.

I feel an overwhelming sense of guilt, but I rest my trust on his word that we are in fact solid when I finally nod.

With a considerable sigh, his whole body goes tense with emotion. I want to reach out and smooth my hands along his muscles, but I'm scared to move. And then a thought occurs to me: What if I'm the one he's mad at? After all, I'm the one who allowed it to happen, I'm the one who put myself in that situation, and I'm the one who stayed faithfully by his side.

Knowing that I might be the cause of his anger kills me. I don't want to be a disappointment to him. The idea stirs anguish inside me, and quietly, I begin to cry. When he sees my pain, he pulls me into his arms.

"I'm sorry," I whimper.

He shakes his head against mine. "No, I'm the one who needs to be apologizing to you."

Confused, I pull back. "For what? You didn't do anything."

"Exactly. I didn't do shit when I knew something wasn't right." He takes a slow blink, and it's now I see the small puddle of tears rimming his eyes. "I didn't know how to talk to you, and every time I tried, we'd end up fighting, so I backed off. I just . . . I had no clue it was as bad as what it was." He rakes his hand through his long hair and pinches his eyes shut for a moment before confessing, "I did nothing to protect you." His voice strains around each word.

"Even if you had done something more than you already had, I wouldn't have listened."

"Why?"

There are a lot of reasons, none of which are easy to admit, but I can see the blame he holds for something he had nothing to do with, so I push past my humiliation and give him a piece of this very complicated puzzle I'm still trying to figure out. "Because it was how I knew he loved me." He starts shaking his head, but I go on to add, "And because I thought I deserved it."

His face pains, and the urge to take it away is immense.

"Tell me you don't still think that."

"I'm getting there," I respond, looking him in the eyes. The aftershock of what Caleb did to me has morphed into a shame I'm trying to find my way out of, but even though I know that what he did was wrong, I still struggle to accept that it wasn't my fault.

With his hand behind my neck, he pulls me into him, and I settle my head along the curve of his shoulder. I band my arms around him and take as much comfort from him as he's taking from me.

As close as we are, I still can't shake the feeling that he's disappointed in me for the choices I made, and I need to know where I stand in his eyes, so I ask, "Are you mad?"

"What?" He draws back. "Why would you think that?"

"Because I did this."

"You didn't do shit, Kate. I'll tell you that for forever because you need to believe me when I tell you that you did *nothing* to deserve what he did to you." Cradling my face, he adds, "I hate that piece of shit for getting inside your head and fucking it all up. What he gave you was nothing even close to love, and I know you think that I don't have a clue about what love is, and maybe you're right, but *this*"—he takes my hand and presses it against his chest—"these feelings I have for you . . . it's fucking killing me to think that you believe someone putting their hands on you is love."

"I know." Another tear drops. "I can see that now, but in the moment, when I was with him, I couldn't."

"I need to know that you aren't still hung up on him."

With my hand still covering his heart, I fist his T-shirt in my fingers and tell him, "No. I was for a while, but I'm not anymore. The only thing I'm hung up on are all the pieces he left me with. I'm still trying to sort through everything and make sense of it."

"I can understand that. This isn't easy for me—letting someone into my life the way I want to let you in."

"It isn't easy for me either."

"I want to be sure that we're on the same page."

Shifting onto my knees, I sit between his legs, and this time, it's me who takes him in my hands. His eyes bore into mine when I tell him, "You make me feel safe in a way I haven't felt before. It terrifies me because you could easily hurt me."

"I feel the exact same way." He takes me by the hips and pulls me on top of his lap, adding, "But I promise that I'm not going to hurt you."

Through fear and hope, I kiss him, and when I do, he drags his tongue along my salted lips, taking my pain and swallowing it whole. Gripping his hair in my hands, I hold on to him as I silently vow to do what I can to heal this damaged heart of mine. Trent deserves the best of me, and I want to be able to give it to him. I know I come with broken pieces, but maybe he's the one who's meant to gather them up, reshape and repurpose them, and then help me put them back together. I have to trust him enough to allow that to happen, and right now, with the stain of him on my tongue, I believe I'm ready to let some of these walls of mine down. Because I'm realizing that whatever hesitations I might have about giving my heart over to Trent, it's too late—I'm already giving it.

Thirteen

KATE

Since the moment I woke this morning, I've had an unexplainable zing of energy. It's my twenty-second birthday today. When I told Trent my plans to go back home to celebrate with my family, I asked if he wanted to come with me. He wanted to know if Caleb had ever been to my house to meet my parents, so I told him about Thanksgiving, that Caleb had come for the weekend. I explained why I lied to him about not being allowed to stay at the house, confided in him about how angry Caleb got when I refused to go with him to the hotel, how he put his hands on me and accused me of choosing my family over him. I was blind to the manipulation, but Trent's been helping me see things more clearly, and now, when I look back, it's easy to recognize that Caleb did that with everything. He always had to be my highest priority, no matter what, and if he ever felt that I was putting someone before him, he'd punish me and call it love.

Clarity is a difficult thing to experience, but it's helping me get to a more rational place inside my head.

Trent couldn't be any more opposite of my ex, and for that, I'm going into this trip with a lot less anxiety.

While I wait for Trent to pick me up, I set my overnight bag next to the door. With Caleb still lingering in my thoughts, I find myself being pulled back into my bedroom. It was during Trent's trip to La Jolla that I finally tossed the picture I'd been hanging on to. It felt good to finally let it go—a release I desperately needed.

Opening my jewelry box, I pick up the diamond necklace Caleb bought me after the fight in Chicago. The sparkly pendant dangles from the delicate chain, and I wonder how I could have ever thought he gave it to me out of love when it's so clearly nothing more than another manipulation.

I've been hanging on to it because I've been trying to decide what I should do with it. Thoughts of pawning it have crossed my mind, but I don't want the money, I just want to be free of the thing.

When I walk into the bathroom and lift the seat of the toilet, I smile at how pissed he would be to know that all the money he spent is going straight into the sewer. I let go and it drops into the water with a soft plop, and for everything he put me through, I flush his expensive token of fake love.

I stare into the bowl as it refills with fresh water and don't think twice about my decision because I'm too busy enjoying the feeling of another broken piece of myself healing.

There is a knock on my door, and I open it to find Trent standing there with a smile on his face and a present in his hands.

"I said no gifts."

He steps inside and closes the door. "I suck at listening," he says, handing me the box, which is wrapped in black paper with a leopard ribbon tied around it. When I give him an inquisitive look, he explains, "I had Ady wrap it."

From the size of the box, I can tell he didn't get me some cheesy piece of jewelry.

"Go ahead. Open it."

I untie the ribbon slowly, but once it's off, I rip through the paper to find a Converse shoebox, and my smile grows when I lift the lid to find a custom designed pair of Chucks. "Oh my god," I squeal as I pull out the shoes and toss the box onto the floor. Maybe some girls would be disappointed to receive something like this for their birthday, but not me. It's so Trent, and the thoughtfulness he put into designing them is beyond sweet. "These are perfect!"

"Yeah?"

"Yeah." With a shoe in each hand, I sling my arms around his neck and kiss him, mumbling against his lips, "Thank you."

After kicking off the plain white Chucks I was going to wear today, I take the new ones over to the couch, sit, and slip them on. The bodies of the shoes are cherry red and the tongues and heel stripes are leopard print. He kept the sidewall and label classic, the way I like them, and added white contrast stitching.

Once I've tied the bright white laces, I stand and admire the shoes before showing them off, asking, "How do they look?"

"Turn around," he requests, and I figure he wants to see the heel stripe, but instead, he playfully smacks my ass. "Looks fucking good."

I jump away and laugh.

After cleaning up the wrapping paper, he grabs my bag and we head down to his Jeep. As he drives north, I can't stop peeking down at my feet, and when he takes my hand and pulls it on to his lap, he asks, "What's that smile all about?"

"These are dope shoes."

He smiles over at me, and it couldn't be more perfect. With each passing day, my heart falls for him a little more.

"Are you excited to see your family?" he asks.

"Yeah, I haven't been home since spring break. Plus, Audrina will be there, and I haven't seen her since last Christmas."

"Where is she going to college?"

"She's at the University of Alabama, but she'll be studying in England for the next year. She leaves in a few weeks."

"England? What made her want to do that?"

"She's always dreamed of living abroad, so she applied to an art conservation program there. It was no surprise when she got accepted. Audrina is a lot like my mother," I tell him. "She has lofty aspirations and likes the finer things, whereas my dad and I are more simple and laidback."

"It's the same with Garrett," he says as he merges off the interstate. "He's always had his head screwed on tight."

An hour and a half later, I lead Trent into my parents' house, but before I can announce that I'm here, my mother calls out, "Kate? Is that you?"

"Yeah."

Trent and I make our way toward where we heard her voice, but she meets us in the hallway and pulls me in for a big hug.

"How was the drive?"

"Same as always." I then take a step back. "Mom, this is Trent."

"It's so nice to meet you," she greets just as footsteps thunder down the stairs.

My sister and I both squeal unapologetically as we run and hug each other. This is the longest we've been apart.

"I've missed you so much," she bellows.

"Me too." Loosening my arms, I pull back and notice her new shoulder-length hair. "When did you chop all your hair off?"

"Earlier this summer. You like it?" she asks.

"I do. You look so much older." She peeks over my shoulder, and I smile as I turn to Trent. "This is Audrina."

The two of them say their hellos before she leans in and whispers, "Is he your boyfriend?"

Trent and I have managed to lay low for the most part, but when I asked my dad if I could bring him with me for the weekend, he obviously wanted to know who this guy was. I explained that we're figuring it out and taking things slow. The last thing I wanted was my family to start forming any opinions before they met him.

I completely dodge her question and turn back to my mom. "Where's Dad?"

"Right here," he announces as he walks in from the backyard. He gives me an endearing smile and then opens his arms. "Come here, sweetheart."

I hold on to him longer than I held on to my mom or sister. Even though we talk all the time, I missed him and the comfort of his hugs that always make everything feel better.

"It's good to have you back home."

"It's good to be home." I smile. "Dad, this is Trent."

The two of them shake hands, and instead of my dad giving him a welcoming hi, he says, "Kate tells me you surf."

"Yeah, she had me bring my board."

"Is that right? What do you have?"

"I brought my Pyzel Bastard with me. Just picked it up a couple of weeks ago when I was in California."

My dad smiles wide. "I have a Bastard myself."

"No shit?"

My mother's eyes widen when Trent cusses, but it doesn't even phase my dad.

"It's old as hell, but it's faithful," he says. "I have a pretty decent collection that I keep in Kate's room."

"You're using my room to store your boards now?"

"Your mom got sick of them being in our room," he explains before turning to Trent. "Come on, I'll show you what I got."

The two of them head upstairs, and I'm happy that my father is holding true to his word to go easy on Trent.

As soon as the two of them are out of earshot, my sister teases, "He's hot, like, in a bad-boy kinda way."

"What? He's far from a bad boy."

"And he's far from your ex too."

That's the truth. When Caleb met my family, he was pristine in his tailored button-up and high-shine loafers. But Trent walked right in wearing shorts and a T-shirt with his long hair hanging out of his backward-facing Hurley ball cap, which is so weathered he really needs to throw it away.

"So, what are the plans?" I ask my mom.

"I think your dad is itching to spend time on the water with you, so I was going to take Audrina out shopping and let you have the afternoon with him. But tomorrow, before you leave, I'd like to take you out without the boys, if that's okay?"

"Yeah, sure," I agree. "Sounds good."

When the guys come back downstairs, my father says, "Get your gear together."

"Where are we going?"

"Juno beach."

"I'll grab the bags from outside," Trent says.

When he returns, I show him to the guest bedroom that's down the hall from my room, and then I go change before we head out.

The day couldn't be more perfect. It's almost always just me and my dad out here on the water, but to have Trent with us makes it all the better. The three of us catch waves, throw tricks, and idle in the water on our boards, making small talk. Seeing my dad and Trent get along so well makes me smile. It's apparent that they have a lot in common, which I already knew, and although my father is a lot less crude with his language than Trent, their free-spirited personalities are very similar.

It's one more thing that reinforces the idea that I'm right

where I should be. Since graduating high school, I've battled with feeling out of place. When I was with Caleb, he vanished that insecurity, yet I still had so much in me that remained adrift. Now that I'm with Trent, everything just feels so right—everything is so much easier with him. I just wonder if I'm as good for him as what he is for me.

Fourteen

KATE

"There you guys are," my mother says. "How was the beach?"

"Perfect," I tell her. "What's for dinner? It smells amazing."

"Snapper, red potatoes, and roasted asparagus." She holds out her arms to collect our towels. "Go get cleaned up. Dinner will be ready in twenty minutes."

Showered and sun-kissed, I take a seat at the dining room table where my mom has already set and served our plates.

"This looks so good," Trent tells my mom.

"Well, I hope you're hungry because I made a lot of food."

"Dude, I'm so starved I could eat a limp biscuit," he says as he picks up his fork and stabs a potato.

My father clearly knows what he meant by that and starts laughing.

"What's a limp biscuit?" my mom questions.

Audrina quickly warns, "Don't ask."

Trent chuckles under his breath as I nudge him, but he ignores me and tells my sister, "You shouldn't know what one is."

"Neither should Kate, but it's obvious she does."

"Can we talk about something else?" I say.

Both Audrina and Trent laugh while my mother lingers in the land of confusion.

"So, Trent," she says, "where did you grow up?"

"Tampa."

"What do your parents do?"

"My mom's a pediatrician," he tells her before taking a bite of his fish.

"And your dad?"

"Don't know. He walked out on us when I was five."

His answer clearly surprises my family, but Trent is so nonchalant about it that they don't seem to know how to react. I asked him once if he ever missed his dad, and he explained that it was hard for him to miss what he'd never had. Still, I think deep down, it bothers him, but he just hides it really well.

"I'm so sorry," my mom responds gently.

"It's cool." He takes another bite. "This shit's good."

"Oh, umm . . . thank you."

My dad pipes in and echoes the compliment, saying, "All her shit is good," slipping in the curse word as a way of telling my mom to loosen up.

Not that my mom should have a reason to be uptight around Trent, after all, she's married to a man who is just like him.

My dad grabs a roll from the basket before asking, "What are you majoring in, Trent?"

"Business finance."

"Oh wow," my mother responds. "Do you know what you want to do after you graduate?"

"Not a damn clue," he admits. "I just figured it would be the best thing to get my degree in since numbers come easy for me."

"Audrina, are you excited to leave for England?" I ask, wanting to take the focus off Trent for a while.

Once she starts talking about the upcoming school year, she

can't stop, and the conversation stays focused on her until the plates are empty and my mom is bringing out a decadent strawberry crème cake—my favorite.

Once we're full and the table has been cleared, my dad tosses his napkin and calls out to my mom, who's in the kitchen washing dishes with my sister, "Honey, can I get a cup of coffee?"

"Oh no," is the next thing we hear before she walks into the dining room. "We're completely out."

"You're slacking, woman," he teases, and she gives him a playful sneer.

"I'll run up to the store because we're going to need some for the morning."

"Mom, I'll go."

"Are you sure?"

I turn to Trent, and he agrees, "Yeah, we'll run and grab some."

"Thank you so much."

"Where are you going?" Audrina hollers from the kitchen.

"We're going to the store to get coffee."

"I want to come."

She emerges from the kitchen and tosses the dishtowel she's holding to my mom.

"What do you need to get?"

She looks at my mom, and says, "Cereal. All you have in the pantry is old people fiber stuff."

My mom rolls her eyes while my father tosses a few bills onto the table, which Audrina snatches up with a perky, "Thanks!"

We head outside, get into the Jeep, and I toss my purse into the back seat with my sister.

"Hey, you have any lip gloss or lip balm?" she asks.

"I should have something in my purse."

"God, this thing is huge," she complains while I give Trent directions to the store.

"Did you have fun surfing with my dad today?"

Trent glances at me with a smile. "It was good. He's chill. It's hard to imagine him as a cop."

I laugh. "Oh, I have stories."

We go on talking, and when we make it to the store, I reach into the back seat to grab my purse, take one look at what my sister is holding, and freak out. "Oh, shit!"

My sister startles as she chews a gummy from the bag she found in my purse. "What?"

I swipe it from her hand as Trent parks. "Why are you eating these?"

"What's your problem?" she snaps. "I'll buy you another bag."

"Relax," Trent tells me, and when I hold the bag up to show him what I'm talking about, his lips break into a devious smile. "Dude."

Turning back to Audrina, I ask, "How many of these did you eat?"

"I don't know, I wasn't keeping count," she scoffs. "Geez, what's the big deal?"

"Oh my god." I drop my head in my palms before adding, "I'm so dead."

"Anyone care to clue me in?"

Trent turns to my sister while I try not to hyperventilate and tells her, "Those are edibles."

"What do you mean?"

My hands fall from my face, and I blurt out, "It's pot!"

"It's what?"

I turn to face her. "It's pot. What you just ate were marijuana gummies."

Her jaw drops. "What the hell are you doing with marijuana?"

"I bought them yesterday and forgot to take them out of my purse."

"Wait!" She holds out her hand to stop me from saying anything else. "You do drugs?"

Rolling my eyes, I groan, "No, I don't do drugs; I do pot."

She looks at Trent and then back to me, utterly shocked. "When did you start using pot?" Trent bursts into laughter, and I slap his arm. "Do you do this too?"

"Uh, yeah," he tells her.

"How long have you been doing this?" she asks me, totally stunned.

"Since high school."

"I can't believe I never knew this about you."

"It isn't like I go around broadcasting it, and in case you forgot, our dad is a cop, so you better not say a word."

She sits still for a second. "Well, I don't feel anything."

"Dude"—Trent chuckles—"you will."

"What's going to happen?"

"You're gonna be fucking lit," he tells her.

"How many did you eat?"

She shrugs. "I don't know . . . four, maybe five."

"Holy shit, girl."

"Oh my god, Trent. What are we going to do?"

"Is that bad?"

"I take one to get high and two to get blasted," I tell her. "So, yeah, in about thirty minutes, you're going to be stoned out of your ever-loving mind."

"You girls stay here. I'm running in to grab the coffee and cereal so we can get home before that shit hits her."

When Trent hops out of the Jeep, she leans forward, and I can see the panic in her eyes. "Am I going to, like, overdose or something?"

"It's pot, not heroin."

"Well, I don't know!"

"You'll be fine. Honestly, you're going to have a pretty epic high."

"What does it feel like?"

"For sure, you're going to be paranoid, but you'll mostly be giddy and talking nonsense. But please, for the love of all that's holy, don't get loud because Mom and Dad will kill me if they find out about this."

After a few minutes, Trent comes out of the store with a whole lot more than coffee and a box of cereal.

"What's all this?" I ask when he gets into the driver's seat.

He hands Audrina the bags and she starts digging through them when he says, "Food for her munchies. I figured having this on hand would keep her from raiding the kitchen." He then looks at my sister through the rearview mirror and tells her, "Hide that shit in Kate's purse."

"This is all junk and loaded with carbs," she whines.

"You're not going to care about carbs in a couple hours," he teases before asking, "Are there any gummies left?"

"No!" I bark. "You are not getting high tonight."

"Dude, you know how painful it's going to be having to watch your sister have the fucking time of her life tonight and not join in."

Grabbing the nearly empty bag, I open his glove compartment and shove it in.

"When we get home, go straight to your room," I tell her.

"You don't think that's going to look suspicious?"

I shrug. "If Mom asks, just tell her you started your period and you're going to lie down for the night."

Trent makes an ick face. "Ugh, fucking gross."

"Don't be such a dude."

"Can't help it. But fine, go with that lady shit, and then tell them that we're all going to hang out in her room and watch a movie, which will explain all the damn snacks if they happen to see them."

Once we're home, no one questions our cover story, and we tell my parents good night before heading upstairs to Audrina's bedroom.

Trent sits at her desk while my sister and I settle on her bed. As I start fishing all the snacks out of my purse and stacking them on her nightstand, I catch Trent watching my sister. He motions his head for me to look at her. When I do, I find she's staring off into nothing. Hell, she isn't even blinking.

Knowing that she's never been high before and with how much she took, I'm worried about her paranoia, and I'm cautious not to rattle her. The last thing I want is her freaking out.

"Audrina." My voice is soft, and her response is way delayed.

"Yeah?"

"How're you feeling?"

She blinks a few times, and when she finally turns her head in my direction, she asks, "Do you think it's happening?"

Trent busts out laughing. "You make it sound like the apocalypse is upon us."

"You think that's a real thing?" she asks him, and there's no doubt her high is setting in. "I mean, it's in the bible, right? So, it must be legit."

He smiles at her, and I shake my head, silently begging him not to egg her on. He ignores me. "You want to know what I question?"

"Huh?"

"The zombie apocalypse."

Her whole face drops, and I roll my eyes.

She flops down on to her stomach and asks, "You believe that could happen?"

He shrugs as he rocks back in the chair. "Depends on whether you believe in zombies or not."

"You know what I wonder about?" she starts. "Okay, so, you know how some dogs will just eat their toys. You know, like how they eat all the stuffing out of the . . . you know those things," she says, motioning nonsense with her hands. "You know what I'm talking about? The soft things . . ."

Trent's brows furrow in confusion.

"Come on! You know what I'm talking about."

"You mean a plush toy?" I ask.

"Yes!"

She then falls silent as we wait for her to finish this very random thought, but there's a total loss in her eyes.

"Go on," Trent encourages.

"Wait. What was I talking about?" She takes another long pause as she retraces her thoughts. "Oh! Yeah, so okay, you know how some dogs eat the stuffing out of the toys?" she repeats, and Trent nods. "What if—" A fit of giggles cuts her words off, and Trent couldn't possibly be enjoying this more as he watches her with a huge grin on his face. "What if—" Another round of giggles hits her, and the girl can barely breathe around them, which has me laughing too. She snorts and then pops up on her knees as if she's finally gotten control of herself, but clearly, she hasn't. "What if, when they poop, it floats out of their butt like little cotton ball clouds?"

She then completely loses it, cracking herself up and toppling over onto her side. She's so loud I have to cover her mouth with my hand.

"Shh, you're being so loud." Next thing I know, she licks my hand. I pull it away from her and wipe my palm on her bed. "Eww."

"What did she do?"

"She licked me."

"You taste salty," she says in all seriousness before flopping onto her back and looking at Trent from upside down. She locks her gaze to his for a long while and then questions, "Are your eyes two different colors?"

"No, you're just fucking blasted."

"I like you," she quips, and I shake my head at him when he shoots her a wink. "I think *Katerina* likes you too," she adds, enunciating my full name with a thick accent.

"Katerina?"

"No one actually calls me that," I tell him.

"She totally likes you," she continues. "Even though she won't tell me."

"You think so?"

"Oh, yeah," she says, dragging out the words dramatically.

"Can we not talk about this," I mumble, but Trent shuts me down when he asks her, "What all has she said about me?"

"Nothing. She's being *super secretive*," she says, whispering the last two words in exaggeration.

"Has she brought home guys like me in the past?"

Again, I shake my head at him, but he's getting so much joy out of this that I let it go.

Audrina rolls on to her tummy with an enthusiastic, "No! The girl is practically a virgin when it comes to guys."

"Audrina!" I scold, but all she does is laugh.

"It's true, you went out with some dude for, what, a month in high school. And then there was that dork you brought home for Thanksgiving a couple of years ago; although, he did have a sexy car."

Trent's eyes shift to mine. He knows she's talking about Caleb.

"I knew it wouldn't last when he said grace before we ate," she adds, and I want to die of embarrassment.

"He did what?"

"Yep," she says. "It's true. I mean, he was cute and all, but he was weird. I don't know. Something about him."

"Okay," I butt in. "Can we talk about something else?"

"Let's talk about Trent," she says before turning to face me as if he isn't even in the room.

"No."

"Oh, come on."

"Yeah, Kate. Let's talk about Trent," he jokes.

"We're not talking about Trent."

She then crawls over to where I'm sitting against the headboard, lies across my lap, and gazes up at the ceiling. It's quiet for about five seconds before she's laughing again. Lord only knows what's going through her head, but she's having the time of her life, and I'm forced to muffle her giggles once again.

This goes on for a couple of hours before she passes out like a rock. It's a little after eleven when Trent and I step into the hall and close her door behind us.

"I never thought it would end," he whispers as we walk down the dark hall to my room.

"I'm just glad she finally fell asleep."

"Dude, I can't believe she murdered all that food."

Trent follows me into my room and shuts the door.

"You can't be in here."

"Says who?"

I tilt my head and perch my hands on my hips.

"The rule was I couldn't sleep in here."

"Exactly."

He strides over to me with a smirk. "I'm not planning to go to sleep yet," he taunts before pushing me back onto the bed.

I stifle a giggle as he climbs over me and starts dropping kisses down my neck. Holding his head in my hands, I grip fistfuls of his hair as his tongue drags along my collarbone. He sends a shiver up my spine while he teases the hem of my shirt before slowly dragging the fabric up and over my bra. His head dips down, and he kisses my stomach.

In the darkness of the room, I close my eyes and get lost in him. His hair tickles along my flesh, and when his hand slides to my breast, he tugs the fabric and exposes me. It's the first time he's seen me like this, and I grow nervous, not because I don't trust him but because I've known him for so long that it's still weird for him to see me this way.

I watch as he takes me into his mouth, and when he begins to gently suck, I let go of a breathy moan as I arch into him. His tongue drags along my sensitive skin, and I feel him growing hard against me. I'm nowhere near ready for this to end, but we can't be doing this with my parents downstairs.

Pushing against his head, he comes up to me and presses his lips to mine, urging my mouth open. Without a word, he takes my unspoken signal and lowers my shirt as he continues to kiss me deeply. His hips grind between my legs, and the pressure sends a rush of tingles through my core.

"Trent," I whisper against his lips.

"Fuck, you feel so good."

Shit, even his voice is turning me on.

He has my body in knots, and I swear if he grinds against me again, I might just explode.

"We have to stop," I tell him, and he drops his head into the curve of my neck. "We can't do this here."

He releases a heavy sigh, and I feel guilty for stopping him.

We've been taking things slow over these past two months, and I'm sure this is the longest this boy has gone without sex.

He's only brought it up once, and that was after he got back from his trip a couple of weeks ago. I explained to him that I wasn't ready, and he understood, but it isn't making this any easier.

Heartbreak sucks and I'm scared to be that intimately vulnerable with another person again.

He tries to lighten the mood by pulling back and rubbing his dick, joking, "If I sneeze, I'm going to blow a batch right here."

He wants me to laugh, but I can't. Pushing myself off the bed, I sit up, and he can tell I'm bothered.

"You okay?"

"I'm sorry."

"For what?"

"I promise, I want to give you more, I just—"

"You think I'm upset?" he asks. "Babe, it's fine."

"I know you can't be fine."

Running his fingers through my hair, he assures, "I'm fine," before nodding to his right arm and teasing, "My muscles have never been this jacked in my life."

And this time, I can't contain my giggle despite feeling like I'm letting him down.

"Seriously, though. You don't need to worry about anything. It isn't like I expected to get in your pants and hit it with your parents downstairs."

I drop my head on to his chest, and he plants a kiss in my hair. With a heavy breath, I lift my chin and look into his eyes. He makes me nervous in a way that gets me all tongue-tied, and I wish I could find the words to tell him what it is he's doing to my heart.

"You're so fucking beautiful," he whispers before giving me a kiss that's so slow, so tender, it borders on torture. He parts his mouth from mine all too soon and drags his hand lightly along the side of my face. "I'll see you in the morning." He then walks out of the room and shuts the door behind him.

I drop to my back, breathless and completely falling in love, I just wish I could find a way to tell him. Fear has a funny way of silencing a person, so I lie here in the dead of night with his taste in my mouth and a thousand unspoken words dancing on my tongue.

Fifteen

TRENT

THE HOUSE IS QUIET WHEN I ROLL OUT OF BED AND STEP INTO THE hallway. When I crack open Kate's door and peek inside, I find her curled up in her sheets, still sound asleep. Deciding not to wake her, I close her door and head down the hall, passing Audrina's room on my way to the stairs. There's no question that girl is still out cold.

"Morning," Steve says when I walk into the kitchen. He's standing by the coffee pot, wearing workout gear, and pouring sugar into his mug.

"I didn't think anyone was up yet."

"I hit the gym religiously at five thirty every morning." Grazing the spoon along the rim of his cup before setting it on the counter, he tells me, "Mugs are up there."

I pull one from the cabinet and pour myself some coffee.

"Did you sleep well?"

"Yeah," I lie. After leaving Kate's room, I found myself tossing and turning for most of the night, wrestling with these damn feelings she's managed to bring to life.

"Come on; let's go out back."

I follow him through the quiet house and out to the large terrace that overlooks the expansive lawn.

"How late were you guys up last night? I'm surprised the girls are still asleep."

"Not too late. Around midnight," I tell him when I take a seat in one of the chairs.

"I think the three of them are spending the morning together before you head back to Miami."

"That's what Kate said."

"You up for a few hours of surfing?" he suggests.

"Yeah, man. I'm always up for hitting the water."

Steve nods and takes a drink before setting his mug on the wicker coffee table. Leaning back in his chair, he asks, "So, Kate hasn't told me much about you. When did the two of you meet?"

"We actually met freshman year."

"That long ago?" he notes, and when he leans forward and rubs his palms together, he asks, "So, you knew Caleb?"

His name catches me off guard because I have no idea what this guy knows about Kate's ex, so I tell myself to tread carefully. "Yeah, unfortunately."

He nods as he looks down for a second. "Unfortunately?"

"I never liked the guy."

He reaches for his mug and takes another sip before turning and giving me a look of no bullshit—a look of a protective father who's ready to drill me.

"Kate won't talk about what happened between them, which doesn't sit well with me," he says. "The fact that she felt the need to run back here after they broke up was troubling—it still is. I just want to make sure she's okay."

"She's doing better."

"Better?"

It's understandable that he would want to know what

happened, but it isn't my place to tell him. "Look, I don't want to say too much because I don't want to betray her trust, but between us, that guy was a total dickfuck."

"In general or to her?"

"Both."

He drops his head and squeezes his hands together. "I'm typically good at reading people. He seemed like a nice enough kid when I met him."

"Nah, man," I say. "He was far from a nice guy."

He lifts his eyes and peers over at me. "What about you? Do I need to be worried?"

"I'd be worried about any guy who comes into her life, but that's only because I care about her."

"Good answer." He kicks his legs up onto the coffee table and leans back. "Do I still need to be concerned about her?"

"No. She's getting past it," I tell him because it's the truth. Ever since she started opening up more, I've seen a huge shift. That isn't to say she still doesn't have moments when the memories come crashing down. But there are fewer and fewer of those as time passes. It isn't because she's ignoring them, either. It's because she's dealing with the damage Caleb did and slowly allowing herself to heal.

"Has she talked to you about any of this?"

"It took her a while, but yeah, she's talked to me about it."

"Anything I need to know?"

The concern is written all over his face, and I can't blame him. I don't know what things were like for her after the breakup, but from the look in his eyes as he asks about his daughter, I get the sense that it was pretty bad, which sends a sharp pang through my chest.

"I don't think there's much to worry about now."

"You'll let me know if there is." It isn't a question as much as a demand, and I give him a consenting nod before he adds, "I've got my eyes on you."

And for the first time, I see the cop in him. I smirk and ask, "What, are you going to pull a background check on me or something?"

"I already have." He takes another sip from his mug, and I laugh.

"Didn't expect me to be so squeaky clean, did you?" I joke.

He chuckles and shakes his head. "It's what you've managed to keep off your record that I'm more curious about."

"You plan on having me followed?"

"Like I said, I'll be keeping my eyes on you."

"Fair enough." I nod and then we settle into a comfortable silence as we finish our coffee before heading inside.

While I'm refilling my mug, Kate comes down the stairs with a cardboard box in her arms.

"What do you have there, sweetheart?" her father asks.

"An old box of junk that was in my closet. I'm just throwing it away," she tells him as she heads out into the garage.

Steve claps my shoulder. "Be ready to go in fifteen minutes."

He heads to his room, and when Kate comes back inside, she says, "You're up early. What have you been doing?"

"Just hanging out with your dad."

"He isn't giving you a hard time, is he?"

"Nah," I respond when she slips her hands under the hem of my T-shirt and wraps her arms around me. I take her head in my palms and drop a kiss onto her forehead. "I need to get ready."

"Where are you going?"

"Surfing with your father."

"Sounds fun. I'm jealous." She grins and fixes herself a cup of coffee before we head upstairs. "I'm going to jump in the shower real fast," she tells me as I head into the guest room and throw on my board shorts.

As I'm tossing my things into my backpack, I grab my leash and notice it's beginning to fray. I go to Kate's room to see if she has an extra I can borrow in case mine snaps. When I round the bed to where her dad's boards are leaning against the wall, I stop and stare down at the pillows, which are still indented from where she slept on them. The first time I was in her room feels like a lifetime ago, and I wonder how different things would be if I had felt for her back then what I feel for her now.

I could've spared her the nightmare she wound up living through.

"What are you doing?" she asks when she steps out of the bathroom, wearing nothing but a towel as her hair drips water onto her shoulders.

"Shit, you need to throw some clothes on."

"That's what I'm doing." She walks over to her suitcase and flips the lid open.

"Hey," I say, watching her rifle through her things. "You remember that time, freshman year, when you faked that headache to get me into bed with you?"

After grabbing some clothes, she rights herself and glares at me. "That's a stretch."

I drop my smile when I think about everything that went down after that day we had at the beach—how everything went south.

"What's wrong?"

I shake my head to expel the thoughts, but they stick anyway as she walks over to me. "I should've made a move on you."

"You were too busy chasing bunnies."

And she's right. I was so busy trying to get my dick wet that I let her go and fall for that cunt, Caleb. Could've, would've, should've's breed regret, and when I hang my head, she presses a gentle palm against my cheek. "What is it?"

"Nothing," I tell her as my stomach sinks in disgust for my own actions. There's no doubt that, had we hooked up, it would've been the end of our friendship. The fact that we never went there is probably the only reason we were able to build what we have now.

Leaning in, I kiss her and push my hand through her wet hair as she moves her soft lips against mine. I could stand here and taste her all day and never grow tired, but her dad is waiting, so I force myself to pull away.

"I'll see you later?"

She smiles and nods before I head out. Tossing my bag over my shoulders, I run into Audrina when she comes out of her room.

"What's up?" I say while taking in her messy hair that looks like a fucking rat's nest.

She stands in her doorway and stares at me with a perplexed expression before her face softens into clarity. "Your eyes *are* two different colors."

I smile and clap my hand against the side of her arm with a proud, "It was a good high, wasn't it?"

As soon as I see the hint of a smile, I nod and head downstairs to meet Steve. After everything is loaded into my Jeep, we drive out to Juno Beach and kill the rest of the morning and half the afternoon in the water.

When he notices I'm struggling with my bottom turn technique, he offers his knowledge and instructs, "You need to squat lower and try digging the inside rail in more than what you're doing."

His advice pays off on my next ride.

When we aren't throwing down tricks, we wade on our boards and shoot the shit, getting to know each other better. It's cool to be able to come out here with him. I've never had a real father figure in my life, and although he isn't mine, he exudes a strong paternal vibe that I'm drawn to. It makes him an easy guy to want to be around.

As we drive back to the house, he tells me, "Make sure Kate brings you the next time she visits."

When we get back, Kate already has her things packed, so I take a quick shower and load our bags into my Jeep. Her family comes outside, and her mom gives me a hug and tells me how much she enjoyed the visit. Then I hang back and watch Kate give her sister a teary goodbye. The girls won't see each other for a while since Audrina is about to spend a year in England, and I know Kate is upset about it.

Steve pulls me in for a bro hug and gives my back a hard pat, saying, "You better take good care of my daughter."

I clap his hand and shake it. "No worries, man."

The drive down to Miami flies by without much talk at all, and when we get back to Kate's condo, the sun is starting to set. "Why don't you park in the garage and stay the night?" Kate asks, and it's an offer I won't ever refuse.

We drop everything on the floor by her door and drag ourselves into her room. Too tired to even think about dinner, we lie down and she curls up in my arms with a heavy sigh.

"You tired?"

"A little," she says.

Taking her hand, I pull it and wrap her arm around me. She nestles her head in the crook of my neck, and everything feels right. Falling for this girl was scary as shit, but it wasn't like I had any control over it. This was never what I thought I wanted, but the more time passed, the harder it became for me to want anything else. Now, it's as if my whole world rights itself when I have her in my arms, and I'm in deeper than I thought I was capable of.

"Your heart's pounding," she murmurs, and I feel it in my chest because that's what she does to me.

She draws back slightly and rests her head next to mine. When I shift to my side, I stare into her eyes and swear I feel something inside me amplify. Nervous and unsure of what to do or what to say because I've never felt this way about anyone before, I fumble. I don't know how to tell her the things that are racing through me. I'm not even sure if she's ready to hear me try.

"What are you thinking about?" she asks, but fear annihilates any chance of conjuring a coherent thought, so I kiss her instead.

As I pull her against me, a war brews inside my chest, causing my anxiety to burst and triggering my pulse to ramp up. Being this close to her has me in a tailspin, and I wish I could just fucking relax.

She senses my tension and parts her lips from mine, breathing a soft, "Hey."

Letting go of a long sigh, I rest my forehead against hers as she combs her fingers through my hair.

"What's going on?"

I'm dangling off the edge of a cliff; that's what's going on.

It's a terrifying excitement I'm unable to temper, and I'm scared to let her know how I feel because I'm not sure how she'll react.

"You have to help me out here because I don't know what the hell I'm doing," I admit with so much uncertainty.

"What do you mean?"

Restless, I roll on top of her, and she runs her hands over my shoulders.

"You have me feeling so many crazy things that I don't know how to make sense of them."

Her brows cinch slightly as she grows timid.

"Tell me I'm not alone."

Slowly, she shakes her head, and when I lift my chest and sit back on my heels, she pushes herself up with me.

"You scare the shit out of me," I confess.

"Why?"

"Because . . ." Battling my thoughts, I go ahead and throw them out there since I don't think I can possibly go another day holding all this in. "Because I never thought I would fall this hard for you, and I don't know how to tell you what I'm feeling."

It wasn't too long ago that Kate told me how scared she was to let herself be vulnerable with me. I didn't have the balls to tell her that I felt the same way then, but I'm trying to now.

"I'm scared I'm going to fuck this up," I reveal.

"I won't let you."

It's exactly what I need to hear, and it gives me the courage to take her in my hands and finally say what's been building for a while. "I think I'm in love with you."

The moment the words are out, her eyes shut for a moment, and when she opens them, they're rimmed in tears. "I already know I'm in love with you," she whispers heavily, and fuck if she didn't just strike a match and toss it onto all the doubt I've been battling.

She pushes onto her knees so that she's in front of me, and then she kisses me with so much fervency it feels like I'm being sanctified. My grip on her tightens, needing more, and she gives it to me, dipping her sweet tongue into my mouth and caressing it against mine. There is no comparison to what this girl does to me, and when she finally draws back, I watch in awe as she peels off her top. God damn, she's perfect. Reaching back, I rip off my shirt and toss it to the floor before dropping my mouth to hers, tasting a love I never thought existed for me, only to find that it does, and it's all within her.

I lay her back on the bed and find myself moving in a way that's completely new for me—with meaningful intentions. It's hard to hold back when it comes to her, but she does nothing to slow me when I slip my hand beneath her and unhook her bra.

Before I can remove it, she slides it down her arms and drops it to the floor, adding it to the pile. She stares up at me, exposed and with no bashfulness at all. Seeing her like this, bare and lying beneath me, has me completely shot to pieces.

She pulls me down, and I take her nipple in my mouth. Last night, she pushed me away, but this time, she pulls me closer as she tugs on my hair. Rolling my tongue over her, I almost fucking lose it when her skin tightens and hardens in my mouth. I take my time because I can't even imagine rushing this.

Her breaths kick up when I slide down her body and unzip her shorts. She lifts her hips, inviting me to pull them off, and when I do, I push her thighs apart. As soon as my tongue is on her, she exhales the sexiest moan, and I lose myself between her legs. She's so soft in my mouth.

Heat radiates in my chest and spirals its way through my body, and when she pulls me back up to her, she kisses me deeply, tasting what I taste. Her hands find the zipper to my shorts, and when there's nothing left separating us and we're skin on skin, I hover over her as she stares up into my eyes with a sincerity that rips right through me.

I struggle to breathe.

I didn't plan for this to happen, and I realize I'm not prepared. "I don't have anything."

"It's okay. I'm on the pill."

I can tell she's lost in the moment and not thinking, so I feel the need to assure her, "I'm clean. I always use protection."

She nods as she reaches down, takes me in her hand, and starts to stroke me.

"Fuck."

My elbows weaken, and I drop down to them, kissing her neck, while she runs her warm hand along my dick. When she starts to guide me into her, I swear my heart ricochets against my ribs.

My head drops to hers as I slowly sink in deeper, and everything about this moment feels completely different from all the others in the past. For the first time, I don't want to fuck just to get off. Never have emotions been involved like they are now, and I'm finding it difficult to keep myself from falling apart as I start to move my hips.

I watch the flush spread over her skin as she moves with me, and she couldn't possibly be any more beautiful. "God, you're perfect."

Her lips lift in a subtle smile before I thrust deeper and steal it away. She moans in pleasure, closing her eyes and pressing her hands into my back, urging me on. I give her everything she's wanting out of me, and when she breathes an emotional, "I love you," I nearly lose my shit.

She hugs her body to mine, moving with me, and I fucking love it. As I work her higher and higher, her ragged gasps grow. When her rhythm begins to falter, I know she's close, and damn it, I'm doing everything not to let myself go just yet because I want to make her feel everything she's making me feel.

She looks at me as if I'm her everything and reaches for my hand to hold. She clutches it tightly as her eyes fill with tears, and I kiss her slowly and deeply, making sure that she *knows* she's safe with me. I doubt anyone could love her more.

Using my other hand, I slip it behind her neck and pull her up to me, lifting her shoulders slightly off the bed because I need her closer, even if it is just an inch.

"Oh, god," she whimpers in pure satisfaction as her hand jerks in mine and her eyes swim out of focus as she falls apart. The moment I feel her tighten around me, I let myself go, and I swear this girl shatters me into a million fucking pieces. Her body tenses, and she grabs me tighter. The room fills with deep breaths and fractured moans as the two of us ride out our orgasms for as long as we can, giving and taking everything we have until there's nothing left.

My head is spinning from what just happened, and I swear she just wrecked me.

She falls back onto the bed, and I wrap my arms around her as I kiss her damp forehead while we struggle to catch our breath. When I look down, I find her cheeks coated in tears before she tucks her head into my chest.

"Don't hide from me," I request. There isn't a single part of her that I don't want.

I touch the side of her face, and her head falls to the pillow before she lifts her eyes to mine, allowing me to see straight inside her heart. All her cracks and broken parts expose themselves, setting me on fire like a thousand suns, and there's nothing I wouldn't do for this girl.

Pushing my fingers through her hair, which is sweaty at the roots, I press my chest against hers and confess, "I never knew it could be like that," and she comforts me when she says, "Me neither."

The very moment I start to pull away, she locks her legs around my hips and keeps me inside her.

"God damn," I breathe. "You feel so good."

And just like that, she has my heart—a heart I never intended to give away but had no hope of keeping from her. I can't imagine another person in this world who could bring me to my knees the way she has.

"Tell me you love me," I request, needing to hear it.

Pulling my lips down to hers, I swear she breathes life into me when she whispers, "I love you," etching the words across my heart.

Sixteen

KATE

"How do we already have a paper to work on? It's the second week of classes," Ady gripes as we walk to our next lecture.

It's our senior year, and there are only two semesters left until we graduate and no longer have to worry about grinding out projects and studying for exams.

"At least it isn't due until October," she says as if it's a silver lining.

"That's only next month, and it's probably going to take that long to write it."

"You think?" she questions as she pulls the door to our lecture hall open and then heads toward the seats we claimed as ours.

"Yeah."

"What's your topic again?"

We settle in, and I turn to her with a huff. "Japanese economical wonder: The reasons and consequences."

Ady's mouth drops open in horror. "What does that even mean?"

"Exactly. I mean, is everyone's topic as crazy as mine?"

Ady shakes her head. "Mine is about the fast food industry and its connection to working-class people."

"What? Are you serious? That's your topic?"

"Compared to you, I lucked out."

With a heavy groan, I slump down in my seat. "I can't believe you're getting off so easy. I'm literally going to have to research my research topic before I can even start my actual research!"

Her eyes glaze over in confusion for a second before she shakes her head. "Maybe it won't be that bad."

When the professor walks in and takes his place at the podium, I flip open my notebook and grumble, "Senior year already sucks."

The next hour drags on, and when my cell phone vibrates in my bag, I pull it out and read Trent's text.

> Trent: I couldn't be more bored than a blind man in a milk sack shack.

Letting go of a silent giggle, I start typing him back when Ady leans over and reads his text.

"Does he ever talk like a normal human?" she whispers.

"You've been living with him for the past three years and you're seriously asking me that?"

"Yeah, but you're dating him. I'm just curious if he has a serious side."

"Of course, he does," I tell her as I hit send on my text.

> Me: Same here. Plus, I think my international marketing professor already hates me.
> Trent: Why?
> Me: Just got assigned a research paper, and my topic couldn't be any crappier. I'm going to be living in the library trying to get this thing written.

Trent: That sucks. Meet you after class?
Me: Yeah.

Sitting in the back of the lecture hall and out of earshot of the professor, Ady asks, "So, how are things going with you two?"

"Good. I honestly didn't know what to expect when we got involved, but so far, everything's been great."

"I still can't believe you guys are finally a thing. I mean, I never thought I'd see the day when Trent would get into a relationship."

"Same here," I whisper. "I thought he'd have a lot more hang-ups about it."

To say I'm surprised would be a drastic understatement. I assumed that, at the very least, our friendship would change, but if anything, it's gotten stronger. He's still the same crass and ridiculous Trent, but I've seen another side of him that is sweet and full of love.

I worried that being with a guy like him would be difficult, but he's made it effortless. After everything that went down with my ex, I just want to be happy, not hurt, not confused, not stressed—just happy. I never imagined he'd be the one to kiss my wounds, but he is, and he does—each and every one of them. He doesn't see them as disasters on my soul, but rather cracks to fill with his love. And for that, I'll never be able to repay him.

It's taken me a good amount of time to let go of the toxic situation I was in with Caleb. It's strange to think about how that volatile relationship became my comfort zone. He fed me poison, and I believed him when he called it medicine. I was standing in hell—yet, he convinced me it was heaven. And when the abuse came to an all-time high and we started going up in flames, he assured me that it wasn't too hot. But it was, and in the end, I'm the one who was left burning amongst the ashes of what I thought was love.

"Finally," Ady grumbles when class ends.

After shoving our notes into our bags, we make our way out of the lecture hall to find Trent waiting for us on the lawn. I walk right into the arms of the man I've fallen in love with and give him a hug.

"Are we still on for tonight?" he asks.

"Tonight?"

"Party at Brody's."

"Crap. I completely forgot." I rub my hand along my forehead. "Are you going to be mad if I bail?"

"Why would you bail?"

"This paper—"

"It's due next month," Ady interjects.

"I know, but I want to get it knocked out now so I'm not stressing about it later. Plus, I have no idea how long it's going to take me."

"What's the paper on?"

Gripping the straps of my backpack, I tell him, "Japanese economics or something like that. I was wanting to get a head start on it tonight."

"Get a head start on it tomorrow."

"It's already stressing me out. Even if I did put it off, I doubt I'd be able to enjoy myself tonight."

"Lame," my unstudious friend pipes in.

"No shit," Trent agrees and then asks Ady, "What about you?"

"Me?"

"You haven't been to a single party the whole time you've been here."

"Yet, she calls me lame," I defend in jest.

"Whatever."

"Are you seriously going to leave me hanging after your girl just ditched me for school work?"

"You're a big boy," she says before turning to me. "I have to run to my next class. See you later."

Trent slings his arm around my shoulders as we start walking out to the parking lot. "You're seriously not going?"

"Don't be mad."

"You gotta stop thinking that I'm going to get mad at you for every little thing," he says with an easy grin.

He's right, I should stop thinking that, but beneath the surface still lives the fear that if I don't put Trent first, there might be a punishment waiting for me. It scares me to think that he could possibly turn on me the same way Caleb did and I hate myself for even considering it. Trent is nothing like that monster, and he doesn't deserve my worry that he could be.

I've been trying to move past those insecurities because I know it bothers Trent. He wants me to trust him, but trust is something I'm still working on.

"So, what's the plan?"

"I'm going to go home, grab a bite to eat, and then come back up here to work in the library," I tell him as we approach my car.

"You can't do your research at home?"

"Possibly, but there are too many distractions there, and I really need to focus on getting this done." I unlock my doors and toss my bag into the passenger seat before turning back to Trent. I tug on the hem of his shirt and pull him closer. The moment before his lips touch mine, I lightly scold, "Behave tonight."

His lips curve into a smirk. "Or else?"

"You act as if you like the idea of me punishing you."

"As long as you don't cockfrost me, I'll take whatever punishment you're willing to give," he jokes before pressing his lips to mine.

I try to play it cool, as if I'm not worried, but I am. This isn't the girl I want to be though—insecure and untrusting. Doubt nags me often, whispering that I'm not good enough, that I'm not making him as happy as what I should. And knowing how girls flock to guys like Trent has me scared that he might find someone better and that he'll realize he's wasting his time with me.

"Text me later?" I ask, pushing down all my uncertainties.

He nods before I get into my car and drive to my condo. When I arrive home, I relax for a couple of hours before eating an early dinner and heading right back to campus. As the sun begins to set, I scan my student ID and enter the university's library. Not quite sure where to start, I stop by the information desk and talk to the guy working. He directs me to the stacks tower and tells me to go to the sixth floor.

Before heading up, I hit the catalog terminal and write down several call numbers for the books I need. Once I have a decent number of resources, I make my way through the massive room filled with countless rows of stacks. It's a maze of bookshelves that nearly reach the ceiling. The silence is eerie, and when I walk along the wall of study carrels, I discover I'm up here with only two other students.

Foregoing a carrel, I go back into the stacks in search of the last few books I need before situating myself on the floor. Settling deep within the room, I crack my first book and prepare for a long night ahead.

Time is illusive as I fill notecard after notecard with facts and opinions, dates and definitions. When my eyes grow heavy, I blink and then look around, realizing I'm sitting in the middle of a chaotic sea of white three-by-five cards covered in my handwriting. Sighing, I start to straighten them with one hand and dig my cell phone out of my bag with the other. When I tap my screen, I find a missed text from Trent that was sent over two hours ago.

I open a photo of him and Brody drinking and flipping me off. I smile down at their faces and then hone in on Trent. A warmth spreads through my chest when I think about how happy he makes me. He offers me more than what I deserve, and after everything that has gone down these past few years, I still can't believe we're together.

Holding the phone out in front of me, I snap a selfie of me returning the sentiment, shooting him the finger.

I get back to my research, and when I find myself stifling a yawn, I leave my belongings and head to the lobby in search of a pick-me-up. I hit up the vending machines and take a short break while I guzzle an energy drink and devour a bag of Skittles. Once I'm amped up on sugar and caffeine, I return to the sixth floor, passing the now vacant carrels and returning to where my things are still scattered on the ground.

Seconds multiply into minutes, which dissolve into hours. Eventually, my lids begin to droop and exhaustion hits hard. Crashing from my caffeine rush, I decide to finish the current book I'm looking at before heading home. I lean against the stack behind me and rest the open book on my bent knees while I continue to jot down important notes, but that soon dissolves into me staring blankly at my hand. I don't even realize the pencil has slipped out from my tired fingers as I begin to nod off.

Something jostles my shoulder, and I jerk awake with a start. It takes me a second to gain my bearings, but when I do, I find Trent standing over me, and I wonder if I'm dreaming.

He squats next to me, and I blink a few times before asking, "What are you doing here?"

"I've been trying to call you."

I drop my head to the side and pull my phone from my bag to see several missed calls.

"I didn't even hear it vibrate," I murmur, my head still clouded in sleep. "How did you know where I was?"

"I didn't. I've been wandering around like a fucking newb,"

he says a bit too loudly, and I quickly shush him. "We're the only people in here," he retorts.

"What time is it?"

"After one. When does this place shut down?"

I chuckle under my breath, knowing damn well this is probably his first time in the actual campus library. "It doesn't."

Grinning, he sits next to me and takes in all the notecards.

"How was the party?"

His eyes come back to mine. "Some trixie mouth shit all over Brody's pool table," he says, and I shudder in disgust. "It was like the damn exorcist." He laughs.

"Gross." I watch as he starts stacking up my notecards. "Why did you leave?"

"I got worried when you didn't answer your phone."

"Seriously?" I ask as my smile grows.

"What?"

"That is so sweet."

He shakes his head. "Don't start that sappy shit, woman."

"Aww," I continue, overexaggerating just to annoy him.

He then tosses the cards, and they go scattering about as he crawls over me, forcing me to lie down on my back. "You better stop that," he warns, smiling deviously at me.

"Or what?"

"I'll show you just how *unsweet* I can be."

A giggle slips out of me when he drops his mouth to my neck, sending shivers along my skin as he tickles me with his kisses. I gently slap his arm. "Stop."

"Why?"

"Because."

He shifts back to sit on his heels, and when he looks down, my eyes follow to see he's getting hard. "I'm like a bitch in heat," he jokes.

"Oh my god."

He then grabs my hand and pulls it between his legs. "See?"

Yanking my hand back, I sit up. "You're crazy."

Excitement brews in his eyes, and I'm shaking my head before he says, "Come on. No one is up here."

"No way!" I whisper sternly.

"Why?"

"Because . . . what if we get caught?"

"By who?" he says, looking around at nothing but the ceiling-high book stacks. "It's one in the morning and this place is empty." He leans forward again, crowding me until I give in and lay back.

"Trent," I hesitate, but when he slips his hand beneath my top and presses his erection into me, I lose all sensibility.

Adrenaline spikes through my bloodstream when he squeezes my breast, and I can't believe we're about to do this as my eager hands slide between our bodies to unfasten his shorts. We both smile as I shove his pants down as quickly as he unfastens mine. Cloaked in nerves, I anxiously shimmy my jeans off one of my legs before grabbing his hips and rushing him inside of me.

"Damn, girl," he says with a cocky smile.

"Shut up."

And just like that, we're going at it on the floor of the library in a frenzy of excitement. We move fast, urgent to find our releases, but when he slips his thumb into his mouth and drops it to my most sensitive spot, I abandon all control and let go of a heady moan.

His smile widens, and I grip his wrist to push his hand away, but he doesn't stop touching me.

"Trent—" I gasp as he sends a radiation of pleasure through my core. "You have to—" My eyes roll back when he strokes me at just the right angle to make me nearly come out of my skin. I can barely breathe as I try to get him to stop before I scream out in pure euphoria. "You have to stop."

"Fuck no," he says on a breath of laughter as he drives me higher. "You look so hot right now."

On the brink of an orgasm, I clench down and grip on to him tightly, doing everything I can to keep quiet as my body peaks.

"I can't hold on," I strangle out on a broken voice.

He swells inside me, and that's all it takes to send me spiraling. His hips buck into me as we both splinter into blissful ravishment.

Nothing can be heard outside of our heavy panting as we ride out our pleasure, and when I have nothing left to give, I go lax beneath him. He doesn't rush to pull out, and although we risk getting caught, I can't bring myself to push him off me.

Instead, I run my hand along his sweaty forehead and grin before he drops it on to mine.

"I can't believe we just did that," I whisper.

But then again, I can. One thing I love about Trent is that he allows me to have fun. He's wild and free, and through those qualities, he's given me the courage to explore that within myself. Trent loves me in ways I didn't know I could be loved, and because of that, it breeds a joy that was once stolen from me.

He plants a kiss on my lips before saying, "You're the realest feeling I've ever known."

And just like that, he melts my heart entirely. There's so much I want to say in return, but all the words get tangled inside a swarm of emotions he sets off. I don't know how to tell him just how much I love him. It isn't the type of love that's felt in my heart—it's in my bones.

He knows I'm often at a loss when it comes to expressing my feelings, but I think he knows. After he slides out of me and we pull our pants back on, I'm still unsettled in my thoughts because he deserves to hear them, to know where my heart is, even though it isn't easy for me to say. Leaning against the stacks, I rest in the comfort of his arms, and he senses my timidity.

"Are you okay?"

Turning to face him, I struggle to gather my thoughts.

"What is it?" he questions as he tucks my hair behind my ear.

"I love you."

"I love you too."

Dropping my head, I muster a bit of courage and reveal, "Before you, I was constantly chasing after approval, thinking all along I was in love, but I wasn't." He runs his hand along the side of my face when I tell him, "I never knew love until you." My eyes fall from his when I shamefully admit, "You give me so much that I sometimes feel like I'm not enough for you."

"You don't have to chase after anything with me. You're more than enough. You're everything."

Seventeen

KATE

I BEGIN TO STIR WHEN I SENSE THE CAR SLOWING. THE BRIGHT SUN PIERCES my eyes, forcing me to squint until they adjust to the bright light.

"You're two for two," Trent says from behind the wheel.

I release a heavy yawn. "What's that supposed to mean?"

"Second time I've brought you to Tampa where you've slept nearly the whole drive."

"Road trips make me tired."

"Weak."

Looking out my window, I watch the scenery pass as we draw closer to Trent's house. We decided to come for fall break. When his mom asked Trent about his "friend"—meaning me—he finally let her know that we're dating, and she insisted he bring me along for the extended weekend. Trent's older brother, Garrett, is going to be there as well.

When we pull into the wraparound drive, Trent parks behind a white car covered almost entirely with love bugs. "That must be Garrett's rental."

"Oh, my god, that's a lot of bugs."

"They must be foaming at the dick to be going at it this late into October."

Trent hops out, but I stay put because these tiny creatures are flying everywhere, a crap-ton more than usual.

"You getting out?" he asks when he knocks on my window.

"Dude, there's got to be a million of them out here."

"They're too busy raw doggin' it to mess with you," he says. "Come on; they're harmless."

As I prepare to make my mad dash inside the house, they begin to accumulate on the windshield. "Gross," I shudder before opening the door and hauling ass to the front door, only to find that it's locked. "Open it!"

"Chill out," he says as he casually strides up.

Flailing my hands to keep the swarm of bugs away, I snap at him once more, screeching, "Hurry up!"

The second the door opens, I dart inside and frantically run my hands through my hair, hoping none got tangled up in it, while Trent stands there laughing at me.

"Hey, dick trickle, what the hell took you so long?" a guy calls out as he walks toward us. He's basically a slightly older version of Trent with blue eyes and shorter hair, and while I've seen pictures of him and know that he's Trent's brother, I haven't actually met him yet.

"Suck it, rat bitch," Trent shoots back as the two of them go in for a hug, patting each other on the backs. "When did you get here?"

"A few hours ago. I've been jacking the beanstalk waiting for you."

Watching them interact is like watching two apples fall from the tree and land in the same damn spot.

Garrett pushes Trent aside and approaches me with a smirk. "You must be Kate."

"Hey."

"Pardon my good graces, but what the fuck are you doing with this fuggnut?"

"Eat dick," Trent says, which earns him a wink from his brother.

"Great, there are two of you," I joke with a straight face.

Garrett drapes his arm around my shoulders and begins leading me toward the back of the house. "Let me give you the grand tour."

"She's already been here, man," Trent says from behind as he grabs our bags and takes them up to his room.

Garrett doesn't acknowledge him at all as we continue our stroll into the living room.

"So, where did you fly in from?" I ask as I duck out from under his arm and take a seat on the couch.

"Los Angeles." He sits in the chair adjacent to me.

"Oh, I thought you were in Pennsylvania."

"I went to college there, but I moved out to California last year after I graduated."

"What do you do in out in California?"

"I work as a film editor."

"Oh, wow. That's cool," I note, having a vague idea of what that actually entails. "What type of films?"

"Right now, a bunch of seasonal movies."

"Tell her the truth," Trent says when he joins us.

Turning back to Garrett, I watch him flip his brother off.

"Garrett works for one of those networks that make cheesy-as-fuck movies for middle-aged housewives," he tells me before looking over at his older brother. "Isn't that right, Mr. Hollywood?"

"Jobs are hard to come by. It was either that or porn."

"Damn, dude, you turned down porn for that shit? You really are a loser."

"Suck it."

"I'll pass."

Garrett shakes his head and turns to me. "So, what are you planning to do after college? Hopefully, you have bigger aspirations than this dipshit."

"I'm hoping to score a job at a PR firm in Miami."

"What kind of PR?"

"I'd like to get into club promotions," I tell him.

"Party girl?"

"Might as well have fun while you're working, right?"

"I'm home," their mother calls out when we hear the front door close. She walks into the room, saying, "Sorry I'm late. All the appointments ran over, and I couldn't catch up for the life of me."

I watch her eyes soften at her boys as she comes in with her arms outstretched.

"It only ever feels like home when I have both of you here," she croons as she gives Garrett a big hug before smothering Trent in affection. After she's done doting on the two grown men, she turns to me with an endearing smile. "And you," she says, "I couldn't be happier to have you here."

I get off the couch, and she gives me a warm embrace.

"I never thought I'd see the day when Trent would have a girlfriend."

"Mom, really?"

She pulls back and smiles at me before telling him, "Oh, stop. Let me have my moment."

"It's good to see you again."

"Well, I hate to rush, but we have dinner reservations in an hour, and I need to get cleaned up," she says.

"Reservations?" Garrett groans.

"Yes. And if it isn't too painful, can you please ditch the flip-flops for one night?"

"Where are we going?"

"Bern's."

"Are you serious?" Trent complains. "That place is douchy."

"Jack made the reservations, so be nice," she scolds lightly before heading to her room, announcing, "Be ready to leave by seven."

I turn to Trent just in time to see him motioning a hand job before asking his brother, "You know anything about this dude?"

"Nah, man. I didn't even know she was seeing anyone until she mentioned it the other week."

They both look annoyed, but I ignore them as I walk out of the room and catch up to Laura. "I hope this doesn't sound weird, but I didn't pack anything for a nice dinner."

"No worries," she says as she leads me into her closet. "Feel free to borrow anything you want."

"You're a lifesaver."

She helps me pick out a long maxi dress that I can easily glam up with the right hair and makeup. I thank her once more before going up to Trent's room. After a quick shower, I take my time getting ready, and when seven o'clock hits, we're all out the door. We decide to take two cars in case we want to go out afterward.

It's a short drive to the upscale steakhouse, and when we walk in, the hostess immediately leads us to our table where a gentleman with flakes of gray in his hair is already seated.

He stands when we approach and greets Laura with a kiss to her cheek before he introduces himself to Trent and Garrett and shakes their hands.

"It's nice to meet you," I say when he leans in to kiss my cheek, and finally we all take our seats. When the waitress stops by, we place our drink orders and then look at the menu.

"It's nice to finally meet you boys," Jack says. "Your mother has told me so much about you."

"Odd, she hasn't told us anything about you," Garrett responds.

She picks up her water goblet and takes a sip. "It's been a little bit of a whirlwind."

"How did you two even meet?" he questions.

"Your mother came in for a root canal a few months ago."

"He's an oral surgeon," she boasts with a smile, and it's obvious she's crazy about him.

The waitress delivers our drinks, and Trent takes a long sip from his beer.

Jack goes on to tell them the whole story, laughing when he talks about how loopy she was from the anesthesia and how he had one of his techs schedule her for a fake follow-up just so he could ask her out on a date. Trent is unusually quiet, but both he and his brother are respectful.

As the evening progresses, Laura gushes to Jack about her sons and how proud she is of them. Everything, aside from Trent being so reserved, is going smoothly, and when we are in the middle of our dinner, Laura sets down her fork, garnering everyone's attention. "I actually have something to tell you." She looks over at Jack, adding, "We both do."

I notice the tension in Trent as he chews a piece of steak.

"We're getting married." She beams before turning to Jack and pecking him on the lips.

"What?" Trent questions, his tone a tad too harsh. "When did this happen?"

"Last month. I've been waiting to get both of you here at the same time so I could tell you in person."

"You just met."

His mother reaches across the table and rests her hand on top of Trent's while looking at Jack, explaining, "Trent has always been a little protective over me."

Annoyance blooms in his eyes as he turns them on Jack. "What do you even know about my mom?"

"I know that she's a hard worker and that she loves you boys." He looks to Laura and adds, "She's caring, vibrant, and the best thing that's ever come into my life."

The clanking of Trent's steak knife dropping onto his plate causes me to jump. "You're seriously getting married again?"

"This time is different."

He nods slowly, not buying it at all.

"Your mother was a little hesitant to tell you boys—"

"I can't imagine why."

"Trent," his mother scolds, but she doesn't see the pain beneath the glare he serves her.

In an attempt to break the tension, Garrett raises his beer. "Congratulations. So, when is this going down?"

His mother's face softens, but Trent remains agitated.

"February," she says. "We thought something intimate at the Davis Island Garden Club would be nice."

Under the table, I lay my hand on Trent's knee, which is bouncing up and down. It has to be alarming to know that she'll be getting married in four months to a guy she barely knows. I give him a gentle squeeze to soothe his unease, but it does nothing. He doesn't attempt to make an uncomfortable situation worse or better. He just shuts down as Garrett and I make our best effort to distract the happy couple from his irritation.

When dinner is finally over and we part ways, Trent scraps whatever plans he had for the night and takes us back home with Garrett in the back seat. He remains shut down, not saying a word for the five minutes it takes us to pull into the drive.

"You okay?" Garrett asks him as we get out and head inside.

"Shit's fucked up," is the only response he gives before heading straight upstairs, leaving me behind with Garrett.

"I'm sorry," I say, unsure of what exactly I'm apologizing for.

"I've grown immune to it all. It's always been hardest on Trent," he tells me. "I'd give him a few minutes."

I nod as he walks away, and I busy myself in the kitchen, getting something to drink before heading up to Trent.

I find him lying on the bed, staring up at the ceiling and sit next to him.

"You okay?" I ask cautiously, unsure of what to expect because I've never seen him upset like this.

"Six times." He releases a heavy sigh. "It's bullshit."

When I run my hand down his arm, he finally turns his head to look at me.

"I can't even count the number of guys she has dated since her last divorce. She doesn't know how to be alone."

"She seems happy," I say, trying to be optimistic because I really like Laura.

"It'll never last." He sits up and leans against the headboard. "She always jumps into a relationship, thinking it's love, only for them to fail. Then she depends on me to help clean up the mess." His head drops, and I can feel the turmoil when he admits thickly, "I love her, but she's so damn selfish."

Scooting in, I slip my arms around him, and I'm surprised when he hangs on to me tightly, as if he's desperate for consolation. I have to wonder if there was anyone around to give him this when he was growing up, but my gut is telling that he was probably alone.

"It scares me."

Loosening my hold, I sit back and wait until he looks at me. "What does?"

"This," he admits. "All I've ever seen is one failed relationship after another."

"Do you doubt yourself with me?"

"I don't want to."

"But do you?"

He drags his thumb along the crest of my cheek, admitting, "Sometimes."

I lean in and fold myself against him when he gathers me in his arms.

"No one has ever been able to love me like you do," I tell him, needing him to know. "I hate that you doubt yourself when I don't doubt you at all."

He pushes his hands through my hair, but it brings upon guilt because he's always doing this—tiny gestures that comfort me when it should be me giving it in return.

I take his hand, pulling it away from stroking me, and lace my fingers with his. "Her lot in life doesn't have to be yours."

His eyes peer into mine, and he lets a span of time pass before he says, "I'm angry at her. It feels wrong to say it, but I am."

"You have every right to feel that way; she's disappointed you."

He nods and takes a hard swallow. Another quiet moment passes before he continues, "Growing up, it felt like I was in the background. I was constantly wishing for it to just be the three of us, that she would stop bringing men home, and that she would make me a priority . . . it sounds really selfish."

"It isn't selfish. It's what every kid wants—to feel important," I tell him, feeling as if I've been taking for granted the very thing he's wished for but was neglected of.

From what I've seen, which I admit isn't much, it's as if his mother comes around more when her world is falling apart. And he's right, she does depend on him to pick up the pieces. But when things are going well for her, she's absent from his life, rarely even calling to check in.

"It worries me that I don't know this guy, that I no longer live here to keep an eye on her to make sure everything's okay."

"You can't always protect people; you can't put that kind of responsibility on your shoulders."

"I've spent my whole life constantly waiting for shit to hit the fan because it always does. The moment things smooth out and everything seems right again, it never fails to fall apart."

"But it isn't your job to keep it all together."

With a long exhale, he tilts his head back, resting it against the headboard. There's so much strife he keeps bottled up, and it hurts me to see him like this. If words could soothe, I'd hand them right over, but they are nothing but a temporary medicine.

"You ever feel like an outcast?"

His question catches me off guard because he's far from an outcast. He's the life of every party and has more friends than I can keep track of. Now he has me wondering if he uses those things as a mask to shield himself, to overcompensate for what he's been lacking. I know all too well what it's like to be surrounded by a ton of people and feel all alone—invisible almost—misplaced.

Leaning in, I press my lips to the thumping of his pulse on his neck, and when he looks down at me, I respond, "All the time."

He threads his hand through my hair, and I reach up to do the same. It's a tender moment that has my love for him expanding boundlessly, floating as if gravity were just a mere illusion—a phantasmal obscurity that only we are able to see beyond.

"I love you," I whisper, but it isn't enough. "I mean, I *really* love you, and I don't want those words to lay on your surface with all the other words you've been told. I want them to sink in, fade into you, and rest in your bones."

His lips fall onto mine in an unmoving kiss, the warmth of his touch seeping into me, and when he pulls back an inch, his breath feathers against me when he murmurs, "God, I love you. You're the truest thing I've ever known in this fake as fuck world."

Eighteen

KATE

"You almost ready?" Trent questions as I tie my hair up.

"Yeah."

"Brogan just texted, he's pulling in now, so I'm going to go load up the jet skis."

"Okay, I'll be down in a second."

Walking out of the bathroom, I pull a pair of shorts from my suitcase and put them on over my bikini before grabbing Trent's backpack he left on the bed. As I leave the room, I swipe my sunglasses off the dresser and head downstairs to toss a few drinks into the bag.

"Good morning."

Peeking out from around the fridge, I see Laura walking into the kitchen. I close the door and toss the bottles of water into the bag.

"Hey."

"Are you heading out?" she asks before she pulls a mug from the cabinet and begins to pour herself some coffee.

"Yeah. We're borrowing some jet skis for the day," I tell her. "Trent's out front getting the trailer hooked up to his Jeep."

"That sounds fun."

Unsure of what else to say, I stand and watch as she takes the carton of creamer out from the fridge and dumps a little into her mug. Although Trent wasn't obscenely obvious last night and did a decent job holding himself together, she has to know that he's upset about the news of her engagement.

She stirs her coffee, sets the spoon down, and turns to face me as she takes a sip.

I hate the unease because I really like Laura, so I break the silence with, "We kind of rushed out last night, so I didn't get the chance to thank Jack for dinner."

"Oh, don't worry about it," she dismisses. "He really enjoyed meeting you all." She pauses, her eyes slipping down for a moment before she addresses the elephant in the room, "How is Trent this morning?"

It comes with a hint of relief that she is, at the very least, aware of his feelings, but I don't want to betray what he confided in me, so I veer left and tell her, "He's just worried because he doesn't know Jack."

She nods and takes another sip. "I can understand that, but this time is different. Jack isn't like any of the others."

"Let's go!" Trent hollers from the front door, putting an end to our conversation.

Laura smiles. "Well, you two have fun."

"Thanks," I tell her as I slip the backpack over my shoulders.

I head outside to find Trent sitting behind the wheel of his Jeep, wearing nothing but a pair of board shorts, and it's a reminder of how badly I lusted after him when we first met.

"Like what you see?"

I roll my eyes at him. "You have a thing against wearing clothes?"

"I'd rather go without them just to watch you slobber," he teases. "Get your ass in, woman."

I throw on my sunglasses as we drive toward the bridge that takes us to the beaches. There's something different about the vibe here in Tampa. It's completely different from what you'll ever find in Miami, but it isn't unwelcome. This place is so chill and laid-back, and even though this is only my second time coming here, I can't deny how much I enjoy it.

With the morning sun glowing down on us, I inhale deep breaths of salty air as we drive over the water. When Trent turns up the stereo, I look over at him and smile. Without a doubt, I'm beyond happy, but there's no ignoring the pang of worry that is still in my chest. It's my wanting to ask questions, to dig deeper, that needles beneath the surface. Suddenly, my smile aches, and I lose the effort it takes to hold it before letting it go.

"You okay, babe?"

"Yeah." It's kind of a lie, but not a big one. Truth is, I'm conflicted and curious, neither of which sit easily with me.

He takes my hand and pulls it into his lap as I try to let the loud music filter out the questions that are clouding my head. When we make it over to the launching dock, we get the jet skis into the water, and head off. It doesn't take long for my smile to return, it's genuine this time as we speed across the water, which is like glass and nothing like you'd find on the east coast.

I glance over at Trent, who is racing beside me, unable to ignore the trill in my stomach. When he catches me gawking, he smiles before cutting a sharp turn and sending a spray of water toward me.

"Ass!" I yell out as he laughs in the distance.

The two of us cat and mouse it around a few small islands before he leads me over to a larger one that backs up to some mangroves. We drag the skis onto the shore, and he pops his seat open to pull out a couple of drinks. He tosses me a bottle of water before I wander around the perimeter of the island, looking at all the shells that have washed ashore.

With the sun now at full peak, heat barrels down on me, coating my skin in a sheen of sweat and illuminating my earlier thoughts. The pang returns. Turning over my shoulder, I see Trent sitting in the sand off toward the mangrove trees.

I go and plop down next to him.

"You seem quiet," he mentions, and when I look at him, I defend, "We've been on the water."

One thing about Trent is that he's learned how to read me well over the years. As much as I don't want to dampen our day, I figure it would probably be best just to talk head on so I can rid this feeling nestled in me.

"There's something that's kind of been bothering me," I tell him. "I mean—well, not really bothering me, but—"

He smirks. "Spit it out, woman."

"It's just . . . I don't want to make you uncomfortable because I feel like I'm about to be intrusive."

His face drops every bit of ease it held a second ago, and I already regret bringing it up.

"Never mind. It's not that important," I recant.

"If it wasn't important, you wouldn't have said anything." Doubt pulls me away, and I squint my eyes as I look out over the water, the bright sun reflecting off its surface. "Whatever it is you want to say, just say it."

Pivoting toward him, I pull my knees up to my chest and wrap my arms around them as I collect my thoughts. Then I second-guess myself, wondering if I'm making too big of deal out of something that might not even be anything at all.

"Say it," he pushes.

"The last time we came here, your mom said something to me, and I've been wanting to ask you but didn't really know how,"

I tell him. "I know you're private about a lot of things so it always seemed invasive to pry."

There's apprehension in his voice when he asks, "What did she say?"

"It might not be a big deal, but—"

"So, what is it?"

"She mentioned how when you were younger you were never home—like middle school age. It just has me wondering why because it's awfully young to just be gone."

Now it's him who avoids me as he looks off into the distance. "She shouldn't have said anything."

"I'm sorry. We don't have to talk about it."

Bending his knees, he drapes his arms over them. There's discord all over his face, and I feel like shit for putting it there.

"I shouldn't have brought it up," I admit. "It's just . . . when we were talking last night, it resurfaced in my head."

"It's okay," he says before telling me, "My mom . . . she hasn't always had the best judgment in men. And yeah, there was a time I left home when I was in the eighth grade."

"You left completely?"

He nods.

"Where did you go?"

"Anywhere I could," he says, and it takes him a beat to finally look at me. "I had a few friends who would sneak me in to their homes to crash after their parents went to sleep." He drifts away from me again when he reveals, "Sometimes I didn't have anywhere to go at all."

"How long were you gone?"

He shrugs. "A couple of months."

I struggle with the question that burns the most, and when he peers into my eyes, I know he sees it, so I go ahead and ask, "Why?"

"She let this guy move in with us; he was an asshole," he

reveals. "He never hit me or anything, but he didn't need to because the shit that came out of his mouth did enough damage. It was a fucked-up situation, so I figured the best way to get my mother to choose me over him was to leave. It took her two months to decide I was worth her breaking up with him."

"Are you mad at her?"

He nods. "There's a lot I'm mad about, but it's the disappointment that bothers me the most."

"She asked about you this morning."

"What did she say?"

"She just wanted to know how you were. I didn't tell her anything except that you were concerned that you don't know anything about Jack."

"She isn't a bad mom."

"I never got the impression that she was," I tell him. I know Laura loves and cares about Trent.

"Come on," he says as he climbs to his feet and holds out his hand for me. He then pulls me up, grabs my sandy butt, and kisses me with a tinge of obscenity, making his point loud and clear that he has no interest in talking about this anymore.

When he starts fiddling with the strings on my bikini, I laugh against his lips and attempt to push him away.

"You owe me," he taunts when he goes for one of the strings, only for me to push his hand away.

"Owe you for what?"

"Forcing all these fucking deep conversations on me."

"I'm not forcing anything."

"Right," he dismisses before quickly snagging the tie from around my neck, pulling it loose.

He's too quick for me to stop him, and when my bikini top falls down, leaving me completely exposed, I rush to cover my boobs with my hands. When I try to scurry away from him, I trip over my own two feet and fall into the sand as he laughs.

"Trent!"

"We're the only ones out here," he says, and as I pull my top back up, he kneels in the sand next to me, grabbing at the string to my bottoms.

I squeal and swat at him, my top falling down again while I shuffle back to get away. Another tie comes apart, and he pretty much has me naked. I yell at him, but as much as I try to feign seriousness, I can't stop laughing.

"You should double-knot that shit," he teases.

"You should have more manners."

At that, he sits up on his knees and pulls out his dick. "Tell that to this guy."

There's no other way around it—his crudeness is such a turn on that we spend the remainder of our time on this little island making love while he eggs me on with his foul-mouthed dirty talk.

We kill the day, drain the jet skis, and by the time we get back to the house, we're starved.

Trent cuts up a pineapple, and we devour the entire thing.

"Leave any for me?" Garrett asks when he comes downstairs.

Trent swipes the last piece, tosses it in his mouth, and flips his brother off.

"Dick," he mutters under his breath when he goes to snoop through the pantry. "Where the hell have you guys been all day?"

"Took Brogan's jet skis out to Clearwater."

He rips open a bag of chips. "Way to leave me hanging, bro. You left me here with mom and her mile-long list of shit she needed done around the house."

"We should go grab some dinner," Trent suggests.

"I think Mom should be home soon. She had to run up to the hospital."

"Dude, I could murder some gyros," he says. "Text her and find out when she'll be here."

Garrett pulls out his phone to shoot her a message and then asks, "Want to take the kayaks out to Caladesi tomorrow?"

Trent looks over at me. "You up for kayaking?"

I'm about to tell him that it sounds like fun when my phone rings.

"Hey, Mom."

"You need to get home," she cries in sheer panic.

"Mom?"

"You have to come now! Your dad—Oh my god!" I can hardly make out what she's saying because she's so hysterical, and it ramps my heart into overdrive as I push away from the island and walk into Trent's living room.

"Mom, what's going on?"

All I get in response is her wailing, and I freak out.

"Mom!" I shout to get her attention. "You're scaring me."

"Is everything okay?" Trent asks. I hadn't realized he followed me, but I can't even focus on him.

"Your dad," she starts before crumbling into more sobs.

My hands start to tremble as I try to calm her down enough to tell me what the hell about my dad has her freaking out. "Mom, stop crying and tell me what's going on!"

Her erratic breathing scares me, but nothing can prepare me for the terror that takes over when she sobs, "Your dad's been shot."

One second. That's all it takes for my body to turn ice cold and paralyze. The phone slips out of my hand. I'm frozen solid as Trent picks it up off the floor and switches the call to speakerphone.

"Hello?" he says, but his voice is deep within a black tunnel.

"Kate?"

"It's Trent. What's going on?"

She's frantic, and it only serves to numb me more, sending a wave of shivers through my limbs when I hear her far off words telling him, "Steve's been shot! She needs to come to the hospital right now. They don't—they don't think he's going to make it."

"What the fuck is going on?" Garrett's voice is a hollow, fading echo as everything blurs into an obscure abstraction of reality.

Warmth touches my face, but I must be dreaming because no sound is coming out of Trent as he holds me in his hands and moves his mouth. All I can hear is a rush of wind clogging my ears.

His lips move, and I nod, having no idea why before he rushes me upstairs. Sitting on the edge of his bed, I watch in a daze while he darts around the room and throws all of our belonging into our bags.

"Kate."

I should respond.

"Kate?"

His eyes tether to mine as he walks straight over to me. His hand slides along the side of my neck, and it's now that his voice begins crystalizing, slowly pulling me out of my trance.

Urgency coats every syllable of every word when he says, "Kate, come on. We have to go right now."

Nineteen

KATE

I ONCE HEARD THAT THE WORLD SPINS AT A RATE OF A THOUSAND MILES per hour. It's a constant force of nature that no one ever questions because it just is—it's always there, always occurring. My question: What happens when it comes to a stop—halts entirely? Does the atmosphere remain in motion, stirring up everything around us in an upheaval of chaotic destruction?

Do we die?

Is that what I'm waiting for as I sit here while Trent speeds through the night along I-95?

He keeps looking at me; I can see him from my peripheral as I stare out the window, watching blinding headlights pass us by. Billboards and buildings paint the obsidian night in streaks of colors, and I use them to create imaginary pieces of artwork in my head—I do whatever I can to distract myself from the what-ifs plaguing me.

Trent's hand has been holding mine for the past hour. I want to pull away because he has it at an awkward angle that caused my fingers to fall asleep shortly after he took it, but I don't move.

I can't.

I haven't spoken either.

"Just hang on," he says for the umpteenth time. "We're almost there."

Please, hurry, the voice inside my head begs. *Go faster.*

His hand squeezes mine, smashing my skin into the million needles prickling beneath the surface. It's the only sensation I can feel and I hate that it reminds me that this isn't a bad a dream I'm going to wake up from.

We veer off the interstate, and it isn't much longer before he's parking the car and rushing me inside and up to the ICU.

"Can I help you?" a woman asks without standing from her seat behind the counter.

"We're here to see Steve Murphy," Trent tells her.

She punches something into her computer. "Are you family?"

"She's his daughter."

"And you?"

"No, I'm her boyfriend."

"I'm sorry, only family is allowed. You'll have to stay out here," she says. "There's a waiting area right over there."

Glancing over my shoulder to where she points, the grim reality sets in even deeper when I see the room is filled with officers—his friends.

Trent turns to me, and I can see he's worried. "Are you okay going by yourself?" he asks. "Your mother texted me not too long ago and said she was back there with him."

I nod, and the lady hits the button that opens the doors. Leaving Trent behind, I walk down the white, sterile corridor that leads me to another desk, but before I'm forced to speak, I see my mother stepping out of one of the rooms.

"Kate, thank god you're here." Her face is splotchy, and her eyes are puffy, and the moment she falls into my arms, she breaks down in a heap of tears. I'm still so numb as she falls apart. I hold her; although, I doubt she can find any comfort within my vacancy.

I let my eyes track to the room she just came out of, and even though the wall is nothing but windows, I don't spot my dad. All I see are a million wires, tubes, and machines. My heart free falls into the depths of my gut.

"Where is he?" It's the first thing I've said in what feels like hours, and it comes out dry and brittle. "Mom?"

She doesn't say anything right away, and the silence scares me.

Oh god. Is he gone?

"Mom, where's Dad?"

Drawing back, she wipes her face and walks into the room as I trail behind. A multitude of sounds from the machines fill my head. My eyes follow her as she goes over to the bed, and that's when I see him. He's buried under a spider web of wires—too many—each one mazing to a different machine.

Somehow, I manage to put one jittery foot in front of the other as I near his bedside. There is a tube down his throat that's breathing for him. His neck is bandaged, and his face is so badly bruised and swollen that he's unrecognizable. The severity hits like a sledgehammer, knocking the wind right out of my lungs and causing me to wince and turn away. It's a brutally disturbing image I can't shake out of my head.

"Oh, honey," my mother says as she steps next to me and lays her hand on my back.

"What happened?"

Before she can answer, a doctor walks into the room to update her on the surgery. While the two of them talk, I take a deep breath and prepare to turn back around and go over to my dad. There's a chair next to his bed, and I collapse into it.

I don't even realize that my mother is no longer talking with the doctor when she asks me, "Would you like a moment alone with him?"

I nod, and she slowly steps out of the room. The doctor is

checking a couple of the machines, and I find myself asking, "What happened to him?"

The older gentleman turns to me with a kind smile on his lips, and I read the name Dr. Guerrero, which is embroidered on the chest of his white coat.

"He suffered a gunshot wound to the neck, which hit a major artery," he tells me, sinking me deeper into my shock. "He suffered extensive blood loss, but we were able to stop the bleeding with the surgery. Because his blood pressure dropped so low, he's now in renal failure, and we have him on dialysis."

"Is he going to wake up?"

"Right now, we have him in a medically induced coma until we can get things under control. At this time, we're unable to explore if there's any neurological damage."

"Is he going to die?"

"That I can't say, but we're doing everything we can," he tells me, thickening the knot lodged in my throat. "The first few days are the most critical."

His words spear a dagger right through my heart, inflicting a pain so unimaginable it renders me silent as I endure its torture. It bleeds freely, dropping acid into the pit of my stomach, doubling me over in agony. I beg to cry, but I can't, so I beg harder because it's too much to hold in—the utter heartbreak of knowing I could lose my dad.

Bones weep, muscles scream, veins rip open, and I beg for mercy, but none finds me as I lay my head on the edge of his bed. I want to touch him, hold him, trade places with him because I can't imagine living in a world where he doesn't exist.

Blades slash through my soul, and as I pray I also question the faith of it all. I offer everything I can as I plead for any semblance of grace.

Just don't take him away from me.

"Honey." My mother's voice filters in through my panicked thoughts. Her hand comes to stroke my hair, and the simple touch makes me feel like a little girl again. Unlike when I was little, her touch isn't able to knit together my broken pieces when life tears me apart. "We just have to pray harder than ever right now." She's weeping, and I nod against the bed.

I don't want to look up, and I don't want to open my eyes to this nightmare. As long as they're closed, it doesn't exist, right?

Fables and fairy tales have me wishing for magic. I'm so desperate, but desperation only breeds more sadness, which remains trapped under my ribs.

My mom stands over me as she continues to smooth my hair and rub my back, and I fold into her. Neither one of us says anything as she consoles me, and after a while, a nurse brings in an extra chair for my mom. I sit with her as she weeps off and on while nurses periodically check on him. The two of us are so distraught that it's easier to remain silent, so that's what we do.

There's no concept of time as I stare at my dad. I've been locked on him for so long that my tired eyes have skewed him beyond focus.

"You look like you're about to fall asleep," my mother murmurs as she runs her hand down the length of my arm.

I take a slow blink. "What time is it?"

"A little after midnight," she tells me. "Why don't you try to get some rest. I'll call you if there are any changes."

"Are you sure?"

Her smile is weak as she nods.

The two of us stand, and I fall into her arms when she embraces me, but it does nothing to lessen the anguish. Now that I'm out of my daze, reality hits again. Each second I'm in this room, the pressure in my chest builds, and I can't take it anymore.

When I step away, she looks into my eyes. "Are you okay?"

I shrug, not knowing how I'm supposed to answer a question like that.

"Are you coming home too?"

She shakes her head. "I think I'll stay here just in case." A fresh slew of tears make their way down her face. "I can't leave him."

The misery inside me creeps up to the surface, but I'm too terrified to let it out, too scared to endure its pain. Quickly, I say my goodbye and duck out of the room.

As I walk down the stretch of hallway, I grow weaker and weaker, so I walk faster, needing to get the hell out of here. Before I know it, I'm jogging to hit the button on the wall that opens the doors. My head fogs as the heat of my unshed tears prick the backs of my eyes. I run to the elevator and start punching the button over and over and over and—

"Hey."

Trent's voice startles me, and I can't believe it slipped my mind that he was here.

"Are you okay?"

"I just want to go home," I tell him, and I see a hint of relief wash over him when he hears me speak.

He tucks me under his arm as we wait for the elevator to arrive, and I'm forced to hide inside myself again when I start feeling too much.

I don't recall the drive from the hospital to the house, and when we walk inside, Trent starts turning on the lights. It's late, and even though I took a shower back at his place earlier, I feel the need for another—maybe I simply need the space.

"I'm going to go get ready for bed."

"Is your mom coming home?"

"No. She's staying the night at the hospital," I tell him before I head toward the steps.

"I'll go get our bags."

Walking into my dark bedroom, I start peeling off my clothes, dropping them on the floor behind me as I go into the bathroom and straight into the shower. I wait for the water to warm up before I step under the spray, and then I move the lever to make it even hotter. It pelts my body, turning it red in its wake. The heat bites my flesh, but it still isn't hot enough, so I push the handle even farther until my skin is burning and stinging, but there's something about the external pain that allows me let go of the internal. Like a hundred paper cuts on the delicate tissue of my heart, I finally give in as the first tear slips down my cheek, melding with the water to create rivers. They stream down my face as I brace my hands against the wall, hang my head, and break down.

I'm quiet at first, but soon, my cries turn into harrowing sobs. The shower is thick with steam, but the scalding isn't enough. Fisting my hands, I rest my head against them, thumping it against my knuckles a few times before slacking against the wall. I cry out, hoping my wailing will wake me from this nightmare, but I'm trapped. There's no escaping this.

A rush of cold air cuts through the steamy fog, and when I look up, I see Trent step into the shower fully clothed. "Christ, that's hot," he bites as he quickly turns the heat down right before grabbing me and pulling into an embrace so fierce I swear I feel every single muscle in his body flexing around me.

Pressing my head against the wet cotton of his T-shirt, I crumble completely. My cries are ugly, but he never wavers as he holds me. I fist his soaking shirt in my hands and cling to him, needy for him to fix this, to make it all better—to tell me this is a sick joke and that it isn't real.

Instead, he stands as a pillar of strength while I drain myself to the point my voice goes hoarse and I have nothing left in me. Trent shuts off the water, opens the shower door, and grabs a towel to wrap around me. He rips off his drenched clothes and slings them on to the shower floor before securing a towel around his waist. When I step out, he holds me once again, pressing his hands along my body to warm me when I start to shiver.

"I'll be right back," he says before going into my bedroom, returning a moment later with pajamas from my suitcase.

Weak and exhausted, I drop the towel, and he helps me get dressed and into bed. With a heart heavier than it should ever be, I curl into his arms as he combs his fingers through my wet hair, whispering, "It's going to be okay."

"What if it isn't?"

"Then I'll be here with you to help you through it."

Closing my eyes, a few more tears spill out.

"I'm not going anywhere, all right?"

I nod against him, and he tugs me even closer, the warmth of his body seeping into mine. And even though he has me pressed flush to his body, it isn't close enough. My neediness overwhelms, eventually bringing me to tears again, because what if he isn't holding on to me tight enough and I slip away?

"I've got you, babe."

"Don't let go, okay?"

"I won't," he assures before dropping kisses into my hair, and not once does he loosen his grip on me as I cry myself to sleep.

Twenty

TRENT

THERE'S A CRICK IN MY NECK FROM SITTING IN THIS CHAIR FOR THE last few hours. A burn slices its way down to my shoulder blades when I pull my head away from the wall behind me and look down at Kate.

She woke me up in the early hours of the morning, crying and asking if I would bring her back to hospital so she could be with her mom. Since visiting hours were over and only her mom was allowed back in ICU with her dad, we sat in the waiting room. After a bit, she stretched out across a few chairs, rested her head in my lap, and fell asleep. A nurse came by shortly after she saw Kate sleeping and offered to get her a pillow and some blankets, but there's no comfort to be had in the ICU waiting room.

My eyes ache from the lack of sleep, but there's no room for complaints when Kate is suffering enough for the both of us. I'm just glad I can be here for her. The thought of leaving doesn't sit well with me, but it's Sunday, and our fall break is over. I slip my cell phone out from my pocket and shoot a quick email to one of my professors who's a total pisspot when it comes to attendance. I explain the situation and then ask if he'd allow me to skip his lectures this week without risking my grade since I've already exceeded the four absences he allots us.

After I hit send, Kate's mother walks by the waiting room again. She's been on the phone all morning, pacing back and forth. A few officers stopped by not too long ago to check in on her and get an update on Steve. After speaking to one of them, I found out that the passenger that was in the car Steve had pulled over for a routine traffic stop had an outstanding warrant and was high on crack. He jumped out of the car and started firing, putting a bullet through Steve's neck.

The only reason he didn't die right then and there was because the driver had enough of a conscience to call 9-1-1 before fleeing the scene. They've both been apprehended, but it's little consolation considering Steve is still in critical condition. I didn't wake up Kate to tell her, but she'll find out as soon as she wakes up because the news playing on the small television in the waiting room has been reporting on it all morning.

"The nurse just said we can go back and see him now," her mother tells me in a hushed voice when she steps into the waiting area. "Should we wake her?"

Looking down at Kate, I run the back of my hand down her cheek. "I think I'll let her sleep for a few more minutes."

Her mom comes over and takes a seat in the chair next to me before stroking her hand over her daughter's hair. "It's good that you're here for her," she tells me.

"I wouldn't want to be anywhere else."

She smiles for only a moment, and I get the feeling she wants to say something, but she hesitates before shifting the focus to her other daughter. "Audrina's flight gets in around noon today."

"You have her flight number?"

"In my email. Why?"

"Send it to me, and I'll go pick her up," I offer, feeling a need to help this family in any way I can.

"Oh, you don't have to do that."

"It's fine," I assure. "You should be here in case anything happens."

Her hand slips out of Kate's hair and onto my knee. She gives it a light squeeze, saying, "Thank you."

"No worries."

When she's gone, I sit alone with Kate. She was so tense yesterday, and I'd never seen her shut down the way she did last night. I wish I knew for sure if I handled it the right way, but I have no idea. I tried to be supportive without being overbearing, but when I heard her crying in the bathroom, there was no thinking. I just went to her. When she let me hold her in the shower, it was a huge sense of relief because she dropped her walls enough to release some of her pain instead of locking it all inside herself like she had after Caleb. It was also one of the hardest moments of my life. I felt entirely worthless because there was nothing I could do to take her suffering away.

She begins to stir in my lap, and I watch as her eyes blink open. The moment she remembers where we are, dread washes over her.

"Hey," I murmur.

She pushes herself up and yawns heavily before slacking her shoulders and staring out the window.

I want to ask her if she's okay, but it's a stupid question.

"Where's my mom?"

"She's back with your dad." I look into her eyes, which are bloodshot, and the overwhelming need to take care of her swims back into focus. "Tell me what I can do."

In a heap of defeat, she shrugs. "Tell me none of this is real."

Wrapping my arm around her, I pull her into me, and she lays her head against my shoulder. "I wish I could."

The two of us sit for a handful of minutes, and I know she's scared to go see her father again, but I encourage her anyway. "You should go spend some time with your dad."

"What are you going to do?"

"I have to go to the airport in a bit to pick up your sister, but you don't need to worry about me. I'll be around. I just want you to focus on your family."

Tired and weak, she gives a solemn nod as we both stand and I pull her into a long hug. I hold tightly and drop a slow kiss on to the top of her head before drawing back and angling her face up to me. She stares for a moment before lifting onto her toes and kissing me. It's the saddest kiss I've ever gotten from her, and it hurts so badly to see this happening when she doesn't deserve any of it.

Hers is the sweetest soul I've ever come across. There's a tenderness inside her that many would be surprised to find, and I'm so thankful that I'm the one she gives it to. I never thought she'd be willing to get involved with a guy like me, never thought she would trust me enough to even give me a chance. I feel undeserving at times because I've been so selfish for so long. But she was who encouraged me to reevaluate myself. She's the only one I've been willing to do that for. And as I stand here, holding her in my arms, fuck, I'd give this girl the world if I could, and it's killing me that I can't fix this for her.

"I love you," she whispers against my lips.

"You have no idea how much I love you back."

Slowly, she pulls away from me, and I watch as she walks through the double doors and down the hall. Heading back to the waiting room, my mom calls me.

"Hey, Mom."

"Hi. I know it's early, but I wanted to check in on the two of you. How's Kate doing?"

I flop down in one of the chairs with a hard sigh. "Not good. I've never seen her like this before. I don't know what to do."

"You're doing all you can just by being there and supporting her."

"It doesn't feel like enough."

"It won't, but I promise you that it is," she says. "How's her father?"

"I don't know. There aren't any updates, but it doesn't look good."

"Well, I'm here if you need me. Please tell Kate that I love her and I'm praying for her family."

"I will, Mom. Thank you."

We say our goodbyes, and I run down to the cafeteria to grab the girls a couple of bagels. Since they don't allow food back in the patient rooms, I leave them at the ICU information desk before texting Kate.

> Me: There are bagels for you and your mom at the desk. I'm heading to the airport now. Call if you need me.

No response comes back, not that I figured any would. I don't want to imagine what she's going through right now being back there with her father.

When I arrive at the airport, I park and go inside to wait for her sister. After a while, she finally appears, looking just as distraught as Kate.

"Audrina," I call out, and she looks surprised to see me here, but she doesn't question anything when she walks into my arms, taking me off guard.

I hug her back for a long minute before she pulls away, and we silently make our way to the baggage claim to collect her luggage and then out to my Jeep.

"Where is everyone?" she finally asks.

"They're at the hospital," I tell her as she continues to wipe at the tears falling down her face.

"I haven't talked to Mom since my layover a few hours ago; have there been any updates on my dad?"

Pulling out on to the main street, I shake my head. "I don't know. But do you need anything? Are you hungry or need coffee?"

"No, I just want to get to the hospital. I'll worry about eating later," she tells me, and I know it must've been hell for her to be stuck on an international flight all night, knowing that her dad is fighting for his life.

After we arrive at the hospital, I walk her up to make sure she's okay before I head back to the house. I take her suitcase up to her room, and as much as I need a nap, stress has me unable to sit still. While I wait to hear from them, I keep myself busy and go to the grocery store to stock up on food since there isn't much at the house. It isn't until I'm unloading everything that I finally get a text from Kate.

> Kate: Visiting hours are almost over. We have three hours before we can come back. Can you come get me?
> Me: Yeah. I'm leaving your house now.

I pick them up, and the two of them are drained and Audrina can't stop crying. Neither says much of anything, aside from Kate mentioning a headache as she and her sister go upstairs to Kate's room.

I grab her prescription for her and make sure they have everything they need before backing out of the room. As I close the door, the last thing I see is the two of them lying in bed and Kate wrapping her sister up in a hug as she cries.

While I'm hanging out in the living room, watching television,

I check my email and see that my professor got back to me. I open his message to find that the rusty old cocksucker isn't going to budge on his attendance policy since it isn't a family related emergency, but rather, my girlfriend's. It never fails that, each semester, I get one asshole professor who actually keeps track of when I show up. He ends the email by reiterating his policy that each absence after the fourth will result in a half a letter grade drop.

"Fucking bastard," I mutter right before I hear the door to the garage open. I stand when I see it's Kate's mom. "Hey."

"Oh, hi," she says. "I just came home really quick to shower and run to the store."

"I already went."

"You what?"

"I went to the store earlier today," I tell her as I follow her into the kitchen.

She opens the fridge to find it stocked. "You didn't have to do that."

"It's the least I could do."

She pulls out the new carton of creamer and then fixes herself a cup of coffee. "Where are the girls?"

"Sleeping in Kate's room."

She brings her mug over to the table and invites me to sit with her. Last time I was here, I spent most of my time with Steve, so I'm not really sure how to start a conversation with her. Thankfully, she doesn't make me sweat. "Steve really loved meeting you this past summer." A subtle grin ghosts her lips as she thinks about something. "You know . . . I wound up googling that biscuit thing you brought up at dinner."

"Too offensive?" I question with a smirk, and she takes a sip of coffee to stifle her giggle.

"It was unexpected, but it brought up old memories." My eyes widen, and she instantly perks up, defending, "No, not about the biscuit thing."

"Thank god!"

She breathes a weak laugh. "It got me thinking back to when Steve and I first met. You remind me a lot of him in his younger years. He had a mouth like a sailor, which my parents did not approve of." She stares down at her hands, which are cradling the mug. "I never imagined I'd fall for a guy like him."

"I think Kate feels the same way," I admit. "I worry she's going to wake up one day and ask herself what the hell she's doing with me."

It's a strange thing to say this aloud, and it's even stranger to say it to her mother, but then she turns to me and says, "I think you're exactly what she's been looking for."

"She's too good for me."

She smiles. "It's okay to feel that way. It'll make you want to be an even better man than what you already are."

It helps settle the doubts I've always had about myself when it comes to her daughter. I often worry I won't be enough, but she's right. I do want to be a better man and give Kate everything I know she deserves. And then the email I just received comes to mind and I worry I'm going to let her down.

"I think she's going to be pissed at me."

"Why?"

"I have to get back to Miami. I have this dickhole professor who's going to drop my grade if I miss any more lectures, and I'm barely hanging on to a C in the class."

"She'll understand."

"I feel bad leaving all of you," I admit. I worry about how the three of them will handle it if things turn worse, and I don't want Kate to be alone.

Her hand finds mine, and she holds it. "You need to take care of your school. I can't tell you how much it means to me that you're here with us, but we'll be okay, and so will Kate."

After that, she makes her way into her room, and I head upstairs. Kate and Audrina are sound asleep, so I grab a few of my things and head across the hall into the guest room to lie down. Unfortunately, sleep doesn't find me, and after a while, my door cracks open.

Kate closes it behind her and slips into bed with me. I cuddle her close and let her heat sink into my body before taking a deep breath and telling her, "I have to go back to Miami, babe."

"Why?"

"I can't miss any more classes. I tried talking to my professor, but he won't make an exception."

She lets go of a deep breath.

"I'm so sorry," I tell her, kissing her forehead. "I don't want to leave you."

She's quiet for a few minutes, and it's just long enough for me to start to worry that she's mad, but then she presses closer to me. "It's okay. You don't have to feel bad about going. I understand."

It doesn't feel right that she's okay with me leaving. In a way, I want her to be upset, I want her to be angry and tell me I'm letting her down by not being here for her when I should be.

"I don't want to be away from you right now."

"I'll be fine."

"Are you sure?"

She nods.

"I'll only be an hour and a half away, so if you need me for anything."

She slides her hand through my hair, grips it into her palm, and presses her forehead against mine before she closes her eyes. "I feel like I'm a burden to you."

"Fuck that." I instantly dismiss the notion. "You're not even close to being a burden."

She doesn't say another word, but it isn't as if she has a chance to before I'm kissing her so deeply I hope she feels it in her bones. She needs to know that I would do absolutely anything for her.

When she lifts the covers and pulls them over us, I'm cautious as she starts to move over me. She slips off her shorts and then starts tugging at mine, but I force myself to stop her.

"Your mom is downstairs," I tell her.

"I don't care."

"Are you sure, babe?"

Her puffy eyes hold too many emotions to count, and when she shifts to straddle my hips, she gives me a timid, "Please."

I know all she wants is to feel safe in this moment, so I don't push her away when she lowers herself and takes me inside her. Despite the fact that her world is in ruins, we manage to console each other as best we can while we quietly make love. Her hands brace against my chest, and I'm entirely consumed by watching her take from me whatever it is she needs. And I swear that I've never felt more connected to another person as I do in this very moment.

Twenty-One

KATE

> **TRENT:** Never heard back from you yesterday. Call me when you get a chance.

I stare at the text I received this morning, the one I've yet to respond to, as a cloud of dread hangs over me. Trent went back to Miami early Monday morning, and the distance this week has given time for guilt and a brand-new fear to emerge through the overwhelming shock and devastation of my dad. For the two days he was with me after my father was shot, I was needy for his comfort, which came on the heel of him telling me how much he had been neglected of that very thing.

Selfishly, I couldn't see beyond the agony festering in my heart, and I wound up taking from him in a very similar way he complained about his mother doing.

She's done it his whole life.

Her world falls apart, and she runs to him to help make it all better.

Realizing I've been doing the same thing hit me out of the blue a couple of days ago, and now I'm questioning myself in more ways than just one.

"Good news," a nurse says when she comes into my dad's

hospital room. "Tomorrow morning, we'll be moving you to the step-down unit."

Still extremely weak, he barely lifts a smile.

Yesterday, they pulled him out of his coma and ran several tests, all of which came back with positive results and with no detection of any neurological damage. Since then, he's been stable, and the news that he'll be moved out of ICU brings a huge sense of relief. He's going to recover.

While the nurse checks his vitals, I go back to ignoring Trent's text and call my mom to tell her the news. My sister and I have been trading visiting shifts with her so we can better take care of ourselves and get the rest we've been severely lacking. It's been one of the toughest weeks of my life, but now that he's awake, hope is more tangible.

"When is your mom coming back up?" he asks when I end the call.

"In about an hour."

"You girls don't have to be up here every waking minute, you know?"

"None of us have a car, so . . . ya know," Audrina teases as if the lack of transportation is the reason we don't go home more often.

I mean, it plays a part, but it certainly isn't the reason.

"You too good for public transportation?" he tosses back, and I smile.

Until yesterday, I was afraid he'd never open his eyes again, that I'd never hear his voice, that he would leave me alone and fatherless in this world, forever putting a gaping hole in our family.

"What about you?" he says, acknowledging me. "When are you getting back to Miami? Don't you have classes you need to go to?"

"I was able to get this week waived, but I have to go back

tomorrow or Sunday because I can't get any more time off," I tell him, hating that I have to leave when he's still stuck here.

The doctor told us that, even if he doesn't experience any setbacks, he probably won't be going home for another couple of weeks. Not only do I not want to leave my dad but also I'm worried about my mother. She's a strong woman, but the stress has taken its toll on her. Hopefully, now that he's being moved out of the ICU, she won't feel as if she has to be here constantly.

"I have pudding," a nurse sing-songs as she pokes her head into the room.

"I'll take it," my dad says, knowing damn well he can't have it.

"Nice try." She looks between my sister and me, holding out the small cup. "Any takers?"

"No thanks," I tell her. "I think I've eaten my body weight in pudding over this past week."

"I didn't want to say anything, but your ass does look bigger."

"Thanks, Audrina," I snark as I flip her off.

She raises her hands defensively. "What? I'm just sayin'. You don't want Trent trading you in, do you?"

I shake my head, wondering if he should. Not because of my looks—Trent would never do that, and my sister knows it. But I have to wonder if I'm able to give him what he needs—what he deserves. Let's face it, a bomb just blew up right in front of my face, and I've been a mess ever since. It's the realization that life is fragile and can be taken away from us at any moment.

I've cried myself to sleep every night this week. This situation with my father has me mentally frail and unable to focus on anything outside of my family. I'm on empty and have nothing left to give, so I'm forced to take.

But I don't want to take from Trent because I wouldn't be asking for a little; I'd be asking for a monumental amount of support and patience. My world has been shaken to its core, and I'm struggling to keep my head above water. The last thing I want is to be a burden to anyone, especially him.

He doesn't deserve another person in his life who does nothing but take.

That's exactly what I would be doing—what I already have been doing—I just didn't realize it until now. I've been relying on his strength to help pull me through the devastation of Caleb. Knowing how much Trent despises him, I can't imagine how frustrating it was for him to have to see me cry over how Caleb shattered my heart.

Trent's too nice of a guy to ever say anything to me about it, just like he's too nice to have ever said anything to his mother about how much her neediness affects him. He has to feel the same way about me. How could he not? He's already told me how much his mother has let him down, how all he wanted was to feel her strength and for her to take care of him. He's never had that. It's only a matter of time until he sees I'm just the same as her. And my biggest fear is that he's going to wind up resenting me—because he will, the same way he resents her.

I shouldn't have been depending on him the way I have been, and it isn't fair for me to use him as my personal crutch.

God, I've been taking advantage of him this whole time. He didn't need me to throw all my baggage on him, but I did it anyway, never bothering to ask if he even wanted it.

I'm just another weak woman who can't fix things on her own.

But I need to. I need to figure out a way to not lean on him so much. Reality is, strength is the one thing I always seem to be in short supply of. Lord knows I didn't have an ounce of it when I was with Caleb, and I don't feel like I have much of it with Trent either, so what makes me think that I'll be able to have it all on my own if I don't have someone next to me to syphon it from?

The desire to resurrect the walls around me that I had built after Caleb, the same walls Trent worked so hard to tear down, is undeniably strong. In a way, I've already started stacking the bricks by avoiding Trent's calls these past two days and not checking in like I should be. I'm putting distance between us because I'm ashamed and disappointed in myself.

He gives, and I take and I take and I take.

We're unbalanced—because of me.

I'm not the right girl for him.

I'm far too fragile.

When the sun trades shifts with the moon and I lay my head on my pillow, I'm forced to hit my vape pen because getting high is the only way I can sleep these days. Without it, I'm an insomniac, crawling the walls and driving myself crazy with frightening thoughts of the people I love dying all around me.

I grew up believing my parents were ever-steady, unbreakable, and forever constant. No one wants to consider the possibility of them dying, so we don't. We put that thought out of the realm of possibilities and allow ourselves to think it will never happen. Having life turn on me so harshly has been a shock to my system, and I'm struggling to cope with the undeniable truth that, one day, I will be without them.

My phone illuminates the room with another notification I can't bring myself to look at, so I don't. Rolling over, I take one more pull from my pen before totally fading.

Another shift change—another day recycled. I wake, shower, and attempt to console the unrelenting pain in my stomach with coffee because I can't eat. I return to the hospital, sit with my dad, and wallow in a swamp of depression even though I'm so grateful to still have him. And then, I come home, get stoned, and sleep just to do it all over again.

Despite the shimmers of light, I'm shrouded in darkness that I can't get out from underneath. My dad was moved to a different floor yesterday, and it brought him so much happiness to see his friends on the force. The nurses had to step in and cut their visits short since he wore out quickly, reminding us all that he still has a long road ahead of him.

"How are you holding up, dear?" my mother asks when she finds me sitting in the living room, staring at the blank television screen and waiting to go up to the hospital.

My response is a painful smile I can't hold for any longer than a few seconds.

"You know, it helps if you actually turn the television on."

Talking is impossible with the pang deep inside my gut today. I have to go back to Miami, and I've been trying so hard not to think about it.

"I spoke with Trent last night."

I can't bring myself to look at her because I don't want to risk her seeing the tears I'm fighting back.

"Is everything okay between the two of you?"

I nod, trying to avoid having to talk about him, but there's no avoiding the obtrusive knot in my throat.

My words strain in discomfort when I finally speak. "What did he say?"

"He's concerned about you. Said he hasn't heard from you in a few days." She lays a hand on my knee. "You know, it's okay to be vulnerable and ask for help."

"I know."

"I can tell he's worried," she says, reinforcing the fact that I'm a burden. "I told him you'd be home tonight. I think it'll be good for you to get some space from all this stress."

"You told him I'm going back tonight?"

"Yeah, why?"

"I'm ready," Audrina announces when she comes down the stairs, ending our conversation, but it doesn't leave my mind.

My sister and I follow my mom up to the hospital in Dad's truck, but I can barely focus during my visit because I'm too consumed with heartache, knowing that Trent will most likely be at my condo at some point this evening. I should be excited to see him and be back inside his arms. Instead, I have sadness blooming inside me.

"What are you thinking about?" my father asks when he notices how quiet I've been.

"How much I don't want to go back to Miami."

"I'll be fine," he says. "I'll be out of here in no time."

I reach over and hold his hand, but the small comfort isn't enough to quell the dread of the minutes ticking down. My mom and sister went to grab a bite to eat, but I stayed to spend some extra time with him before Audrina drives me back to my place.

"I'm worried about Mom too," I tell him. "Audrina booked her flight back to London. She leaves in three days, and Mom won't have anyone at the house."

"Your mom is a tough woman; she'll be fine. All of you need to stop fussing over me."

"Dad, you were shot," I remind him, needing him not to be so dismissive of the severity of his injury. "We almost lost you."

"But you didn't. I'm still here, kicking and breathing."

Shaking my head, I hold his hand a little tighter, dreading the day I'll no longer have him. The thought weighs on me every second of every minute of every hour. It never leaves my side. The inevitability of that fact has changed me this past week, and if I could, I'd hold on to him for forever.

When it's time to go, I break down, leaning over him and crying as I do my best to hug him with all the machines he's still hooked up to. He continues to act as if everything is fine and I have no reason to be concerned, but that's just his stubbornness talking.

"I'll come back next weekend to see you," I tell him before I kiss his cheek. "I love you."

"I love you too." Then he looks at Audrina, saying, "Drive carefully."

She gives him a hug and then tugs me from the room.

The trip back feels shorter than it should, and when we arrive at my place, Audrina decides to hang out for a little while. She's just switching out the laundry for me, when the expected knock happens.

She's quick to rush to the door, and the moment I hear his voice, the desire to run and hide consumes me. When I step out of my room, he looks over my way, and I'm sure my sister can feel the tension between us.

"I should probably get back," she says.

"No, you don't have to leave."

She glances at Trent and then to me. "It's fine. I told mom I'd be home in time to have dinner with her."

A fresh shot of sadness washes over me as we hug each other. I hate that she's leaving for London and I won't see her for a while. She cries in my arms, and I struggle to keep myself together when she blubbers, "I'm going to miss you so much."

"I'm going to miss you too."

She pulls back and wipes her eyes. "Promise you'll call or text me every day."

"I promise."

After one more hug, she turns to say bye to Trent, who pulls her into a warm hug as well. It kills me to watch because the two of them are growing closer.

The second the door shuts behind her, Trent takes me into his arms with a heavy breath. His warmth is a comfort I want to cling to, but I know I can't, and I pull away.

"What's going on?"

I turn and take a few steps back, growing nervous because I don't know how to do this when I don't want to do this at all. I wish he would be the one to let me go just to spare me the agony of having to hurt him.

"Kate, talk to me," he says. "Tell me why you've been avoiding me."

A sharp pain slices down my throat, and I lose all my strength when tears begin slipping down my face. He walks over and I quickly turn around before his arms fold around me so he's hugged against my back. It's in this moment a whimper slips out.

"Baby, don't cry."

And this is it, this is the reason we have to put space between us. It's wrong of me to keep taking when his affection only makes me want more. It isn't fair to him.

His head presses against the side of my cheek, and when I move my hands to grip on to his arms that are crossed around my chest, I whisper cowardly, "I can't do this."

The moment the words are out, his arms constrict, holding me tighter. I want to stay forever in them, but that's only because I'm needy.

"Everything's going to be okay," he tries to assure.

Shaking my head, I pull his arms from around me and turn to face him. Staring into his eyes, all I see is his concern, and I know he won't ever understand.

"I need you to talk to me."

"I can't do this," I repeat.

"Can't do what?"

I take a step back. *"This,"* I state. *"Us."*

"What the fuck are you talking about?"

Dropping my eyes because I'm too scared to look at him, I tell him, "We need to stop seeing each other."

His hands come to find my arms, and I wish he wouldn't

touch me. It's only making this harder. "Look, I know you're going through a lot of shit right now, but . . ."

When his words fall short, I finally open my eyes. Devastation surrounds me, and there's no avoiding it.

"I'm sorry," is all I can manage.

"Why are you doing this?"

"Because I love you," I tell him from the most honest place inside my heart.

"Then why are you trying to break up with me?"

"Because I'm not right for you," I admit as my heart crumbles into pieces that I will never be able to fit back together again. "I wish I was, but I'm not."

"What the fuck are you talking about? You're perfect for me." He speaks with undeniable fervency, but how the hell can he say that when I'm the very thing he complains about?

"I'm just not good enough."

His teeth grind, and he's furious when he says, "Caleb's the one who made you doubt your self-worth, not me!"

"This has nothing to do with him."

"Bullshit!" He catches his anger and takes a beat to calm himself before he comes back softer, saying, "I've done everything to show you that your perfect just the way you are."

"That's just it . . . you've done *everything*." Another drop of agony rolls slowly down my cheek. "You've done more than what you ever should've."

Confusion deepens the lines across his forehead. "What's that supposed to mean?"

"I'm weak and I use you for your strength. I've been taking advantage of you." I pause and then add, "My life falls apart, and I turn to you to get me through it. Sound familiar?"

"Are you seriously comparing yourself to my mother?"

"How is what I'm doing any different?"

He steps closer to me. "Because it is."

"How?"

"Because it just is, Kate."

"Then tell me how."

"I don't fucking know, but it just is!"

The fact that he can't argue the difference reinforces that I'm seeing things for exactly what they are, and it makes me want to fall to my knees in heartbreak.

"Kate, please."

"You say I'm not a burden to you, but—"

"You aren't."

"You wouldn't tell me even if I was."

"Yes, I would," he states fervently, but I'm already shaking my head at the truth we both know.

"Have you ever told your mom?"

"What the fuck, Kate." He turns on his heel and paces away from me.

"I'm sorry," I cry. "I wish I didn't need as much as what I do, but *I do*."

"Then let me give it to you," he says, stepping back over to me.

"You'll only wind up resenting me. I can't do that to you."

He's at a loss for words as he shakes his head ever so slightly in disbelief.

I feel it too. I can't believe it's come to this, and as much as it hurts, it'll hurt worse if we allow the bitterness of resentment to rip our love apart.

"You said it yourself when we were in Key West. You told me nothing lasts forever."

"Really? You're bringing up shit I said years ago?" He rakes his hand through his hair as he stalks away from me. "This is bullshit. You're just scared."

"I am," I agree. "And because of that, I have no business being in a relationship—in *any* relationship."

Lacing his fingers behind his head, he stalks across the room as he lets go of a heavy breath that's dripping in frustration.

When he looks at me, he drops his arms in defeat, nearly begging, "Tell me how to fix this."

I blink, and tears fall again. "You can't." Those two words are a guillotine to my heart, splitting it right open, spilling everything it ever held inside it. "I'm doing this because I love you and it's the right thing to do."

"None of this makes any sense." He comes back over to me and takes my face in his hands, pleading, "I can't lose you."

"I can't lose you either," I cry. "I want to keep you for forever, but I'm not enough to be what you need—what you *deserve*." As more tears spill out, he pulls me against his chest so tightly I can feel his heart beating erratically against my cheek, and I hate that I'm not stronger. I wish he could just admit it to himself because this is killing me to break his heart like this. "I'm so sorry."

"You're good enough. I swear to you, you are."

I shake my head at the lies he's trying to convince himself are truths.

"Don't do this," he begs.

Pressing my cheek against his warmth, I hug him tighter when I weep, "I'll forever love you for everything you've done for me."

"Please, don't do this." His voice cracks, and when I look up, there's heartache welling in his eyes. He shakes his head, pleading once more, "Don't," and I have to force myself to step out of his arms, and the moment I do, his sadness spins into anger. He raises his voice, demanding, "Don't fucking do this!"

"Trent, please," I beg. "Please don't be angry, just try to understand that—"

"Understand what?" he snaps. "That some guy fucked you up, and now I'm paying the price for it?"

I open my mouth, but too many words collide, preventing me from saying anything.

Fuming mad, he walks straight to my door, and when he turns around, tears are running down his cheeks.

"Trent."

"Fuck you," is all he leaves me with before slamming the door behind him.

Twenty-Two

KATE

The murky gloom of a new day greets me as I wake, despite the sunshine and palm trees that make a mockery of my mood. As I go through the motions of my morning routine, I'm nothing but a vacant body getting from point A to point B. This past week, between my father and Trent, I've been pushed to my breaking point. I'm dangling from a withered thread, all the while depending on it to save me.

Because that's what I do—I depend on everything other than myself.

After Trent stormed out yesterday, I spent the whole night crying before reconstructing my walls. Self-preservation drives me to shove down all that threatens to break me.

I'm sick of feeling too much.

I try not to think about Trent, but he's everywhere I look. There's a hole in the pit of my heart where he belongs but I forced him from—yet, he's still there, clinging to the edges, refusing to leave. I did the right thing—for both of us—*I think*.

Why does it feel like my story is constantly filled with broken pieces, terrible choices, and ugly truths?

"You did the right thing," I reassure myself, but heartache holds me in its claws.

After a quick call to get an update on my dad, I grab my backpack and head to campus. It seems pointless though. How in the world am I supposed to concentrate with so much on my mind?

When I walk into class, Ady is already sitting in her seat. I drop my bag next to her feet, and she pops her head up from her book. "You're back."

I force a smile as I plop down in my chair and dig my notebook out from my bag.

"How's everything with your dad?"

"He made it out of the ICU," I tell her.

"Oh, thank god. I've been so worried." She reaches over to give me a quick hug. "I wanted to call, but I knew you were dealing with a lot, so I've been relying on Trent for updates."

She speaks his name, and it triggers a pain I have to force myself to ignore.

"You should come over tonight, just hang out and take your mind off everything."

I'm not sure I'm ready to say the words aloud, but I don't have a choice because she lives with Trent. It isn't something I'm going to be able to hide, so I go ahead and get it over with. "I don't think that's a good idea."

"Why?"

Anxiously, I scribble on the corner of the notebook paper in an attempt to avoid the sadness. "We broke up."

"What?"

I can't bring myself to look at her as I nod.

"What happened?"

With a dismissive shrug that's a complete sham, I respond, "It just didn't work out."

"I didn't even know you guys were having problems."

Not wanting to go any deeper, I continue coloring the edge of the paper in black ink.

"Kate." Her voice is laced in worriment.

Looking up, I remain expressionless when I say, "I don't want to talk about it."

She nods with a gentle understanding. "Okay."

As the hour passes, I don't hear a single word of today's lecture, and by the time class ends, my page is covered in so much ink that the paper curls. Ady barely speaks to me as we go from one class to another, and I love her for that. Love that she isn't forcing conversations on me that I'm not strong enough to have.

After our last class together, I follow her over to the student center, and before I break away to head to my car, I give her a simple, "Thanks."

Her eyes soften, and I know she gets it. "You'll call me if you need anything, right?"

I nod and drive back to my place while she remains for one more class.

Loneliness torments me more and more with each day that passes—one fading into the next. I find myself losing track of time as I sit alone inside my head, watching the sun die every night, only to witness its rebirth the following morning. Days drag slowly, nights last forever, and weeks pass at a suffering pace.

I miss him.

I constantly fight against wanting to call him just to hear his voice.

Thoughts of him are consuming, and I have to remind myself that maybe my journey isn't about love. Maybe, right now, my journey is about being alone, about waking in the middle of the bed and finding hope in the vacancy, hope in the quiet, hope in the way I stretch into my life and give myself permission to take up the space within it. Ever since I came here to Miami, I've been searching to find the place where I can fit in and feel settled. Maybe this is the time for me to learn that I don't need to depend on others for that, that I can be my own place of sanctuary.

Maybe, just maybe, there's a whole other world waiting for me on the other side of myself where nothing ever burns.

"There you are," my mother welcomes when I walk through the front door.

It's Thanksgiving break and the first holiday where it's only the three of us since Audrina is in England still.

I was hoping to come home and feel normal again, but nothing has been normal since my father almost died.

"Where's Dad?"

"Lying down in the living room."

After three and a half weeks in the hospital, he was finally released, but he's still going to physical therapy to regain his strength after being bed-ridden for so long.

As he sleeps on the couch, I move quietly to slip the remote out from under his hand. I'm impressed with his quick reflexes when he clutches it tightly and pulls it away before his eyes even open.

I laugh, and he looks at me, teasing, "Don't mess with a man's football game."

"You're not even watching it."

He smiles before struggling to sit up. When he groans in discomfort, I slip my hands under his arms to help him. "You make me feel like an old geezer."

"Stop."

Once he's situated, he pats the spot next to him, and I take a seat before leaning in for a long hug.

"How are you doing?" I ask.

"You mean aside from being annoyed with everyone fussing over me?"

"I can hear you," Mom calls out from the kitchen, and Dad chuckles.

"People just want to help."

"I'm sick of lying around this house," he grumbles, and I can totally relate. Time moves at a snail's pace when the world leaves you idle. "I'm ready to get back to work."

"Work?"

My mother enters the room with a platter of snacks, shaking her head as she sets the food on the coffee table. "You need to be thinking about retiring."

"Are you hearing your mother?" he says, and she shoots him a glare, but I know it stems from a place of love. He turns back to me. "I'm too young to retire."

"You're not *that* young," I tease.

"Those are fighting words, girl."

I laugh.

"It isn't about your age," my mom nags. "It's about your safety. Do you have any idea how close we came to losing you?"

"I took a bullet to the neck," he responds as he scoops a pita chip through the hummus. "I'm well aware."

She flops down in one of the chairs, mumbling, "You are a stubborn man."

Dismissing her entirely, he finishes his chip before asking, "Where's Trent?"

"He's at home with his mom," I respond, not that I know for sure.

It's been weeks since we broke up, and I've yet to tell my parents, but I wonder if they can see through my stone wall to the truth. I wonder how well I'm hiding the pain from hearing his name. It might as well be a lance across my heart that inflames these self-inflicted wounds—wounds that scorch like fire, sending flares up into the night sky, alerting the world that I'm in distress.

"Do you mind if I go upstairs and rest for a bit?"

"You just got here," my mother says with a hint of concern.

"I know, but I didn't get much sleep last night."

She nods, and when I stand, she tells me, "The turkey will be coming out of the oven in a couple of hours."

"Okay."

I make a beeline to my room, needing space to digest the sadness his name just reawakened without them noticing that something is wrong. Closing my door, I lie on the bed and sink into his memory.

Drowning is a quiet, desperate thing.

I close my eyes to keep the tears inside, and when I convince myself that it's safe to reopen them, I wake to the ghost of him hanging on the other side of the sky. He's beyond my reach, and my heart plummets in the wake of his effervescence. Shutting my eyes again, I see tiny specs within the darkness behind my lids—stars of iridescent light that shine over me. Maybe it's him. I try to convince myself that it isn't, that stars are only phantoms of the nighttime.

Rolling over, I look out my window to see tall stacks of billowing clouds, and I wish for them to open, beg the universe to send in the rain to cry for me because I can't do it on my own without sacrificing myself.

My head won't shut up while I search for placidity, and I become irritated. Sitting up, I throw a pillow onto the floor and drop my head into my palms—hating myself.

"What am I doing?" I murmur when doubt peeks over my shoulder and whispers into my ear.

How the hell am I ever supposed to leave Trent behind when

he grew roots inside me? Roots that remain even when he's gone. There's no point of pushing him away when he's forever with me.

Maybe I was wrong.

Maybe my skies are painted in his stars for a reason—a reason perhaps I should pay attention to. There's no question that he became my center of peace, my most calming place in the world. So, why am I trying to avoid the very pain that's found its home within me?

I pick up my cell phone and then hesitate as I try to avoid all the reasons this is a bad idea. Somehow, I'm able to push those thoughts aside long enough to tap his name and send the call through.

Each ring jostles my heart, sending it into overdrive as my anticipation of hearing his voice grows. Eventually, the ringing stops, and his voice mail picks up. My heart comes to a stop, dropping down a few ribs lower as I end the call and toss the phone aside.

Blue devils return, dumping their despair all over me again. Perhaps him not answering is a sign—the universe telling me that letting him go was the right thing to do.

I would've never been enough for him. He was too good for me.

Lying back down, I do everything I can to keep him out of my thoughts, but no matter how long I stare at my ceiling, I can't help but wonder what he's doing in this very moment.

Twenty-Three

TRENT

Five months.

That's all she gave before giving up on me.

Never has my heart ached the way it has since she ended things. I knew better than to get involved with her or anyone for that matter, so I take responsibility for my own pain as well. For the first time in my life, I handed myself over to another person, trusting that I was doing the right thing, only to wind up hurt—wallowing in sadness like a pussy. Heartbreak is a bitch, and it's no joke. I can't even explain the depression I'm unable to get out from underneath.

I miss her.

I miss every goddamn thing about her.

She let me get used to how it felt to be loved, and she gave it to me in the most perfect way. There was no avoiding falling for her, it was as if she were created for me to love, and now she's gone.

Days melt together, pushing time forward, yet I'm stuck as the world moves all around me. I'm in the eye of an unrelenting hurricane. For now, I sit idle while vicious storms brew from every direction, and it's only a matter of time before the storm closes in on me.

I heard her voice the other day—it was a jackknife to my gut. She stopped by to pick up Ady, and I hid in my room like a coward because I didn't trust myself to see her and not do everything possible to convince her to be with me.

Desperation blows ass, but that's where she has me trapped.

I hate that she thinks so poorly of herself, but it isn't as if I don't understand why—I do. The girl has gone through a lot. Life hasn't been gentle with her, but I thought I was doing everything I could to prove that I was her tether, her constant. In the end, she turned all that against me. She let self-doubt take her hand and pull her away from me because she believed she wasn't enough.

But she was.

I can't rid myself of her because I'm marked by her, but I'm conflicted if I even want to be. My head has been fucked since she pushed me away, and I want to hate her just to lessen this pain, but I can't because I love her, and I don't want to love her because that hurts too.

But how do I unlove a girl like her?

How do I vanquish the memory of her when starving it to death feels like such a sin?

I ponder that question while I sit like a little bitch on my mother's couch. Jack is here, and to see them making Thanksgiving dinner together irks me. Everything irks me at this point.

"Pull the tampon out, dude."

"Fuck off, Garrett."

"Boys," my mother calls from the dining room. "Let's eat."

I spend the next hour pushing food around my plate and listening to my mother's wedding plans before I ditch out and head up to my room. Lying down, I get stoned and lose myself in memories of having Kate in this bed with me.

Fuck, that girl was every version of amazing.

My cellphone rings in my back pocket, and when I pull it out, I see her name. The letters feel like nails driving through me.

The ringing only serves to reopen wounds that refuse to heal and remain in a constant state of tenderness.

When the phone goes silent, I close my eyes, only to reawaken in December, staring at the same ceiling and thinking the same thoughts. It's Christmas morning, and my mom is blasting obnoxious holiday music downstairs.

"Fuck me," I groan to myself.

Looking out the window, I find a heavy blanket of gray clouds in the sky, giving the illusion of a cold wintery day.

Was she an illusion too?

She left a gift for me at the condo last week.

I threw it away.

Strength abandons me when my phone chimes with a text.

It's from her.

Kate: Merry Christmas.

Knowing her fingers typed out the message only a minute ago, the very fingers she used to cling on to me with, rips my heart open. It bleeds the fuck out all over again, forcing me to numb the pain she just inflicted. I hit my vape pen, get high, and throw on a T-shirt before heading downstairs.

Dragging myself into the kitchen, I pour myself a cup of coffee, and when my mom notices my stoned, bloodshot eyes, she gives me a smile dripping with pity and hugs me.

"You're going to be okay," she encourages softly while she holds on to me for a few more seconds. "The first broken heart always hurts the worst."

I spend the rest of the day on the couch, getting drunk off the spiked cider Jack made and staring mindlessly into the Christmas tree.

Jack offers me a distraction when he turns the television onto a James Bond movie marathon. We shoot the shit while one movie bleeds into another, and when my phone chimes again, I see it's a text from Micah followed by a photo.

Micah: Am I crazy?

I then click on the photo to see an impressive diamond on Ady's left ring finger.

Me: No shit! Is this for real?
Micah: Yeah, man. I'm going to marry this girl.
Me: Congrats, brother.

As happy as I am for the two of them, I can't disregard the bitterness staining the back of my tongue. It seems everyone is moving on and making plans. We graduate college in May, and I don't have anything to look forward to because I'm still stuck in this turnstile of misery.

Memories of Kate follow me everywhere I go: from my bed in Tampa to my bed in Miami where I now sit and fight the urge to call her. Goddamn, today is a tough one, and all I can think about is how badly I want to hear her voice, talk to her, and ask if she's in as much pain as I am.

A part of me hopes that she is, that she's still suffering and can't stop thinking about me. If she is, then maybe we still have a chance. I don't make the call, though, because I'm scared I'll find out that she's happy and resolute in her decision.

I wish school would fucking start back up; I really need the distraction.

A knock on my door pulls me out of my thoughts.

"Yeah," I say before Ady steps in. "What's up?"

She walks over and sits next to me. "You going out tonight?"

"Why? You want to come out with me and have some fun?" I tease, knowing all too well that she is the last person anyone would expect to turn up at a party. "Or are you trying to get rid of me so you and my boy can pound like rabbits and be as loud as you want?"

She slaps my arm. "You're disgusting!"

"You sure you want to get married? I heard that shit dries up fast once you're locked down."

She cocks her head. "Is that all you think about?"

I laugh, but shit, it's been two months since I got laid, so yeah, it's been on my mind a lot lately.

"Seriously, though, you've been moping around here like a beaten dog."

"Nice."

"You know what I mean," she says. "It's New Year's Eve."

"So?"

"So . . ." She drags out the word before asking, "What if I told you that I want to go out with you?"

"Micah's cool with us hooking up?"

"I meant to a *party*," she stresses through an amused smile.

"What are you talking about? You never go out to parties."

"Well, I want to go to one."

"What's the catch?"

"No catch," she tells me before settling on a more serious tone. "I hate seeing you like this."

"You can thank your friend for that."

She shoots me a glare and dodges my comment. "Come on. I doubt I'll make this offer again."

"Where are we going?"

"Micah said Brody is throwing a party."

Lifting my brows at her. "You're really going to hit up one of Brody's parties?"

"Only if you go with me." She smiles as if she's daring me.

I want to tell her to forget it, but I'm also going insane sitting around here with nothing to do when Kate used to occupy so much of my time.

In need of a pick-me-up, I concede, "Okay."

Her eyes brighten. "Seriously?"

"Yeah, but I'm not taking you anywhere looking like *that*," I joke, and she sneers at me while looking down at the sloppy outfit she's been lounging around in all day. After she leaves to get ready, I hop in the shower and throw on a fresh outfit. Knowing Ady doesn't drink, I pull a beer out of the fridge, call out, "You're DD," and get a head start on the night.

She walks out of her room, wearing a pair of short black shorts and a strappy dark green top, and I give her a wink.

"Stop flirting," she warns, pointing her finger at me.

"You guys ready?" Micah says as he trails behind her.

"What the fuck?"

Ady looks over her shoulder and then back at me. "What?"

"You didn't tell me this douche was coming along."

"You think I'm sending Ady to a party with you—*alone*?"

"Dude, I'm not into being a third wheel."

"You're not," Ady pipes in. "Micah's the third wheel." She takes my hand. "You ready?"

Dropping her hand, I opt to sling my arm around her shoulders while shooting Micah a smirk and taunting, "Sucka!"

The three of us head out, and as Micah drives to Brody's place,

Ady keeps a death grip on his hand. He glances her way and gives her an encouraging grin, but damn, the girl looks tense as shit just to be going to a party.

After he finds a spot to park along the curb, we hop out, but before I go around to the passenger side to open Ady's door, Micah pulls me aside, saying, "Watch over her."

I note the worry in his eyes, but I don't question him—I never have. I'm not blind to the fact that something serious went down with her and that it's most likely the reason she came running to Miami and has lived with us ever since.

"I got her," I assure, and he nods before I open the door. Taking her hand, we walk up the sidewalk and I try to ignore how her grip tightens the closer we get. It's a similar grip Kate used to have on me when situations would make her nervous.

"You're good," I encourage as we head inside.

With no intention of letting go, I tuck her under my arm as we push through the crowd of people, stopping short of the kitchen to chat with a group of mutual friends. Ady may not party, but she still runs deep in our circle, and she relaxes into a conversation with some chick Brody has been spending time with lately.

"Here," Micah says when he hands me a drink, and I'm quick to guzzle it and shove it back into his hand for a refill. "Do I look like your bitch?"

"Yo, man," Brody hollers over the music. "You made it."

We clap hands, catch up, and when I get another drink, I take Ady aside to dance like we always used to do in high school, which feels like forever ago. As alcohol dilutes my blood, I'm able to free myself from the weight I've been carrying on my shoulders for the past couple of months. In this moment, I actually feel human again. Tossing back another drink, I look down at Ady, who smiles up at me.

"You having fun?" I shout over all the noise.

"I actually am," she says as if she's surprised.

As we continue to dance, she appears to be distracted. She keeps skating her eyes around the room and glancing over my shoulder.

"Looking for my replacement?"

She laughs. "No."

When I turn to see who's caught her eye, I go still.

"What the fuck is she doing here?" I ask, not taking my eyes off Kate, who's against the wall hanging out with a small group.

"Don't be mad," Ady says from behind me.

Too late.

She stops dancing when I face her. "You fucking set me up?"

"The two of you are miserable without each other," she defends.

"Yeah, she really looks miserable."

"Maybe if you just talked to her."

"Fuck this shit." I grab Ady's hand and pull her out of the room and away from Kate because it hurts too much to look at her. "Hey," I call out when I find Micah at the front of the house. "Here." I pass her off to him. "I'm out."

"Trent," she calls, but I'm not down with this and keep walking. "Trent, wait!" She rushes after me, and when we're outside, she catches up and reaches for my arm. "I'm sorry."

I turn around, pissed the fuck off that she'd do some dumb shit like this.

"I'm sorry," she says again.

"Did she know I was coming?"

She shakes her head with remorse in her eyes. "I didn't mean to upset you. I just—"

"You just what?" I push. "Thought if you got us in the same room everything would go back to how it used to be?"

She shrugs.

"I don't know what the hell she's been saying to you, but she let *me* go. This was *her* doing, not mine."

"She's just scared."

"Tough shit!"

"Trent."

Her voice in unmistakable, but it comes with a spiked dagger that immediately impales me, sending a violent pain through my ribs. I turn to find Kate standing on the steps. She's so beautiful despite the look of disbelief on her face, as if this were the very last place on Earth she'd expect me to be. Suddenly, all the anger is eclipsed by my love for her, which floods my system, preventing me from looking away from the only thing I want. It's hard enough having to avoid her texts, but to see her standing in front of me, speaking my name, is a completely different battle.

"I'll let you two talk," Ady says before scurrying back inside.

Timidly, Kate walks down the steps to where I am, and it takes everything in me not to grab her and tuck her back inside my arms where she belongs.

"Did you get my present?"

"I didn't open it," I tell her.

She nods, looking at me with the saddest eyes. "Why won't you respond to any of my texts?"

I shove my hands into my pockets as a thousand reasons slam into me, and I wish I could look away from her. It's torture to have her here, but not *have* her. "I don't know how to talk to you."

"I'm still me," she says, but she isn't.

She feels different in a way I can't describe, and I hate it. Hate this tension and space between us.

"I don't want this," I admit. "I don't want to feel this way around you."

"I don't either."

"Then what are we doing?"

She blinks a few times, fighting back her emotions.

"Tell me you've come to your senses. Tell me we can stop this shit so we can just be together."

Her eyes well with tears that tell me she feels the heartbreak too.

I step closer to her, wanting to touch her, but I don't. "You know this is bullshit."

"I can't," she says, her voice trembling.

"Can't what?" Her stubbornness gets under my skin, and I grow frustrated. "What the fuck do you want from me? Just tell me. Whatever it is, I'll do it. I'll give you whatever you want."

"I know you will."

"Why is me wanting to love you such a fucking problem?"

She blinks and a tear falls.

"Look, I know you've been through a lot," I tell her. "Your ex fucked with your head, but I'm telling you right now, you're enough and you aren't taking advantage of me. I swear to god, you aren't." She's headstrong, and I don't see her budging, which irritates me even more. "Fuck this shit," I fume. "Fuck this whole white-picket-fence idea you've built in your head about how life should be easy and simple and fair. It's nothing but a glorified cage, and it isn't always safe, but I swear to you that *I am*. You have no reason not to trust me. I'm not going to hurt you, Kate."

"But I'm hurting *you*." Tears spill down her face, and when I move in closer, she shuts me out, wrapping her arms across her chest. "I need you to just trust me when I tell you that."

A swarm of anger rushes over me for how she's single-handedly ripping my heart out of my chest and throwing it away. I love her so damn much, but fuck if she isn't pissing me the hell off and making it so that it's *me* who needs space from her.

"Go back inside," I bite harshly before walking away, calling a cab, and going home.

I wish I didn't love her so hard—embarrassingly hard—but I do. I can't shake it. I hoped that going back to school would offer me a distraction, but it hasn't. I stick to my side of campus, never venturing over to where most of her classes are. Everything about her makes me uneasy, and I can't be myself, I can't do the things I used to without nerves constantly tormenting me. Everywhere I look, I'm scared I'll see her. I go surfing, but there's no enjoyment because I'm too worried she'll show up. Miami is a large city, but we both run so close to each other that I'm surprised we haven't crossed paths since the night of the party.

I'm going crazy, and no matter how many weeks pass, my hurt still remains.

January creeps along slowly, achingly slow, eventually rolling over and dumping me into February, and I'm done.

I can't keep going on like this.

It's been months, and I'm no better. Nothing is better. Life still sucks, and I'm still miserable.

I'm so over feeling like shit because of her, because of what she did to us.

The hope that she'll come around is fading, and as much as I want to keep hanging on, I can't do it anymore. I'm drowning, trapped in the undertow of *I want yous*, *I love yous*, and *I miss yous*. I've been clutching on to faith in my hands where her fingers belong. I've been holding on to hope in my throat where her lips should rest, but instead, it wraps around my neck like a noose, strangling the life out of me.

I just want to breathe again.

I want to be free of this pain, go back to having fun, and enjoy life again. And why shouldn't I? She's the one who threw *me* away.

The answer is easy: Because I love her.

But at the same time, this isn't fair to me.

In a last-ditch effort to see if I should continue holding out for her, I send her a text.

Me: I need you to tell me if I still have a chance with you. I still love you, but if this is truly over, you have to let me know. Hanging on to you is killing me.

Scared of what she might say, I turn my phone off and head into my last lecture of the day. When class ends and I go back outside, the sun is now hidden behind dark storm clouds that split open as I walk out to the parking lot and get into my Jeep. It's now, with the rain pouring down, that I turn my phone back on. While I wait for the screen to come to life, I allow my heart space to beat freely as anticipation grows within the fibers of optimism.

Kate: You can stop hanging on to me.

And just like that, she fucking shreds me.

Twenty-Four

KATE

'M FREEFALLING FROM THE HIGHEST POINT OF VELOCITY, STRAIGHT toward the concrete below, and it's my own fault.

After all, I'm the one who sent the text a couple days ago, telling him to stop hanging on to me.

Now, all I'm left with is the unrelenting fear as I wait for the impending impact.

I had to delete the text from my phone; I couldn't look at it without enduring a barrage of regret. Depending on the day, hour, minute, or second, I sway back and forth in my conviction to walk away from the best thing I've ever known. I'm like a little kid lost in one of those wacky carnival mirror mazes. There's no telling if it's me I'm looking at or if it's a reflection of a reflection of a reflection, and no matter where I turn, I can't find my way out. I often have the urge to slam my fists against the glass to break free from this atrocity I've thrown myself into.

"Thank god it's Friday." Ady flops down in the chair across the table from me in the student center. "I don't know about you, but I'm starting to get sick of this place."

Immediately, I want to ask her about Trent, ask how he's doing, but I'm scared of the answer. Scared he's back to living his single life, relieved to be free of me—the weak and indecisive girl he probably regrets getting mixed up with.

I wouldn't blame him.

"Where have you been?"

"I was on the phone with Micah," she tells me, and I brace myself for what I know is coming.

"So, what's the verdict?"

"It's official. We're moving."

Sulking back in my seat, I sigh. "I can't believe you're leaving me."

"I'm not leaving you yet," she rushes to assure me. "I'll be back all the time."

It didn't come as a total shock when she and Micah got engaged over Christmas. We all saw it coming, but knowing that after we graduate in a few months, she'll be moving with him to San Diego sucks. I've been doing my best to mask how I really feel and put on a happy face for her, but it finds a way of seeping out. Selfishly, I want her to stay.

Without Ady, I really have nothing in Miami. Looking back on these past four years, I have so many regrets. All of my friendships suffered when I got involved with Caleb, and when I ran back home and didn't tell anyone, it created an even bigger wedge. Now, all the people I used to hang with are hanging with Trent, while I'm alone on a sinking island.

Everyone is moving on with their lives while mine is going nowhere. I should be excited and wearing the same smile as Ady, but it's hard to find anything to be happy about right now.

"Have you told your mom?"

She cringes. "No. She's going to be so sad when I do that I don't want to tell her over the phone," she says. "Micah and I have to find a weekend to go visit her and break the news."

Sarcastically, I tell her, "Have fun with that."

"Gee, thanks." She reaches for the cup of coffee that's in my hands and takes a sip. "Ugh, gross. What's in this?"

I laugh when she hands it back over. "Stevia."

"What's wrong with sugar? Lord knows you need the calories."

I sneer, but she's right. I haven't been taking care of myself, and it's been hard to stomach food.

"Seriously, you need to be eating donuts with your coffee," she jokes, but it's hard to smile when even the mention of donuts holds memories of Trent.

"Yeah, yeah."

Her face straightens. "So, how are you doing? I feel like I've been so flighty the past couple of weeks."

"It's fine. You have a lot going on," I respond, dodging her question, which, of course, she notices.

"Are we still not talking about Trent?"

"Nope," I confirm with a shake of my head.

Even though we broke up almost four months ago, I never told her about the conversation I had with him at the New Year's Eve party or the text I sent him two days ago, so I understand why she thinks the topic should be safe. But it isn't.

"So, what are you doing for the rest of the day?"

I take another sip of my coffee, and she's right, this stevia tastes like shit. "I think I'm going to hit the water. I haven't been on my board all week."

"Want to grab dinner afterward?"

"Yeah, I'll call you when I leave the beach."

We hang out for a little while longer until she goes off to her last class of the day. Before I head home, I run over to the university bookstore to grab an exam book for a test I have next week.

I walk inside and stop the instant I see Trent standing with a small group of people. Seeing him steals the oxygen right out of me, and I know I should duck out and grab my exam book later, but I can't bring myself to move as emotions take over me.

He talks to a couple of buddies of his who look familiar, but it's the girl standing next to him who has my heart drumming out of rhythm. It's a complex feeling to watch him, the person I came to know so deeply has become a stranger I don't talk to anymore.

It isn't right that I'm not going up to him, saying hello, and kissing his lips. I should be the girl at his side—not her. And then the thought of who she is, who she might be to him, sucker punches me. The impact is aggressive, and I have to bite my cheek to quell the overpowering jealousy growing inside.

Trent stays back when they start to disperse, and a small portion of my heart is comforted when the girl grabs his friend's hand as they head out. My breath catches in my throat the moment he looks up from his phone and sees me staring. I don't know if I should be relieved that he finally notices me standing here or heartbroken.

He's emotionless, and it hurts that I'm the one who put that look on his face. I wonder when my feelings for him will begin to fade. Timidity spirals through me with each step I take as I walk over, but he remains unmoving.

"Hey." My voice comes out uneven, a noticeable tell of my nerves, but he doesn't respond. Looking into his eyes, which have captured me since day one, I fight the gravity trying to pull me closer to him because he's no longer mine. "How are you?"

"How the fuck do you think I am?"

I hate that he's so angry. I open my mouth to speak, but I'm clueless as to what to say or how to talk to him anymore.

"What do you want?"

Shrugging, I shake my head, uncertain of everything as I stand here, shattered, heartbroken, and despising myself for not being strong enough for him. "I just miss you," I admit honestly.

His only reaction is a humorless laugh, which he drops a moment later. "Do me a favor," he says, his tone firm with annoyance. "Leave me the fuck alone."

He doesn't give me a second look before he walks away. My heart screams for him to come back, but I know better than to call out because this is exactly what my heart does. It leads me down foolish paths lined with hopeless hopes and uncertain certainties, so I let him go, despite the yearning to chase after him and all his perfection.

Perfection is a myth though. I'm weary of roses because of their hidden thorns. Trent thinks I dream of white picket fences—he calls them glorified cages. But cages keep us safe from the scary world that lies on the other side of the bars—the unforeseen, the unpredictable, the inevitable. The thought of walking through life without any protection scares me more than walking through life not entirely sure my heart is still in my chest.

A tiny voice inside me whispers, *"What if his love is enough to shock the beat back to life inside you, making you stronger than what you ever were before?"*

Never have I felt more lost than I do right now. Turning around, I exit out the same door I just came through and go straight to my car. Each step I take illuminates more fears, more doubts, more questions, and I realize I'm running in the wrong direction. These past four years have led me nowhere but backward. I'm more alone, more lost, more confused than ever.

What the hell am I even doing?

Getting behind the wheel, my hands tremble beneath the weight of my fucked-up world. My keys slip out from my fingers and fall onto the floorboard. Looking to where they landed by my feet, it all becomes too much, and a tear slips down my face.

I'm so lost.

Pulling my cellphone from my bag, I reach out to the one person who might be able to shine some clarity down on me.

"Hey, sweetheart."

"Dad, I really need to talk to you."

"Is everything okay? You sound upset," he says, and his voice is so much of a comfort that I begin to cry harder.

"Everything's falling apart."

Twenty-Five

KATE

After I called my dad yesterday, he decided to take today off work so he could come to Miami and talk to me. He could tell how upset I was, but he felt we should have this conversation in person rather than over the phone, so he did what he could to assure me that whatever was going on would be okay as I sat in my car and cried.

Anxiety fuels my body as I pace my condo, waiting for him to get here, and as soon as the knock comes, I rush to open the door.

"Hey, sweetheart." He smiles tenderly and wraps me up in a hug I've been in desperate need of.

My body slacks into his comforting arms. "Thanks for coming."

Although I'm dreading this conversation, I know it needs to be had. I can't continue holding all of this inside me, and I need his advice so badly.

"Let's sit," he says, and when we're situated on my couch, he lays a hand on my knee. "So, what's going on? What has you so upset?"

With a defeated sigh, I tell him, "I don't even know where to start. I'm just so lost."

"What is it you're trying to find?"

His question makes me think a dimension deeper about what it is I'm searching for, and I sag my shoulders. "I don't know."

I wait for him to speak, to guide me through this, but he doesn't. He simply peers into my eyes, imploring me to dig even deeper and find for myself what it is I'm trying to say.

"It's like . . . the whole universe is in motion, and I'm being left behind."

He nods. "You're in a moment of transition. It's normal to feel that way, to be confused about where you're going and how you're going to get there," he says. "You're about to graduate. That can be a scary thing for some people."

"I feel like I can't find the path I'm supposed to be on," I admit. "Everyone around me is moving forward, making plans, getting engaged, finding jobs . . ." Dropping my head, I mindlessly fidget with the hem of my T-shirt. "I walk out of my condo, and I have no clue which way to turn."

"Life doesn't come with a road map. I wish it did so that I could give it to you, but we have to figure it out on our own."

"That's just it," I respond. "I'm scared of not knowing what to do or if I'm going to go down the wrong road."

He chuckles lightly. "That's inevitable, honey. Everyone winds up traveling down the wrong road at one point or another. If you never take the wrong one, you would never appreciate the right ones. It's part of the adventure."

With a weak smile, I shake my head. "An adventure I don't want to go on."

"Unfortunately, you don't get that choice. You're on it whether you like it or not."

I blow out a breath of frustration as I lean back into the couch and stare at the ceiling. "Why do I feel like I don't know who I am anymore?"

"Because these are the years when nobody knows who they are. You aren't the same person you were when you came here four years ago, and you probably aren't going to become the person you thought," he tells me, and when I lift my head and look at him, he continues. "That's the natural order of life. It's going to take you places you don't want to go and kill off parts of you that aren't meant to stay."

His words sink into me, through my skin straight down into my bones, where they penetrate my fears. The unknown is a scary place for me to be—yet, here I am in the thick of it.

"What does Trent say about all this?" he asks, still unaware that we aren't together anymore. "Have you talked to him about how you're feeling?"

I shake my head when a wave of sadness washes over me.

"Why not?"

The moment my eyes prick, I close them. My father's hand cups my shoulder, and I swear he cracks the bone beneath. I try not to whimper, but it comes out anyway.

"Is everything okay between the two of you?"

I sniff, and his grip on me tightens when I finally reveal, "We broke up."

After blinking open my eyes, I wipe my face.

"When did this happen?"

"When you were in the hospital after you got shot."

His brows lift in surprise. "That was four months ago; why didn't you ever say anything?"

Cowardly, I shrug. "I don't know."

"Do you want to talk about what happened?"

"I just didn't want to wind up heartbroken."

Confusion etches lines in his forehead. "What does that mean?"

I take a deep breath and let it out slowly, dreading having to tell him the truth, to expose a side of myself I seriously doubt he knows even exists. It takes a second for me to admit, "I was becoming a burden to him."

"He told you that?"

"No. He would never tell me that; Trent's too nice of a guy to ever admit to feeling that way."

"Why would you be a burden to him?"

I give a weak shrug because I'm scared to admit the truth to my dad.

"A shrug isn't enough," he says. "You're going to have to spell it out for your old man."

I crack a feeble smile, but it quickly vanishes. "I kind of went through some things after Caleb and I broke up, and I put a lot of that on Trent's shoulders."

"He didn't like that?"

"What guy wants to deal with his girlfriend's ex-boyfriend baggage?"

"A guy who's in love." I shake my head, and he adds. "Everyone has baggage, sweetheart."

"I have a lot," I mutter.

"But you said he never complained. So, why are you assuming you were a strain on him?"

"Because . . ." I hesitate to say anything more because a part of me feels like it would be a betrayal of Trent's trust. But at the same time, I need my dad's help to sort through this mess, and I can't do that if I'm not honest.

"Because why?"

"Because of his mom," I reveal. "She relies on him a lot for emotional support. Ever since he was a kid. Every time something goes wrong, she depends on him to pick up the pieces, and it's been really hard on him. He's never said anything to her about how he feels, but he's told me."

"But how can you compare you trying to get over a break up to years of what she's been doing?"

"Because it was more than just a breakup; I don't really want to get into it. It's just been a rough time for me and then with you getting shot . . . I guess I didn't realize just how much I had been depending on him."

"Did you try talking to him about it?"

"He never would've told me the truth, but I know I was wearing on him and I didn't want to be that person."

"What person?"

"A needy person who can't deal with her own problems."

"No one expects you to deal with them all on your own. We all need help sometimes," he says. "Relationships are all about giving and taking."

"Exactly. And all I've been doing is taking."

"It's a balancing act. Look at your mother and I, ever since I landed myself in the hospital, that woman has been doing nothing but giving while I've been taking," he explains. "It's the season we're in right now because I need her, and when it's her turn to need me, guess what? I'll be doing all the giving and she'll be doing all the taking. Between those unbalanced moments, the give and take will even out. You just have to give it time."

His words make me take a pause to reflect back on my time with Trent, and even though it's mostly overshadowed by my leaning on him, moments appear when maybe he was leaning on me. I examine those instances deeper, and wonder why I never saw them before right now.

Maybe it's because he comes about it from a different angle

than I do. Maybe I was giving him what he needed when he confided in me about the things he'd gone through as a kid, when he opened up about his feelings toward his mother getting engaged and the abandonment of his dad. Perhaps he was looking for compassion and advice, both of which I gave. If I take a step back, I wonder if we're not as far off as what I convinced myself of.

Sulking into the cushions, I sigh heavily.

"What is it?"

"I don't know. Maybe it was almost losing you that got everything so messed up for me."

"Yeah, things like that can screw with your head."

"I was just so scared."

"But you can't shut people out when you get scared."

"That's not what I did."

"That's exactly what you did," he states. "Don't you think it was unfair to assume that you were a burden to him."

A whole new version of guilt blooms in my stomach.

"You took the thoughts in your head and convinced yourself that they were in his, and then you didn't even talk to him about it. You broke up with him."

"God, you make it sound so cold."

"Because it was," he says, almost scolding me. "Kate, what the hell are you doing?"

I stare at him because I don't have the answer.

"Why would you sabotage something that was going so well?" he questions and then continues without giving me space to respond. "When he came to visit over your birthday, the two of us had several really good chats, and let me tell you something, that boy loves you, and never once did I get the impression that he felt you were too needy," he says, but he doesn't stop there. "Your mother also told me how he stepped up for you girls when I was in the hospital. I'm just shocked that you threw away a relationship that appeared, from my perspective, to be a solid one."

And then something clicks.

What if Trent was right? What if my not feeling good enough isn't coming from him, but rather Caleb?

What if this has nothing to do with Trent at all? The man who saw past my faults, resurrected my heart, and brought me back to life.

Memories of Trent slip down my cheeks like faded cracks of thunder as I sit in a constant state of heartbreak. After everything I've destroyed, I still sleep in the comfort of how it felt to be loved by him, in the gentle moments of his purity. I miss him and I don't know how to make myself stop.

"I was scared," I confess on a damp whisper.

"Of what?"

"Of losing him."

"So why did you break up with him?"

"I guess I figured it would eventually end anyway, and I thought it would hurt less to do it sooner rather than later."

"It doesn't make sense," he says, lifting my chin so he can look into my eyes.

"First I lost Piper and then Caleb and then when I almost lost you . . . I just wanted to protect myself."

His eyes soften. "If you were scared of losing him, why did you force your fears on yourself instead of holding on to him tighter?"

"Because I didn't want to be blindsided the way I always am."

"So, this is about you being scared of not being in control?"

There's a shift inside me when he says this, and slowly, more pieces start coming together.

"You think nothing can break your skin if you throw walls in front of you? Because that's what you did when you pushed him away. That was you putting up a wall," he says, brushing a stray tear from my cheek. "Look at you. Look at the pain you're in. That alone should tell you that your walls mean nothing in this world. No matter how far you run or how many walls you hide behind, you can't protect yourself from feeling the effects of life's hardships. They will always find you. They find all of us."

He's right. I've been fighting myself for months, and for what? To be sad and alone and hating myself for hurting Trent the way I did just to protect myself, only to wind up running into the exact heartache I was trying to avoid? I'm a wreck.

"But you know what you can do? You can surround yourself with people who love you enough to walk through the shit storms with you so you don't have to do it alone. And let me tell you something, there is nothing worse than walking through life alone."

The weight of what he is saying slams into me, shattering everything I convinced myself of into infinite fractals of regret. I drop my head into my palms, and he pulls me into him and hugs me as I digest his truth.

"I miss him so much," I cry as he holds me.

"Then stop being a foolish girl and be honest with him."

"He hates me."

"I don't believe that."

Pulling back, I dry my tears with the sleeve of my shirt. "He does."

"So what?" he dismisses. "Do you love him?"

"Yes."

"Are you willing to let go of your insecurities in order to be with him?"

I nod.

"Then he deserves to be able to make the decision of whether he wants to be with you instead of you forcing that choice on him."

"What if he doesn't want to be with me?"

"Then you've learned a hard lesson, and you move on and grow from it," he tells me. "But you need to let go of these fears you have, sweetheart, because you're going to wind up pushing everyone away from you." He tucks a lock of hair behind my ear. "But if you're so scared of loss that you throw away someone who clearly adores you, what's the point? I'm not saying you shouldn't fear losing things in life, what I'm saying is that loss is inevitable, but it won't destroy you."

"It scares me though."

"It scares everyone," he says. "Do you have any idea what your mother has been going through, knowing how close she came to losing me? But you don't see her running, do you?"

I shake my head.

"Just imagine what that would do to me if she did."

There's no question he'd be devastated—crushed—entirely heartbroken. I doubt he'd ever be the same. Then my thoughts drift to Trent, and guilt punctures like a thousand daggers being thrown at me from every direction for what I've done.

"It's okay to be afraid. Most of us are because life guarantees us nothing." He takes my hand again. "Do you know how terrified I was when you had your surfing accident in Hawaii?" I nod, dreading the truths he's about to give me. "You were under water for so long I was certain that, by the time I could get out to you, you'd be dead."

I watch his eyes rim in unshed tears as I start to realize that life is surrounded with moments of risk—that each day poses a threat.

"As cheesy as it sounds, life is nothing without the people we love, and here you are, throwing them away."

It hurts to hear, but the truth is rarely painless. I never meant to throw Trent away, but I let my insecurities take over and skew my heart, and I fought against his gravitational pull. I flung everything at him to push him away—stars and planets and moons—I used them in my defense. And then I left, never giving him a chance to catch them, hold them in his hands, and hang them back up in my sky to show me that, with him, I was home.

I'm matter and he's space.

I feel stupid now, that I would fight against us when we're useless without each other.

Twenty-Six

TRENT

"No bow tie?" my mom questions when she walks into the kitchen to find me drinking a beer with Garrett.

"Is it really necessary at this point? The tux is enough." I push the top two buttons of my shirt out through the holes, opening the collar.

My mother is getting married today . . . again, and I've been in a shit mood since I ran into Kate yesterday. Seeing her managed to drag me right back down the black hole of misery I've been trying to dig my way out of. Yet, here I am, stuck with her roaming through my head.

I keep catching myself thinking about her and what used to be. I don't know why the mind does that, takes you back to the places you can't really go back to.

Maybe it's to heal.

Maybe it's to punish.

"You look beautiful, Mom," Garrett tells her when she shows off her understated nude dress, which doesn't look like something a bride would wear.

"Thanks, dear." She looks at me and brushes her hand along

the shoulder of my tuxedo jacket, saying, "And thanks for pulling your hair back. You look very distinguished."

I laugh. "Don't get used to it. I hate wearing these things. They make me feel like something a Lacoste sewer fart shitted out."

With a heavy sigh, she shakes her head and Garrett raises his beer bottle, toasting, "Cheers to that."

"You boys are going to be the death of me."

"Not if these suits kill us first," he tells her.

"Are we ready to go?"

"Let me grab my keys," Garrett says before rushing upstairs.

She turns to me, softly asking, "How are you doing? You were really quiet last night at dinner."

"I'm fine." I try to smile. "Garrett's right, you look really nice."

She nods, taking my hint, and drops the topic of me.

"Let's do this," my brother announces as he clamors down the stairs and my mother shoots me an excitedly anxious smile.

"Sixth time's a charm, right?" I tease.

"I really hope so."

When we arrive at the Davis Island Garden Club, it's nothing like her past weddings that looked like a floral shop barfed all over everything. It's small, with only close family and friends, no more than fifty people in attendance. It's as low-key as she wanted it to be, and I keep a mostly pleasant expression on my face as Garrett and I stand by her side while she and Jack exchange their vows of foreverness, which seem like bullshit to me. I look across at Jack's three kids, who are standing by his side, and wonder if their smiles are genuine. His daughter brushes a tear away, and I scoff on the inside, not that I don't think love has the ability to be everlasting but because it failed me and now I'm bitter.

I never considered the idea of settling down with anyone, never believed love wasn't anything other than an illusion people created to serve as placeholders for their shortcomings. I was happy and content on my own; I didn't need that shit to come in and complicate my life.

That was before Kate.

That girl knocked me on my ass.

She was an unexpected surprise—a defining moment. A collision of stars slamming into me and sending my neat little world plummeting into the ocean. I never expected a girl like her to change me, but she did. Now there's nothing left but the memories that continue to haunt me, memories I wish would die.

A light applause pulls me out of my thoughts, and just like that, the ceremony is over.

For the next hour, I fake a smile as we take photo after photo that will likely be trashed in a year or two. Garrett and I are on our best behavior for Mom's sake, but I know he's itching as badly as I am to get to the reception and hit the bar. He's already been eyeing some chick on Jack's side, and I don't blame him. She's fucking hot, but I can't get myself right in the head to nail anyone when all I can think about is Kate.

She's like the phantom cockblock I can't get rid of.

As everyone slowly heads into the ballroom, I grab a beer and sit alone on the veranda fighting reckless thoughts. The band plays in the background while laughter and celebration fills the air, but I keep it out of my headspace. I know I'm shitty company right now, so I hammer back my drink before grabbing another.

When the sky goes black, my mom makes her way outside, and I shove down my shit.

She sits next to me. "I haven't seen you all night."

I take another swig of my beer.

"Is everything okay?"

"I just hope this one works out," I tell her honestly because even though I'm wrapped up in my own crap, I worry about her and this guy, who she's only known for a handful of months but is now her husband.

"Jack is safe," she says. "I truly believe he is."

"And what about the others?"

She looks out over the water of the bay that shines beneath the moon. "I don't know how to explain it, but with him, I feel at peace."

I watch as her smile grows slowly, and when she looks at me, she reaches over and tugs the elastic band out of my hair before loosening the strands with her fingers.

"Better?"

I nod and down the rest of my beer.

"Jack and I are about to leave."

"It's already time?"

"It's almost ten," she says. "You've been sitting out here for hours."

"Weddings aren't my thing, you know that."

She grins, but it doesn't reach her eyes. "You know I'm here for you, right?"

"Yeah."

"You can always talk to me."

"There's honestly nothing to talk about." I take another sip. "You go have fun in Switzerland and don't worry about me."

"I always worry about you; I'm your mom."

"It's time," Jack says when he steps out onto the veranda, and I stand before taking her hand to help her up from the bench.

"Trent," he acknowledges, shaking my hand and giving me a hug. "It's always good to see you."

"Congratulations," I say, hoping my mother is right about him. Then we head inside, and when the singer of the band takes the mic to announce their send off, everyone claps as Mom and Jack smile and wave goodbye before getting into the car that drives them away.

"A few of us are heading over to SoHo," Garrett says. "You coming?"

"I'm not into partying tonight, man."

"You sure?"

"Yeah. I'm beat."

While everyone starts to disperse, I pull out my phone to call for a ride. I've had it off all day, and when I power it up, I pause when I see I have three missed calls and one new voice mail from Kate.

I wish she would just leave me alone.

After deleting the voice mail, I open my app to request a driver to come pick me up. As I wait, I stop by the bar and guzzle another drink.

It's a short five-minute ride back to my mom's house, and when we pull up to the wrap-around drive, I notice a silhouette of someone sitting on the front step of the entryway. It isn't until I get out of the car that I realize Kate's car is parked on the far side of the driveway.

As the driver pulls away, his headlights illuminate her as she stares at me from the porch, but the moment he turns onto the street, she goes dark again.

She stands, but she doesn't move, and the hole she shot through my chest expands, forcing me to fill it with anger because the sadness she evokes is intolerable.

"What the hell are you doing here?" I snap as I approach the door, but I don't bother to look her way when I shove the key into the lock and open the door. "You should go back to Miami."

"Trent, wait."

I shouldn't, but I do.

"I was wrong," she says, and when I finally glance over, I see her face is splotchy from crying.

Her words are everything I've been hoping for, but they irritate all the same.

"I know you must hate me, but I need to talk to you, to tell you I messed up."

I hesitate to say anything I might regret as frustration claws its way through me. Her unrelenting presence in my thoughts has left me an utter mess, and I want to yell at her, but the agony in her voice has me weak. I open the door wider and motion my head for her to come inside.

After flicking on the lights, I shrug off my tux jacket and toss it onto the entry table. I don't lead her in any farther than the foyer before I turn and say, "I don't hate you."

Her eyes fall shut, sending a current of tears through the streams already coating her cheeks. The urge to comfort her is powerful, but I keep to myself.

"So, what is this? Why did you come here?"

"To tell you I made a mistake and that I never should've pushed you away."

Defensiveness erupts because this girl has no clue how much power she holds over me. "I don't need you running back to me because you're lonely."

My tone is scathing, but she doesn't waver when she says, "I came to apologize and to explain things to you." Her eyes drop for a moment before coming back to me. "I was wrong" she admits. "And I'm so sorry it's taken me all this time to realize that what I'm most afraid of is losing you."

"What does that even mean?"

Wiping her face, she goes on to explain, "When I was with Caleb, I'd never felt so powerless in my life. I had no idea how much of me he actually destroyed, and I should've never turned my insecurities on you the way I did. But after what happened to my dad . . ." Her face crumples as sadness consumes her, and it takes everything inside me not to grab ahold of her. I want to—God damn, all I want is to love her. "My head got so warped with all these thoughts. They scrambled together and threw me into a spiral, and I got scared. But what scared me most of all was how quickly the world can turn on me."

"It turns on all of us, Kate. All of us."

"I know."

"But you threw me away so carelessly, like you never even gave a shit."

She shakes her head, and her voice grows desperate. "My doing that didn't come from a place of carelessness. I swear to you it didn't." She takes a step closer to me. "That was me putting up walls that I never should have put up, and I don't expect you to understand but—"

"You don't think I understand? You think you're the only one who hides behind walls?" Needing her to seriously hear me, I take three strides to close the gap between us before telling her, "I've been living behind walls my whole life, Kate. And, yeah, it's scary to let them down and to show our weaknesses. I never wanted to, but you didn't give me a choice. From the moment I met you, you dug into me, which was terrifying. But guess what, I took them down—*for you*. You're the only one I've been willing to do that for."

Her tears are unrelenting, but this girl allows herself to get so tangled in her irrational thoughts that she can't understand she doesn't have to hide from everything.

"I trusted you," I add. "And you hurt me in a way no one has ever been able to do. But it was worth it just to love you and feel you loving me."

"I'm so sorry," she cries into her hands and it's all too much for me. I gather her in my arms and hold her tightly as she breaks down. "I felt so lost and scared and it made me insecure. And then I felt guilty for everything you were doing, which only made me feel weak."

I tilt her head to look at me and tell her, "Of course, you were weak. Your father almost died. You're allowed to be weak." I drag my thumbs through her tears. "You're allowed to be devastated and broken, and you're allowed to need me without having to feel guilty about it."

"I felt like a burden."

"I know you did, but you needed to believe me when I told you that you weren't."

"I just didn't know what to do, and I didn't know how to talk to you."

"That's fine if you can't talk to me, but you don't have to push me away." To have her back in my arms and no longer fighting against me, I'm able to breathe again. I swear I can feel my heart lift to a place where gravity doesn't exist. "I know there're a million thoughts in your head that you will never speak to me because it makes you nervous to be vulnerable. I'm willing to accept that side of you, but I need you to promise that if you start doubting yourself, you won't run because I'm not an abandoned house here for you to come and go in and out of as you please."

"I promise," she says, and I wipe more of her tears away. "Losing you was excruciating, and I know it was my fault and that I'm not perfect, but I'm here now, and I'm so sorry." She lets go of an emotional sigh before giving me everything I've been hoping for, telling me, "You're what I want—you've always been. I'm just praying that you can forgive me because it's killing me to know I hurt you and that I can't take it back."

Without a breath of hesitation, I tell her, "Of course, I forgive you." Holding her in my hands, I stare into her teary eyes.

"But I can't do this again unless I have your whole heart this time."

"You have it. It's yours," she says freely. "It doesn't beat without you."

And with that, I kiss her—I kiss her so deeply, licking the salt from her lips and wondering if she can taste my own pain. Her grip tightens, and I swear I'll spend the rest of my life twisting her heartstrings around my wrists to keep her close to me because I don't want to ever experience life without her again.

I tried to let her go, and I failed miserably. As much as I wanted to hate her and move on, I couldn't. This girl found a way to make herself a home between my ribs and become the rhythm of my damn pulse. I never thought I needed someone as much as I need her.

Drawing back slightly, I look deep into her eyes, needing her to feel my words in her soul when I tell her adamantly, "I don't ever want you to think that you aren't good enough for me because you're the best thing that has ever happened to my life."

She nods and breathes a heartfelt, "I'm sorry," and I feel it, the guilt for ripping us apart.

I want to take the pain away because it serves us no good, so I let go of the seriousness for a moment and chuckle under my breath. "You had me moping around like a little bitch."

She draws back, allowing me to see the slightest tug at the corner of her lips.

"I was miserable without you," I add more seriously.

Unwilling to waste any more time, I take her up to my room and show her how much I love her in the most honest way I know how. We lock ourselves away, and with our defenses down, I make love to her. She reaches into my infinity, silently crying as I move inside her. Clinging her arms around my neck, she begs for more, needy to mend her heart's fault lines, all the while confessing our shortcomings and regrets so that we can move past them and be stronger.

And, in the moment her body splinters beneath mine, she kisses me before giving back the same words I once gave her when she whispers, "You're the realest feeling I've ever known."

Epilogue

KATE

Four months later...

Letting go of insecurities doesn't come easily. My past has scarred me in ways I'm still trying to cope with. As much as I love Trent and trust that he loves me, it's sometimes challenging not to let my mind wander into the worry of *am I enough*. I'm trying to be more open, to share more of my thoughts and feelings with him, to say the words that expose me to vulnerability. He deserves it and so much more after the crap I put him through. Guilt for hurting him manifests at random times, and the need to apologize weighs heavily on my shoulders, but each and every time it gets too heavy, he's there to assure me he's over it and that I should be too.

I'm moving forward, and even though I've been racked with nerves about my future, I'm also excited. The two of us graduated a couple of weeks ago, and I start my new job at one of Miami's top entertainment groups as a club promoter next week. It's a dream job to nail fresh out of college.

Along with the anticipation of this new chapter in my life, I'm also dealing with losing Ady. She and Micah are already packing to move to San Diego in a few weeks, and I'm dreading having to say goodbye.

"I can't believe you're moving," I tell her as I help her box up a few belongings.

"You'll have too much fun at your new PR job to even know I'm gone."

"Doubtful." The moving boxes are already starting to pile up around the condo, and I hate it. "Have you decided what you're going to do for work?"

As she tapes up the box, Micah comes up from behind and nips her neck, joking, "She's going to be my wife, so she'll be busy cooking, cleaning, and doing laundry."

She laughs and pokes him in the ribs. "You wish."

Suddenly, the door swings open and Trent steps into the condo with his arms spread wide open. The three of us stare as he boasts a grand smile, wearing a suit and tie.

"Dude," Micah says. "Why the fuck are you dressed like that?"

"Interview day, young pup." Trent saunters into the room, adjusting his tie that doesn't need adjusting. "My people, you are now looking at the future of Tate and Nixon Investments."

"The future *what*?" I ask, stifling my laughter because he looks so damn proud.

He's overly dramatic as he falls back into one of the chairs and crosses his leg over his knee. "The future *everything*, my unemployed friend."

I sneer when I remind him, "I got a job last week."

"Peasant work." He brushes imaginary lint off his shoulder before wagging his hand at me. This time, I do laugh because his phony arrogance was nowhere to be seen earlier today. He isn't one who really ever gets nervous, but his anxiety as he was getting ready for his interview was undeniable.

"So, what's your job title?" I ask.

"I'll be a financial analyst."

"Entry-level?" Micah inquires when he closes the fridge and pops the cap off a bottle of beer.

"A man can be defined by his capacity to be humble, so yes, I accepted an entry-level position."

"Congrats," Micah says as he raises his beer in salute. "You're one step above an unpaid intern."

"Eat dick."

"No thanks."

"God, this place is depressing," he says as he looks around and notices how much Ady and I were able to pack up while he was gone.

The four of us spend the rest of the day just hanging out, knowing our time together is ticking down. When evening falls, we order in pizza and find a movie to watch. It's nearing midnight when Micah and Ady call it a night and head to bed, leaving Trent and me out in the living room.

Curled up on the couch together, I roll over to face him and smile.

"What?"

"Congrats on the job."

"Yours sounds like more fun."

"Jealous?"

He smirks. "Fuck yeah."

"I'm nervous," I admit.

"You'll be great."

He tugs me in closer, pressing our bodies flush against each other, and I kiss him, tasting a love I once feared I'd never have again. My hands lose themselves in his hair when his hands begin to roam. There was a time I believed I would never have him this close again. I was so foolish, but if I had to do it again just so I could appreciate him as much as I do now, I would. I'm stronger than I was before because it allowed me to finally see the truth to my faults. I hate that we both had to suffer for me to get here, but in the end, it was worth it.

His hand slides under my shirt, and he hooks his fingers into the cup of my bra, laughing when he yanks it down and my breast spills out.

"You're such a child," I tell him as I roll my eyes, but it's when he lifts my shirt and shoves his head under it that I bust out laughing.

Playfully, he takes me into his mouth, and the moment he starts sucking, I go silent as my eyes fall shut and a breathy moan falls from my parted lips. Far too soon, he pulls his head from beneath my shirt.

"Why are you stopping?"

He looks so sexy with his devious smirk and mussed hair.

"Don't be a tease."

He then grabs my ass and pulls my hips roughly against his hard dick. "Trust me, I'm gonna give it to you, but I want to ask you something first."

"Ask me later."

"I'm not a cheap toy for you to use for your pleasure."

With a fast hand, I pinch his nipple, and he flinches away, cupping his pec. "Damn, girl."

I giggle, but when he settles back down, his easy smile is gone.

"What do you want to talk about?" I ask.

"You know I have to be out of this place in three weeks, right?"

I nod.

"I checked out a vacant unit on the sixth floor the other day that I'm going to sign a lease for, and I was thinking that, for the environment's sake, we should put your name on it too."

"What does that have to do with the environment?"

"Isn't there a global water crisis or some shit like that?"

"Not that I'm aware of," I respond through a light chuckle.

"Okay, then, but I still want to shower with you," he says and then winks. "We could bang it out every morning before work."

"So, you want me to move in with you for the sole purpose of shower sex?"

"Oh, don't worry. There will be other perks too," he says suggestively.

As exciting as the idea of living with him is, I don't agree right away, and slowly, my smile falls.

"What's wrong?"

"I don't know, it just . . . it seems like a big step."

"You scared?"

"I'm not sure what I am," I tell him honestly.

Putting all jokes aside, he takes my hand in his, lacing our fingers together. "I love you," he states without a hint of doubt. "And we've known each other for four years."

"I know."

His eyes drop down to our entwined hands, and he goes quiet for a moment before looking back at me. "I want to be with you."

"You are with me."

"I want more."

And I do too. It's been a rocky year for us, but to expect perfection when we're both trying to figure out our relationship would be foolish. Yeah, we had a hiccup there in the middle, but he's been one of my closest friends. As I look into his eyes, I see his love for me, a love he has proven to be reliable. Change unsettles me, and I don't think that will ever go away, but without it, I never would've found myself here with him. And it's with him that I've finally found a place of security, a place where I belong, and a constant in my life that makes all the other changes I might face a lot less scary.

I know that, with him, I'm planted on a sturdy foundation.

So, I ignore the unease that comes with taking this next step. So long as he's by my side, I'm exactly where I'm supposed to be.

"Are you sure about this?"

"I never would've asked if I wasn't," he tells me. "What do you say?"

Happiness expands within my heart, and although I'm nervous to take this step with him, I'm also rooted in my faith that he's my forever. So, with a smile, I hold his hand as I take this leap. "Yes. I'll move in with you."

His eyes light up, and I swear it's the most beautiful vision in this world. I kiss him because he's mine and I can, but it only lasts a moment before I pull back in wonderment, asking, "Who are you?"

His brows furrow, and where I would normally hold back the emotions roiling through me, I share them with him, when I go on. "Who are you to walk into my world without a key, knowing nothing about me, and make yourself at home?"

He stares into my eyes, which are now open paths to my soul, only for him to walk upon, and on a faint whisper, I ask again, "Who are you?"

He smiles. "I'm the fucking love of your life."

Note From the Author

Did you love the Secrets & Truths duet?
Follow Ady's story in the Crave duet!
Keep reading for a sneak peek.

National Domestic Violence Hotline

If you are worried about your relationship or have questions about your partner's behaviors, contact an Advocate.

They are available 24/7/365.

It's free and it's anonymous.

Call 1-800-799-SAFE (7233)

or chat online at
www.thehotline.org

Sneak Peek of CRAVE

CRAVE
part one

CHAPTER
one

Kason

I often find myself wondering if I have always been like this, if I ever existed without being afflicted with this craving. When I think back, I reach static before finding a time where I was free. Maybe I've never been free. Maybe I was born with some sort of displacement. A wiring gone wrong.

I was six years old when I saw my first set of tits.

I woke up in the middle of the night, thirsty for a drink of water, when I walked into the living room and saw my babysitter naked from the waist up while kissing her boyfriend. I didn't understand at the time exactly what I was seeing, but I knew I liked it. Not in a sexual way, but the visual intrigued me.

Her name was Shannon.

I don't remember much about her. She was one of a number of babysitters that would stay overnight while my mother worked her second job. I often found myself staying up late, hoping Shannon's boyfriend would show up. To this very day, I can still remember the excitement I felt when I saw her on the couch with him, when I heard the sounds they made. I would crouch on my hands and knees and watch them as I hid behind a fake ficus tree that sat in the far corner of the living room.

The excitement of watching her dry hump her boyfriend didn't make my dick grow like it does now as I clench my hand firmly around myself. Memories play behind my eyelids, and I cum quickly, shooting my load into a wad of toilet paper before flushing it.

I wash my hands and then run damp fingers through my hair as I look at my reflection in the mirror. I stare into green eyes, eyes that bear no resemblance to my mother's, and tell myself under my breath, "Seven hours," but I already know I won't be able to last that long. I only set these trivial goals to give myself the illusion that I'm being proactive about controlling whatever this is.

The idea that maybe I'm uncontrollable has been weighing heavily on me lately, but I shrug it off as I walk out of the bathroom.

"Bye, Mom," I shout and then grab my backpack and the keys to the shitty old Camaro I recently bought. I was finally able to save enough money from the part-time job I've been working after school to buy the damn thing. It's old and rundown, but it gets me from point A to point B.

The car fits in with the apartment complex, but I tell myself that I don't. The thought of this being my life has never sat well with me. I've grown up threadbare with an absentee mother who works herself to the bone for every penny she makes, only to fall short every month. She's drowning in debt, and I refuse to go down that same path.

I toss my backpack into the passenger seat and pump the gas a few times before cranking the ignition and bringing the car to a grumbling start.

Most would look at a kid like me and make the stereotypical

judgment call. But I'm smarter than the other dopeheads that live on this side of the tracks. The only way I have a chance of getting out of here is by going to college and making something of myself. All I have going for me is academics, so I've made them my priority, and in return, I've maintained a solid four-point-oh GPA semester after semester.

Pulling into the parking lot of South Shore High, I park in my usual spot next to Micah's pristine truck where he and our buddy Trent are already waiting on me.

Micah claps his hand obnoxiously against the old metaled hood of my car and gives me a shit-eating grin. "Kason, what the hell happened to you last night?"

"Got tied up with stuff."

"Speaking of stuff," he hints as we head into the school building.

If it weren't for my association with Micah, I'd be just another roughneck outcast. But with his money and popularity and my ability to score him weed on a consistent basis, we've forged a friendship that benefits my social standing in this school. I guess that's one of the perks of living where I do—pot is an easy score for the rich kids. I've never touched the stuff myself, but I'll happily buy it off my neighbor, inflate the price for the naïve Micah, and pocket the profit.

"I gotta work this afternoon, but I can meet you when I'm done."

He turns to face me as he walks backward down the crowded hall, telling me, "Indian Rocks. The guys and I will be skimming there."

"Dude."

He smiles, ignoring my irritation, and then turns the corner and rushes to his class.

"That's way outta my way, man!" I holler before colliding into another student. "Fu—"

"I'm so sorry." Her voice comes before I'm able to gather my bearings enough to see who I bumped into. When I do look, she's already kneeling and grabbing the books she dropped.

"I'll get those." I squat next to her, and when I hand over her books, I finally get a look as we stand.

Long blonde hair frames her face, which is soft in color compared to most of the overly tanned girls in this town. But when you live in Tampa and the beaches are the main hangouts, what else can you expect? Her cheeks flush with embarrassment, and when she looks me in the eyes, she apologizes again, saying, "I'm sorry. That was my fault."

"I wasn't paying attention either, so no need to apologize." She shifts nervously on her feet and hoists her backpack higher on her shoulder. "What's your name?"

"Adaline," she responds and then shakes her head as she corrects herself. "I mean Ady. People just call me Ady."

"You new?"

"Is it that obvious?"

"Not in a bad way, but yeah. You have that lost look in your eyes."

"And here I thought I was blending in," she says and then smirks. "That is, until you ran into me and sent my books flying across the floor, causing a scene in front of everyone."

"I thought you said it was *your* fault? You even apologized for it."

"I was being polite. You know, new girl and all. Wouldn't want to make any enemies on my first day, but you should really watch where you're going."

Her humor cracks a smile on my face. "All right then. I'll take the blame if it'll make you feel better."

"It will. And thank you," she responds with modest perk.

"I guess I'll see you around then."

I start to head to class but only make it a few steps when she shouts, "Wait." I turn back, and she adds, "You never told me your name."

"Kason. People just call me Kason."

"Very funny."

"See you around, Adaline."

"It's Ady," she corrects as I head down the hall to first period, and I chuckle before making a detour that causes me to show up tardy.

I knew I'd never make it the full seven hours.

The day moves along in the same pattern as every day before, but it isn't until sixth period that I see her again. I sit in my usual seat at the back of the classroom and watch her eyes skitter around the room to find an unoccupied desk. She tucks a lock of hair behind her ear while kids file in behind her.

I typically mind my own business with girls, avoiding interactions that could possibly lead to an interest on their part. It's safer that way. But for some reason, I decide to put the poor thing out of her misery.

"Adaline."

She raises her chin and smiles when she spots me.

"I told you, it's Ady," she says when she approaches, but I ignore her reminder.

"No one has ever claimed the desk in front of me."

"Seriously? It's March."

"Your point?"

She hangs her bag on the back of the chair and shifts to the side to look at me when she takes her seat. "No point. Just wondering why you've sat back here for nearly the whole year by yourself."

"Maybe I'm a loser."

She laughs. "That's a stretch."

"How so?"

"I saw you at lunch. I can tell you're not a loser."

"Spying on me?"

She unzips her bag and takes her notebook out. "Don't flatter yourself. I'm the new girl, remember? It's kinda my job to be observant."

I catch Micah from the corner of my eye as he walks down the aisle, and Adaline looks up, following my line of focus.

"You again," he says to her before taking the seat to my right.

"You've already met?"

"Third period English," he tells me and then turns to her, saying, "And for the sole purpose of you being new, I won't hold it against you that you're sitting in my desk."

She shoots me an annoyed glare, to which I smile.

"In my defense, he told me no one sat here."

"Figures. This dick would throw anyone under the bus for a good-looking blonde."

"You think I'm good-looking?" Her tone is playful and full of mockery.

"His words, not mine."

"That isn't a denial."

She then turns in her chair, closing off the conversation, and I'm already somehow intrigued with the new girl and her air of confidence. Looking to my side, Micah mouths *she's hot*. I shake my head at him and then open my notebook, trying to redirect my focus when I feel the fangs of urgency bite.

I shift in my seat, hyperaware of my surroundings, but as I take a quick scan of my classmates, I find them all lost in their own conversations.

The teacher calls everyone's attention and begins her instruction while I struggle to pay attention to the lecture. I take notes and listen, all the while counting down the minutes until the final bell. When the last tick hits, I grab my bag, scrape the legs of my chair against the floor, and rush to get my fix.

"Dude," Micah calls. "Don't forget. Indian Rocks tonight."

"Got it," I throw over my shoulder, not wanting to look back and risk the chance of catching another glance of her. Sitting behind her and smelling the sweet scent of her shampoo was torture enough. So, I hightail it to my car and speed home to quell what's starting to feel like a curse.

C R A V E
a hauntingly profound love story

"Captivating! E.K. Blair has woven magic into this deep tale of love."
-SL Scott, *New York Times* bestselling author

"Tender, sexy, and unputdownable. Heart-pounding with tears in my eyes, E.K. Blair blew me away!"
-Jessica Hawkins, *USA Today* bestselling author

"E.K. Blair's ability to write about incredibly difficult situations is stunning. I was captivated and glued to the pages. E.K. gave one hundred percent to this book. It's unlike anything else out there right now, I promise."
-*Carlene Inspired: Literature and Life*

Explore other titles from

E. K. Blair

Follow
E. K. Blair

Instagram:
www.instagram.com/ek.blair

Facebook:
www.facebook.com/EKBlairAuthor

Twitter:
twitter.com/EK_Blair_Author

Goodreads
www.goodreads.com/author/show/6905829.E_K_Blair

Bookbub:
www.bookbub.com/authors/e-k-blair

TikTok:
www.tiktok.com/@ek.blair

Acknowledgments

This duet has become so close to my heart. It wasn't always the easiest to write and many tears were shed during the process. My goal was to write an honest and respectful story about an abusive relationship, and I have to thank to following people for helping me bring this story to life.

To my fans, I cannot thank you enough for continuing to love my characters and support my stories. Your loyalty means the world to me. The greatest joy is being able to open my heart and share what's inside with you.

To my husband, none of this would be possible without you. I know I say that a lot, but it is so very true. You are my support, my best friend, my partner in crime for life. Thank you for all you sacrifice in order for me to follow this passion of mine.

Sally Gillespie, you are one of my biggest blessings! The time you give me is simply incredible. Thank you for helping me in the creation of this story. It was such a memorable journey for me.

Ashley Williams, wow! Just WOW! How do I even thank you properly? The hours upon hours you have devoted to this duet are downright incredible! You make my words strong, even though you bust my balls to do so. From the early mornings to the late nights, and everything in between, you are always there for me. You are an amazing editor and friend!

My sister, Kelley, thank you for, once again, advising me on all the medical situations that arise in this story. You always take the time to clarify and explain everything I need to know to create an accurate storyline.

Bloggers, there are too many of you to name, but each and every one of you are equally important. Thank you for your undying support.

As always, when I end a story, I must turn to my characters and say the most heartfelt thank you of all.

Kate, you are so strong and courageous—a bright light that was momentarily dimmed. My wish is that women will read your story and find hope within it.

Trent, my crude and inappropriate Trent, you're a true friend—selfless and strong. You care so deeply for the ones you love and have so much depth to you. Your personality shed light on this painful tale, and because of who you are, you brought Kate back to life. I don't think you will ever know just how special you are to me. I am so heartbroken to say goodbye to you. I will miss spending my days with you, but I will revisit you often. Thank you for simply being you.

Ady, it was such a treat to see you blossom through this side of the story. I hope that people will read about everything you survived in the Crave Duet. You are a fighter and exactly who Kate needed to help her find herself again.

Thanks to each one of you!

www.ingramcontent.com/pod-product-compliance
Ingram Content Group UK Ltd.
Pitfield, Milton Keynes, MK11 3LW, UK
UKHW040636290425
5678UKWH00013B/142